Laura gra_____led

The door cr_____s. At the same time she was almost physically assaulted by an unpleasant odor, which seemed to be charred wood, mold and something indistinguishable but repugnant.

Realizing she'd made a mistake, Laura was about to draw back and slam the door. Some impulse she couldn't identify compelled her to take a tentative step, and then another, into the dark interior. A cold wind blew from somewhere, making her shiver, and she thought she caught a faint whistling sound that set her teeth on edge. As she put one foot before the other, she was seized with a sense of unreality. It was as if some unnamed force was drawing her forward against her conscious will....

REBECCA YORK

A *USA TODAY* bestselling author, Ruth Glick published her one hundredth book, *Crimson Moon*, a Berkley Sensation, in January 2005. Since 1997 she has been writing on her own as Rebecca York. Her novel, *Killing Moon* was a launch book for Berkley's Sensation romance imprint in June 2003. Her latest 43 Light Street book was *The Secret Night*, in April, 2006. In October she launches the Harlequin Intrigue continuity series SECURITY BREACH with *Chain Reaction*.

Ruth's many awards include two RITA® Award finalist books. She has earned two Career Achievement awards from *Romantic Times BOOKclub*—for Series Romantic Suspense and Series Romantic Mystery. *Nowhere Man* was the *Romantic Times BOOKclub* Best Intrigue of 1998 and is one of their reviewers' "all-time favorite 400 romances." Ruth's *Killing Moon* and *Witching Moon* both won the New Jersey Romance Writes Golden Leaf Award for Paranormal.

Michael Dirda of the *Washington Post Book World* says, "Her books...deliver what they promise: excitement, mystery, romance."

Between 1990 and 1997 Ruth wrote the Light Street series with Eileen Buckholtz. You can contact Ruth at rglick@capacces.org or visit her Web site at www.rebeccayork.com.

43 LIGHT STREET

REBECCA YORK
Whispers in the Night

HARLEQUIN®

TORONTO • NEW YORK • LONDON
AMSTERDAM • PARIS • SYDNEY • HAMBURG
STOCKHOLM • ATHENS • TOKYO • MILAN • MADRID
PRAGUE • WARSAW • BUDAPEST • AUCKLAND

ISBN-13: 978-0-373-36056-7
ISBN-10:   0-373-36056-8

WHISPERS IN THE NIGHT

Directory

4 3 L I G H T S T R E E T

	Room
NOEL EMERY Paralegal Services	311
ABIGAIL FRANKLIN, Ph.D. Clinical Psychology	509
O'MALLEY & O'MALLEY Detective Agency	518
KATHRYN MARTIN, M.D.	509
LAURA ROSWELL, LL.B. Attorney at Law	311
SABRINA'S FANCY	Lobby
L. ROSSINI Superintendent	Lower Level

CAST OF CHARACTERS

Laura Roswell—A weekend at Ravenwood stood her luck on its head and put her in grave danger.

Jake Wallace—This ex-football player knew all the right moves...but there was a deadly secret in his past.

Sam Pendergrast—Had he lost Emma to Laura's father and taken an opportunity for revenge?

Andy Stapleton—How far would this real-estate developer go to hide the Ravenwood secret?

Emma Litchfield—When she couldn't get what she wanted with her feminine wiles, had she turned to blackmail?

Timothy O'Donnell—He talked like a con man. Was he working on some kind of scam?

Martha Swayzee—She knew all the gossip and wasn't afraid to spread it.

Jo O'Malley—Could this detective dig up the dirt on Ravenwood before it was too late?

Hiram Pickett—This small-town chief of police didn't want any outsiders messing up his case.

Warren Ketchum—He was a law-and-order judge with more than justice on his mind.

Julie Sutton—She started the Ravenwood investigation, and it cost her dearly.

Prologue

Twenty years in the past

Falling sleet bit into Dorian's skin like shards from a broken whiskey glass. Gusts of wind buffeted him toward a stand of tall pines. The first storm of the season. Why did it have to be tonight of all stinking nights?

His arms ached from the hundred pounds of dead weight he was carrying. When he tried to pull his coat tighter, he almost dropped the bundle he'd hastily wrapped in one of the damask tablecloths. Cursing, he staggered forward.

In the moonlight, bare branches rose up in his path like the outstretched arms of bogey men. Stopping, he listened for footsteps above the howling wind. All he heard were the faint strains of a Beatles tune drifting out into the darkness. "Nowhere Man." He shivered.

Somehow out here in the cold, he'd forgotten about the others in the house. What if one of them came out? They could circle around. Grab him. Drag him back. Terrifying images slithered through his head—a man with a net leaping out from behind a tree. The net disappeared. The man's arms stretched impossibly long as bony fingers curved toward Dorian. Claws at the end tore into his face.

Shrieking, Dorian staggered back, clutching the table-cloth-wrapped bulk like a shield. Sweat poured off his skin and froze into droplets of rancid ice.

He filled his lungs with a deep gust of the cold mountain air, but wicked visions still flickered on the backs of his closed lids. Slowly, slowly, reason penetrated his fear. He was safe. Nobody had followed him out here. The guests inside were havin' a good time. Plenty of bunnies. Plenty of juice. Plenty of hash.

Special party. Special for the nosey blonde who had thought she was so smart. But he'd tumbled to her game.

Just a little farther from the house. The old quarry. Nobody's been there in years.

In the moonlight, he almost missed the rim. Only the branch of a tree kept him from pitching off the edge of the cliff into oblivion. Staggering back, he flung the bundle onto the ground.

As the cloth gaped open, a slender arm flopped out and lay across the rocky ground like a white exclamation point. Panting, he stared at it.

Some unnamed compulsion forced him to stoop and pull the material farther back. Sucking in a jagged breath, he peered down at the girl. A strand of long, corn-silk hair lay across her pale face. Once her expression had been mobile. Now it was rigid.

She'd been witty. Manipulative. Devious. At the end, she'd been afraid. The look of fear was still there—erasing everything else. Something deep inside him had responded to that fear. He'd liked it. Her defenselessness had been exciting. His mastery had been a power trip. Once he'd gotten started, he hadn't been able to stop.

Now the sightless eyes accused him. With a shudder, he reached out and closed them. That was better. He'd never have to look at her again.

Too bad he'd had to kill her. She was such a pretty chick. And sexy. Damn sexy. But it was her own fault she was dead.

A gust of wind picked up the edges of the tablecloth—whipping up the fabric like a ghost trying to claw its way out of the ground. Dorian moaned and would have run, except that he wasn't finished.

With stiff fingers he started to wrap the girl once more in the makeshift winding sheet. Then he stopped. No. He'd almost made a big mistake. If anyone found her down in the ravine, they might think she'd stumbled and fallen over the edge. But not if she was all wrapped up. He pulled the cloth away before dragging her to the edge of the cliff.

He didn't see the cross-shaped crystal slip from her grasp and bounce down into the gully; he only saw the girl as he sent her plummeting into space. Like a soul taking flight from its body.

Frozen moments later, she disappeared into the gaping chasm.

Chapter One

Sights and sounds were muffled by the cloth wrapped around her face, but Laura Roswell knew where she was. She'd been trapped in this nightmare landscape before. Chill air stung her skin. The wind moaned around her like a chorus of lost souls. A man's rough hands crushed her body, shifted her limp weight over his shoulder as if she were a sack of oranges—not a person.

No, not a man. It was death that held her in his icy grip.

She tried to scream. The terror clogged her throat, clamoring for release, but no sound escaped from her numbed lips. She had to get away or die, but her muscles had stopped obeying her urgent commands.

God, no. Oh, please. No.

The words were frozen in her soul along with the horror.

She was helpless. At his terrible mercy. He could do anything he wanted with her, and no one could save her. No one would even know where he'd taken her.

Then, in an instant, everything changed. She was falling, plummeting into space, spiraling down, down, down into a midnight chasm.

In that moment, she knew she had a choice. She could either wrench herself from the dream or crash against the rocky ground below. The immobilized scream tore from her throat. Even as she catapulted from sleep, Laura realized it had been her own voice crying out in the shadowy bedroom.

She struggled to a sitting position, half expecting chilly air to sting her lungs as she gasped in a ragged breath. Ordering her body to relax, she unclenched her death grip on the covers. Her death grip on reality. Yet her fingers still trembled as she smoothed them across the crisp flowered sheets and soft wool blanket.

Darting a hand out from under the covers, she snapped on the light beside the bed. The yellow glow from under the fringed shade warmed the room she'd redecorated in Victorian splendor after her husband had moved out. She looked around at the polished mahogany dresser, the fainting couch piled with its lace pillows. The dried flowers. The cluster of framed photographs on the marble washstand. Bill would have hated it. That as much as anything had made her fall in love with the style.

Just as she'd clutched the covers, she clutched the familiar surroundings. This was her world, the cozy nest she'd made for herself, where she felt warm and comforted and in control of her life.

As she plumped the pillows behind her head, the last wisps of the dream dissipated like the scent of wildflowers drifting away on the breeze. The flowers were so out of kilter with the rest of the half-remembered images. Yet their perfume tantalized her. Dreams didn't leave an aroma. Maybe she was smelling the perfumed soap she hadn't been able to resist at Sabrina's lobby shop yesterday.

But an unidentified scent was the least of her worries. For months, she'd been congratulating herself on how well she'd gotten back on track after the separation and the divorce. Then the nightmares had come creeping up on her like evil spirits lurking in the dark corners of her mind.

Laura shuddered. No, not just ordinary nightmares, she corrected herself; the same dream, over and over. Even if she couldn't quite remember what it was, she was sure of that much. And sure of the terrible feeling of defenselessness that always left her sick and trembling when she awoke. Maybe her good friend Dr. Abby Franklin would tell her she really didn't have it all together. Or maybe she'd just been working too hard. But it was getting more and more difficult to deny that something was seriously wrong.

She wanted to sink back into the warmth of the bed covers and catch up on some of the sleep she'd been missing, but it took only a few minutes to acknowledge that she wasn't going to turn her brain off. On a sigh, Laura swung her legs over the side of the bed and stretched. She'd brought home several folders of work last night and only gotten to two of them. The extra time this morning would give her a chance to go over the Rutledge custody case before she got to the office.

Two hours later Laura arrived at 43 Light Street, the turn-of-the-century building where she worked. The offices were large and the rent was cheap for downtown Baltimore, but there were inconveniences, she mused as she waited to see whether the ornate brass elevator was working. As it arrived, Jo O'Malley joined her. Not only was the small but successful private investigation firm of O'Malley and O'Malley housed in this building, but its owner was one of Laura's closest friends.

"How are you doing?" Jo asked.

"Fine," Laura answered automatically, smoothing her shoulder-length blond hair and casting the woman a sidewise glance. Talking about personal problems, even to her friends, was never easy for Laura. And it was particularly difficult with someone like Jo, who was newly married and bathed in the warm glow of happiness.

"How's Cam?" Laura asked.

Jo launched into an enthusiastic account of her husband's

latest electronic gadget, and Laura murmured quiet responses, wishing she could change the subject.

Unlucky in love, lucky in law, Laura characterized her own situation as she headed down the hall toward her third-floor office. In the year and a half since Dr. William Avery had left, her legal practice had really taken off. Probably because she now had the time and the need to pour herself into it. When she'd married in her second year of law school, she'd been naive enough to think she could have it all.

Having it all had lasted five years.

"And good morning to you, too," a familiar voice intoned.

"Oh, sorry." Laura realized that while she'd been deep in thought, she'd opened the door and come to a halt in front of her paralegal's desk.

"Sara Spencer canceled her appointment for this afternoon," Noel Emery said. She'd come to work as Laura's secretary but had upgraded her skills in night school. Now she handled much of the routine work in the office.

"Darn! This is the second time. She's afraid her husband is going to beat her up again if she goes ahead with the divorce. Or take it out on their daughter."

Noel nodded.

"Okay. I'll have another go at seeing if social services can get her and Emily into a group home. Or if they can't do it, we'll hit one of the private shelters. When I've found a place where she can stay, I'll call her back."

Laura was heading for her office door when Noel called her back. "Wait. You've got a special-delivery letter." The petite brunette handed a thick envelope across the desk. "And the Jacobson petition is ready for your signature."

"Thanks." Laura slit the seal on the envelope with her fingernail.

"What is it?"

"A letter from a land development company called ASDC. They want to buy my property in western Maryland. Only I don't have any."

Then the context clicked into place. Years ago, her father had been conned into investing in a limited partnership in the middle of nowhere. Because the location made the property unsalable, it was about the only thing he'd left her when he'd died. But she'd been surprised that she'd been mentioned in his will at all. He'd walked out on the family twenty years ago and hadn't called, written or visited.

The letter from ASDC was like a hand reaching out from the past to grab her by the back of the neck. That was why she suddenly felt cold and clammy, she told herself. She wanted to simply toss the communication into the trash, but she was too disciplined to let her emotions overcome logic.

"Did a ghost walk over your grave?" Noel asked.

Laura realized her assistant had seen her reaction. She laughed. "Kind of. My father always did clomp through people's lives with combat boots." She bent her head back to the correspondence. "After thirty years, it looks like his mountain is finally worth something. The company that wants to develop it is dying to wine and dine the investors at a mansion house in Garrett County. A place called Ravenwood."

Laura wondered why the name sent another shiver up her spine. She'd never heard of the place.

"Sounds good to me," Noel observed.

"I think I'll pass. Write them a letter and ask for more information about their proposal." She tossed the correspondence into Noel's in basket and went into her own office.

SIX-FOOT-TWO, two-hundred-pound Jake Wallace usually stood out in most crowds. It wasn't just his size that made both men and women give him a second look. It was the easy way he moved, the ready-for-anything expression on his square-cut face and his animal energy. Until you engaged him in conversation, you didn't encounter the offbeat sense of humor that made his sports column in the *Baltimore Sun* so popular. If you looked deeper, you realized something had given him a deep understanding of human nature. You didn't perceive the pain. He kept that too well hidden.

Wednesday morning, however, only a couple of staffers glanced up when Jake sauntered into the news room at twelve fifteen. The rest of the crew was used to his irregular hours—and too aware of their own deadlines.

Sports reporting was a bit like being on the swing shift. When you covered night games and had to turn your copy in for the morning edition, you weren't expected back at your desk before lunch.

The previous evening Jake had filled in at a Capitols-Fliers game. He'd composed the story in his head on the hour drive back to Baltimore, banged it out on his laptop while waiting for a Hungry Man dinner to heat in the microwave and filed the copy via modem.

Jake had just settled into his chair when Brenda Montell, the intern from Essex Community College, sidled up. "How was the game last night?" she asked.

He gave the girl what he hoped was an avuncular smile. The kid was centerfold material, and she had a crush on him. For about ten seconds, he'd considered inviting her to O'Grady's for a private little party after work. Then he'd given himself a silent lecture on robbing the cradle mixed with a strong reminder that trolling for dates at the office was asking for trouble.

When she came on to him with one of her sports questions, he always answered as if he were shooting the breeze with one of the guys. "Sobolov, the Caps' new goalie made three incredible saves that kept us in the game. Lucky for us we finally scored in the last thirty seconds.''

"That must have been really exciting.''

"Yeah, but I have to work on my high school football forecast.'' Brenda left, and Jake began pawing through the press releases and wire-service reports on his desk, looking for his notes on the area's best young players. Four years off the field, and something inside his chest still went tight when he realized another season was starting and he was on the sidelines. But he'd had a good career while it had lasted.

Jake flexed his bum knee. He would have had surgery and tried for another couple seasons—if Holly hadn't needed him. Staying with her at the end had been more important than his career. Except that he hadn't exactly been there at the end.

As always when that terrible memory surfaced, he felt as if he'd been tackled by a two-hundred-and-fifty-pound linebacker. But just like on the field when you were the bottom man under a pile of heavy bodies, you learn to pick yourself up and go on.

Actually, he was surviving a lot better than most former players. Thank God he'd had the sense to major in journalism and that he had some small talent for putting words together.

He located the football material and started going over the players' stats when a messenger from the mail room showed up.

"Special delivery.''

Jake examined the envelope. "This looks like it was meant for the real-estate section.''

"It's addressed to you.''

The messenger left, and Jake inspected the letterhead. ASDC? He'd never heard of the outfit. However, by the second sentence, he felt excitement expanding in his chest.

It was a development company offering to buy the land his uncle had left him, the tract in western Maryland that he'd always assumed was worthless. He sure as hell could use the money. Maybe he'd finally be able to pay off Holly's medical bills. And if he was really lucky, there'd be some change left over so he could take a leave of absence and finish the research for his book.

Except there was probably a catch somewhere. There usually was.

Jake looked over at his calendar. No harm in taking a little trip up to Garrett County. If he didn't like the setup, he could always get a head start on the article he was planning on the western Maryland ski resorts.

BECAUSE SHE WANTED to finish the notes on an abandonment case before going home, Laura didn't get out of the office until almost seven, long after she'd sent Noel home. Thinking about how much her life had changed, she made a quick stop at the gourmet section of the grocery store on her way home and picked up some of her favorites—marinated vegetables, curried chicken and tabouli.

Twenty minutes later as she sipped a glass of wine and savored the goodies, she read a chapter of the historical romance she'd started the day before. Reading was a lot more relaxing than listening to a running report on the tremendous profit margin on lab tests. Of course, there was no one to hear about her day, either—not that Bill had really given a damn. And she did get stuck with all the chores, she admitted, as she transferred the morning's load of laundry from the washer to the dryer. At least, she didn't have to drop a bundle of shirts at the cleaners on the way to work.

Laura's energy reserves gave out while she was folding towels. Leaving them in the basket in the guest room, she flopped into bed and turned on the TV hidden in the antique armoire.

Her eyelids drooped in the middle of a miniseries. Flipping the button on the remote control and settling down under the covers, she was asleep in less than five minutes.

It took a bit longer for the dream to snare her. At first it was as refreshing as a windswept meadow. She was standing in the wilderness in her nightgown. Tiny flowers as delicate as baby's tears glistened in the moonlight. Her bare feet crushed them as she walked and the fragrance wafted upward like a cloud of incense. Music floated toward her on the wind.

It was coming from a mansion house. Ravenwood. That was the name. Ravenwood. She'd been here before, long ago. As Laura approached, she could see the lights, hear the laughter. A party, and she'd been invited. The letter had come this morning.

Suddenly she longed to join in the merriment. But someone barred her way. She couldn't see him in the darkness. Yet he was there. And he was coming to get her. Coming to kill her. No, not just kill her. Worse than that.

Please, somebody help me. The mute plea died before she could give it voice. If she called out, she would only give herself away. On silent feet, she turned and fled into the dark woods, blond hair streaming out behind her. In the blink of an eye, midsummer warmth changed to bone-numbing cold. The white flowers were snow, biting into her bare feet. She slipped, fell, picked herself up with desperation born of panic. Horror closed the gap behind her— puffing and crashing through the underbrush.

Closer. Closer. Until merciless fingers dug into her shoulder. He stopped her in her tracks and whirled her toward him. They were face-to-face. No! He had no face. Only red, glowing eyes that burned into her, windows into the depths of hell.

White-hot terror zinged through every cell of her body. *Run. Save yourself.*

But flight was impossible now. The hand on her shoulder pressed. Under his touch, her flesh grew cold and numb. Like evil magic, the paralysis spread until her whole body went limp as a dead flower stalk. Gagging and choking with revulsion, she sagged against him. She was helpless. Trapped. At his mercy. Night after night he had come for her. Now he had her again, and she knew exactly what he was going to do to her.

Chapter Two

Somehow, from some reservoir of strength deep within her, a scream welled up and tore from her lips. A scream that released her from the paralysis and the bondage of the dream. Once more Laura had wrenched herself from the clutches of evil forces.

Again she sat up in bed and wrapped her arms around her knees. Her skin was clammy. Her heart threatened to pound through the wall of her chest. Her breath came in labored gasps. But this time she wasn't simply overcome by mindless panic. This time the dream memories were more distinct.

With a determined effort, she brought her terror under control as her mind scrambled to make sense of the midnight phantom. Taking slow, calming breaths, she grasped at the only explanation available. The faceless man chasing her in the nightmare was Bill. She'd felt so helpless in the dream. Just the way she'd felt helpless as she tried to keep their marriage from falling apart.

Bill Avery had hurt her more than she'd ever believed she could be hurt. He was the one who'd wanted out of their marriage, and she'd had sense enough to acknowledge that there was no way to heal the breach. But much as she longed to put the past behind her, she was still preoccupied with what had gone wrong.

As the idea caught hold, she began to fit facts to the dream's symbolism. It was convoluted, but maybe subconsciously she was letting the aftershocks of rejection bar her path to what could very well be an entertaining weekend in the country. Then, for good measure, she turned Bill into a murderer pursuing her through the frozen wasteland of her imagination. *Shades of Little Eva,* she thought with a wry laugh.

Well, she tried to keep her clients from playing the victim role—and she'd worked hard to keep from playing it herself. She wasn't going to give her ex-husband any power over her now. Bill was probably planning a great time for himself, starting with a T.G.I.F. party Friday night. She could darn well do something similar. Tomorrow she'd call ASDC and tell them she accepted their kind invitation.

THE MOUNTAIN AIR WAS CLEAN and crisp. The fall leaves were bright enough to have been cut from red, yellow and orange crepe paper. Along with the impossible china blue of the sky, they foretold a glorious fall weekend.

She should be feeling marvelous, Laura thought as she unconsciously tightened her hold on the steering wheel of her new Dodge Shadow. Yet somehow, the farther she got from Baltimore, the more unsettled she became. Probably bad memories were taking the edge off her anticipation. The last time she'd driven to western Maryland, she and Bill had been on a skiing weekend. After the first morning, he'd been in a snit because she had no difficulty with the expert trails while he'd been more comfortable on the intermediate runs. She'd forgotten about the episode until today.

The exit ramp dumped her onto a two-lane road that wound through picture-postcard mountain scenery.

"No wonder you sunk some money into the area, Dad," she muttered as she rounded yet another curve and gazed out across another jewellike valley. "You always had a weakness for beauty."

There was little sign of human habitation, only an occasional house or trailer set well back into the trees. Laura could understand why development had taken so long to catch up to Ravenwood. Probably you had to drive for forty-five minutes to buy a quart of milk.

She had started wondering if the directions ASDC had provided were correct when she finally spotted the town of Hazard. Luckily, she didn't blink on the way through or she might have missed it.

A couple of rustic motels. A grocery. Three gas stations, two of them with convenience stores attached. Thankful for the chance to fill up her tank and stretch her legs, she turned in at the station that took her credit card.

A sleepy-looking beagle eyed her car as she pulled alongside the one unleaded pump, but the mechanic leaning into the jaws of a Jeep's hood didn't emerge. Self-service apparently wasn't an option, and Laura was wondering how to get some attention when another man came sauntering out of the office. Fishing-rod thin, he had a face remarkably similar to the beagle's.

"Help you, ma'am?" he asked as he wiped blackened hands on a pair of green overalls. The name embroidered on the breast pocket was "Cully."

"Could you fill my tank and check the oil and water? And I'd like the key to your ladies' room."

"Ain't locked."

Laura got out of the car and stretched. Following the sign around the side of the building, she found a stoop-shouldered old woman with her hair pulled into a wispy bun mopping out the little room.

"Be out of your way in two shakes of a lamb's tail, honey."

"That's all right. Take your time."

Two minutes later the washroom was spotless.

"What a wonderful job you've done," Laura said to her.

"Why, thank you kindly." The woman smiled, displaying uneven yellow teeth that sported several gaps.

Maybe she should tip her, Laura thought as she closed the door, but when she emerged several minutes later, the attendant had vanished.

"Right pretty day you've got," Cully observed as he ran Laura's gas-company card through the machine. "Your first visit up here?"

"I've been to Western Maryland before. But not around here." Laura opened the door and pulled out the directions. "Is this the road to Ravenwood?"

Cully had been about to give her the credit slip. Now his hand hung suspended about six inches from his body. At the corner of her vision, Laura caught a sudden movement and turned slightly. The mechanic who hadn't budged from under the Jeep's hood the whole time she'd been at the gas station straightened up and stared at her.

The friendly smile had evaporated from Cully's face. Laura saw his eyes narrow as he gave her a ruminating look. "Ravenwood. Didn't know the place was back in business."

Uncertainly, she took a step back. "I'm—uh—spending the weekend there."

"Ain't got no directions to that place."

"Well, uh, thanks anyway." Laura opened the car door. Cully had already turned his back, but the mechanic was still watching her with hard eyes.

Suddenly anxious to depart, Laura inserted the ignition key. She was just about to turn it when a bony hand clamped itself over hers.

Laura gasped and tried to jerk away.

"Wait."

The fragile-looking blue-veined hand held her with surprising strength. In the next moment, the old woman who'd mopped the restroom was leaning in the window of the car, her wrinkled face only inches from Laura's.

"A sweet girl like you shouldn't be goin' to Raven-wood."

"Why not?"

"Bad doin's up there. Bad doin's. I should know."

"Leave her be, Ida." Cully had come back and was tug-ging gently on the stooping shoulder.

"She's a nice girl." The old woman was still leaning in the window, but she'd let go of Laura. She seemed to be fumbling in her pocket. "You take this, child." Her hand was trembling slightly as she held out an ivory-colored crystal shot through with gold streaks. About an inch and a half long, it was shaped like a cross.

"It's a good-luck piece, a fairy cross," Ida answered Laura's unspoken question. "Go on, now. Take it. Maybe it'll keep you out of trouble."

Wanting to get away from this bizarre scene and not sure what else to do, Laura plucked the crystal out of the old woman's grasp. It felt warm and smooth in her fingers.

Ida straightened. "You take care."

Laura nodded uncertainly. In the next moment, she dumped the fairy cross onto the passenger seat, turned the key in the ignition and pressed her foot to the accelerator. With a screech of gravel and a jerk, the car shot out of the gas station. She didn't understand what had just happened, but it seemed important to put as much distance as possible between herself and the station.

It was strange. At first, the people had been friendly. Then everything had changed—when she'd mentioned Ravenwood.

A creepy feeling washed over her, the same creepy feel-ing that had been haunting her all the way from Baltimore. Her foot eased up on the accelerator, and she pulled over to the shoulder of the road, strangely uncertain about continuing the trip. Slumping forward, she wrapped her arms around the wheel. What was she getting herself into? Was something funny going on at the estate where she was supposed to spend the weekend?

Perhaps she should listen to the old woman's warning, turn around and go back where she belonged. Just then, a flash of light caught the corner of her eye, and she turned her head. The crystal. What had Ida called it? A fairy cross?

The gold vein running down the center had captured the sunlight like a stained glass ornament hanging in a window. Feeling a strange compulsion, Laura stroked a tentative finger across the smooth surface. The stone had felt warm before. Now it was hot, probably from the sun. Picking up the talisman, she turned it back and forth, watching the gold vein shimmer in the light. The crystal was shaped like a perfect little cross, with the four arms of equal length. It was intriguing and beautiful. Was it also valuable? Maybe she should return it to the old woman. But she didn't want to go back to the gas station. And she couldn't bear the idea of giving up the charm.

Laura continued to rotate the crystal, almost mesmerized by the light dancing and quivering in the depth of the strange trinket. It seemed to tug at her in some curious, unexplained way. At the same time, it had a calming effect on her frazzled nerves.

On Monday, she'd have to show the charm to Sabrina and see if she'd ever heard of a fairy cross. Sabrina Barkley had opened a herb-and-dried-flower shop off the lobby of 43 Light Street. Laura had stopped in a number of times to buy pomander balls and fresh basil, and she and Sabrina had gotten into some fascinating conversations about the uses and history of herbs. Sabrina also seemed to know a lot about new-age stuff, too. Maybe she could explain something about the powers of crystals.

Smiling, Laura closed her fingers around the cross, imagining for a moment that it pulsed in her hand. It did seem to have some sort of power—at least, to make her feel more confident. Or perhaps that was simply the strength of the old woman's suggestion. She'd sounded so earnest when she'd said it would bring good luck. After slipping the little talisman into the zipper compartment of her purse, Laura pulled back onto the road.

About five miles farther on, she spotted a newly painted green-and-white sign incongruously attached to a faded white gatepost. The elegant gold letters said Ravenwood.

Laura peered up the drive but could see nothing except trees. After checking her odometer, she started up the track. Someone had spread a layer of new gravel over old ruts. But the cosmetic application didn't do much for the uphill ride. After she'd jounced along for almost two miles, she still didn't see any signs of habitation. In fact, the lane was losing a battle to the underbrush encroaching from either side.

There was no place to turn around, and the prospect of backing down the mountain was daunting. Rounding a sharp curve, Laura was rewarded with her first sight of the house.

It was a massive stone structure, built on the lines of a baronial castle with diamond-panel windows, turrets, balconies and steep gables decorated with Gothic bargeboards cut in incongruously lacy patterns.

Stopping the car, Laura sat for several minutes, fascinated by the romantic style and the way the disparate combination of elements produced an intriguing harmony. Yet for all its charm, there was something forbidding about the sprawling mansion. Perhaps it was the sheer massiveness of the stone walls that looked as if they might have been built to hide dreadful secrets. No, that was just a silly fancy.

As she cleared the woods, Laura noticed a rectangular

area where several cars were already parked. An Eldorado, a Mercedes, a faded Chevette, and an old but well cared for 280Z. The guest list encompassed a considerable economic range, she surmised as she pulled in between two of the cars. It would be fun to match the people with their vehicles.

She was getting her overnight bag out of the trunk when the arched front door opened and a man came down the stairs, smiling hospitably. Dressed in a three-piece suit with a paisley handkerchief that matched his tie, he managed to cover the distance between them quickly without looking as if he was exerting himself.

"You must be Laura Roswell. I'm Andy Stapleton." His handshake was straight out of an executive salesmanship course—firm but friendly. Unfortunately his diamond ring pinched her hand when he squeezed.

"Nice to meet you," Laura responded automatically, allowing him to take her overnight bag and close the trunk.

"I hope you didn't have any trouble finding us. We're a little off the beaten track."

He swept Laura toward the house as if he were afraid she might change her mind. In truth, she did hang back slightly when she stepped across the threshold and took in the contrast between the bright sunlight outside and the gloomy interior. The effect was heightened by the decor, which carried through with the Gothic theme. The dark woodwork and tiny panes of glass were more oppressive than charming.

"Why does the house have a bad reputation in town?" she asked. Springing a question out of the blue was one of her proven courtroom techniques. It often elicited a revealing answer. This afternoon she felt as if the entrance hall had swallowed up her voice.

"The house was leased by a Baltimore industrialist who had extensive renovations done. When he went bankrupt, he had a lot of outstanding bills with local merchants and contractors.''

The explanation was plausible, but the pat delivery made Laura wonder if Stapleton had had the answer ready all along, just in case one of the investors asked.

Further speculation was cut off by an emphatic male voice that boomed out from a doorway just ahead of them along the hall.

''Never give advice. Sell it. That's what I always say.''

Looking inside, Laura saw that the speaker was a short, rotund man with a florid face who appeared to be in his midsixties. His hair was wavy, thinning and a vivid shade of red that had to have come out of a bottle.

He was standing under a brass chandelier and addressing a tiny, gray-haired woman seated on a wine red velvet couch. But when he sensed the movement in the doorway, he turned.

''Laura!'' he greeted her like a long-lost daughter. Crossing the room, he squeezed her in a bear hug and then stood back to give her a closer inspection. ''Darlin', I'd recognize that blond hair and those blue eyes anywhere. You're the spittin' image of your old dad.''

She stared at him, feeling as if she were acting in a movie for which she didn't know the script.

''It's Uncle Tim. Or at least that's what you used to call me when you were a wee mite and I bounced you on my knee. I'm Timothy O'Donnell.'' He turned to include the woman on the couch. ''And this is Martha Swayzee, another of the old gang.''

Laura crossed the room and shook the old woman's hand. It was dry as a starched doily and about as resilient.

''We were so sorry to hear about your father, dear. It's so tragic to die alone, cut off from your friends and family,'' Martha murmured. ''Too bad your mother wouldn't have him back when he tried to reconcile with her.''

Before Laura could dredge up a response, the old woman was rattling on. "How is your mother, anyway?"

"She died several years ago."

"I'm sorry to hear it. Such a long-suffering woman. We'll get a chance to talk later, dear, and you can fill me in on all the details of your divorce."

"Umm," Laura responded noncommittally, unconsciously backing away.

Andy touched her shoulder. "Why don't I show you your room so you can freshen up."

Laura followed him gratefully down the hall. When they were out of earshot, he leaned closer. "Martha is quite an old busybody. Don't say anything to her you wouldn't want to see on the front page of the *Baltimore Sun*."

"Don't worry, I won't." The confident promise belied the agitation churning in Laura's chest. She hadn't thought about the other investors when she'd decided to come. Now she realized that at least some of them had been close friends of her father's.

Laura had always told herself she wasn't the least bit interested in what Rex Roswell had done after deserting his family. But her mother's accounts of his defection had never included a chapter on attempted reconciliation. Was she going to hear the other side of the story, Laura wondered as she climbed the circular stairs that wound through one of the turrets.

Stapleton ushered her past a door at the top and down another long hall. They took another turn before he stopped in front of a door, inserted a key in the lock, and stepped aside so she could enter the room beyond.

Inside, the furniture was antique, but the moss-green-and-peach carpet, upholstery and wallpaper were new. The wall opposite the bed was covered with elaborately carved paneling.

"The ladies have private baths," Andy said as he set her

suitcase on the stand under the window. "The gents are going to have to share."

"I'm sure I'll be very comfortable."

"Remember, we'll be serving high tea in about twenty minutes."

Alone at last, Laura sat on the bed for a moment, but got up again quickly. The room was pretty enough and should have made her feel welcome. Instead, she was edgy. Probably because she was wondering if Martha was going to be the only unpleasant surprise, she told herself as she hung her dresses in the closet. Yet she knew that wasn't all of it. Something about the chamber filled her with a sense of anticipation and dread—the way she felt in the seconds before a judge rendered his decision.

The bureau drawers were a bit musty, so after hanging her dresses in the closet, she left the rest of her things in the overnight bag. But she had too much energy to rest. Instead, she wandered around the room, picking up knick-knacks and putting them down again in different places, as if the new arrangement were somehow more suitable. She didn't touch the fruit basket ASDC had left. But she moved the statue of Psyche and Cupid from the dresser to the nightstand and the ceramic flowers from the nightstand to the shelf along the paneled wall where she paused to trace the garland pattern carved into the wood. It was delicate and beautiful, the craftsmanship of a bygone era.

She had started to move the overstuffed chair away from the window when she stopped herself in midpush, wondering what had gotten into her. She wasn't the kind of person who rearranged other people's belongings.

Shaking her head, she went to wash up. The renovation hadn't extended to the bathroom. The black-and-white tiles were cracked in several places and the faucets moaned when she turned them on.

After changing into her raspberry knit dress, Laura freshened her makeup. Locking the door behind her, she stepped into the hallway again. In the waning late-afternoon light, the long corridor was dark and gloomy, and her imagination conjured up the image of a woman holding a candle. Either Stapleton *should* have given out candles to the guests, or he could have put in higher wattage bulbs, she thought as she made her way down the hall. Everything was ghostly quiet, except for the creaking of the floorboards. It was just her own feet making them squeak, Laura assured herself. Yet the farther she got from her room, the less able she was to shake the eerie feeling that someone was following her—almost breathing down her neck, in fact. When she spun around to look, no one was there, although she did see a flicker of light, as if a door had silently opened and closed.

All at once, Laura couldn't keep herself from quickening her steps. However, when she came to the turn she and Stapleton had taken, she hesitated. She'd never had a great sense of direction and she wasn't sure where to find the stairs. Although both ends of the hall looked identical, instinct urged her toward the right. As she hurried along the passage, she strained her ears, trying to catch some hint of conversation from below. But the mansion was so large, she might as well have been alone. She was almost running by the time she reached what she hoped was the entrance to the stairs.

When she grasped the knob and pulled, the door creaked open on rusty hinges. At the same time, she was almost physically assaulted by an unpleasant odor that seemed to be composed of charred wood, mold and something indistinguishable but repugnant.

Realizing she'd made a mistake, Laura was about to draw back and slam the door. Some impulse she couldn't identify compelled her to take a tentative step and then another into the dark interior. A cold wind blew from somewhere in the darkness, making her shiver, and she thought she caught a faint whistling sound that set her teeth on edge. As she put one foot before the other, she was seized with a sense of unreality. It was almost as if some unnamed force were drawing her forward against her will.

Reality slammed back into her as a Hulk Hogan-sized hand clamped down on her shoulder. Laura's heart stopped, and the breath froze in her lungs.

"I'd stay out of there if I were you," a whiskey-smooth voice advised.

For a moment, she was paralyzed. Then she whirled around to find herself confronting the owner of the outsized hand. He was blocking what little light came down the hall and she couldn't see him well. She sensed, however, that the body was as large and sturdy as the hand.

Although she wasn't a short woman, this man towered over her. When she didn't move or speak, he pulled her back with surprising gentleness for someone so large. Then he reached to close the door. As his body brushed by hers, Laura caught a quick impression of powerful thighs and well-honed muscles under his jeans and nubby sports jacket. His after-shave was a no-nonsense masculine scent.

"Whoever forgot to block this entrance off is two bricks short of a load," he said as he pushed the door firmly shut. "I stumbled in there, too, thinkin' it was another way out."

She couldn't quite picture him stumbling. "I was looking for the stairs."

"You'll have more luck at the other end of the hall."

When he stepped back and gestured, Laura got a better view. His face wasn't pretty—but it was rugged and square and certain of its basic values. She imagined a lot of women would find the combination appealing. But she wasn't going to acknowledge the interested look in his dark eyes, not when she was feeling foolish at having the wits scared out of her. Besides, she was no longer attracted to male self-confidence. And whatever else you could say about him, this guy was very confident and all male—from the natural waves of his chestnut hair to the tips of his size-fourteen Reeboks.

"Thanks for your help." Breezing past him, she started for the other end of the hall at a rapid clip.

He followed. With his long strides, he didn't have any problem keeping up.

"You can't be one of the original investors because you're under sixty-five," he observed in a conversational tone.

"I inherited a share from my father," she tossed over her shoulder.

"Then we've got something in common. I inherited mine, too."

"Umm."

She effectively squelched further conversation until they reached the ground floor, where Andy Stapleton emerged from the drawing room.

"Ms. Roswell. Mr. Wallace. I was just about to send a search party."

"Ah, the two eagerly awaited ingredients." The observation came from a wiry man who'd followed Stapleton into the hall. At first, Laura would have guessed that he was in his late forties or early fifties. As she drew closer, she decided that he was probably older—but very well preserved.

"Sam Pendergrast." He held out his hand.

Laura shook it. So did the Wallace character. Pendergrast's arm was hard and muscular, as if he worked out regularly. From the way he looked her over, Laura also got the distinct impression that one of the ways he stayed young was by keeping company with women half his age. However, in this case, she had the feeling that the man couldn't decide which of the newcomers he wanted to talk to more.

She was both a bit relieved and a bit irritated when he turned to the giant who stood beside her.

"Jake Wallace. Ohio State. The Buckeyes. Your team won the Rose Bowl, didn't they? And then you made All-American and went on to the Broncos."

"It's nice to be remembered," Wallace returned modestly.

"A lot of football players wait too long to retire. You opted out a little too soon."

"I—uh—decided the odds weren't too good on knee surgery."

"Damn shame. But football's loss is journalism's gain."

"Thank you."

Laura had been following the conversation. She'd never heard of Jake Wallace, but she gathered he was an ex-football player of some notoriety. Now he was some sort of journalist, although she was pretty sure she'd never read him.

Pendergrast led the famous Jake Wallace into the parlor, where Tim O'Donnell joined the admiring circle of men around him. They began quizzing him about the Redskins' chances for the play-offs.

Laura had no interest in joining the Jake Wallace fan club. She was left with the choice of looking as if she were sulking in the corner or approaching Martha Swayzee, who was sipping a cup of tea beside a table on which a maid was setting out little sandwiches and scones.

At least it wasn't going to be a one-on-one gossip session. Martha was talking to another woman of about the same vintage.

It was interesting to see the way different people aged, Laura thought. Martha had dried up like a milkweed pod, while her friend was fighting a rear-guard action. Like Tim

O'Donnell, she dyed her hair. It was too dark to be flattering to the deep lines grooved in her face, although she'd tried to compensate with a liberal application of makeup. The pink cheeks, blue eyelids and red lips were garish rather than youthful. Her dress, too, was flamboyant. And the whole effect was emphasized by a pair of gold party slippers.

"Laura," Martha called out. "Come over and meet Emma."

Something about the tone of voice put Laura on the alert. The watchful look in Emma's eyes was another indication that the two other women knew something she didn't.

"I'm Laura Roswell," she murmured, wondering what had possessed her to drive up here from Baltimore. The weekend certainly wasn't turning out the way she'd anticipated.

"Emma Litchfield."

"Doesn't she look just like Rex?" Martha asked.

"There is a resemblance."

"The eyes. The hair color. The shape of her face," Martha continued. "Of course, you can see some of her mother, too."

"Really, you don't have to prattle on." Emma's voice was quiet, but her words put an abrupt stop to the other woman's critique.

"I take it most of the investors knew each other," Laura said as she poured herself a cup of tea.

"Oh, yes. We were such good friends," Martha answered. "But you know how it is. People go their separate ways. And at our age, they're more likely to be written up in the obituary column than in the gossip column. It's a shame Rex and Arthur couldn't be here. Then we'd have a real reunion. Arthur was Jake's uncle. But then, it is nice to meet you two young people."

The men had drifted toward the tea and food and had

begun helping themselves with more enthusiasm than the ladies. But they were less adept than the women at balancing both cups and plates of little sandwiches and miniature pastries.

"Well, let's all pull up seats and get comfortable," Andy suggested, bringing up side chairs and arranging them around the oriental rug.

He escorted Emma toward a settee that had been pulled up under the brass chandelier, but she shook her head. "A straight chair is better for my back, young man."

Sam took the settee. Laura found herself not so subtly maneuvered into sitting next to Jake on the couch. How sweet, she thought. Everybody probably thinks I'm just dying to hear about his exploits with the NFL.

When the guests were settled, Andy cleared his throat. "I thought I might start outlining the opportunity that's become available to the Ravenwood investors. After twenty years of tax write-offs, you finally have a chance to make a tidy profit on land that hasn't appreciated in ten years."

"Why the sudden change in the picture?" Jake asked, leaning back and stretching out his left leg.

"The shortage of recreational land closer to the city. Progress is finally moving out this way."

"Then why wouldn't it be better for us to hold on to the property and develop it ourselves?" Tim asked.

"It might be, if you had the monetary resources and the expertise to—" Andy never got to present the rest of his argument.

Laura was aware of a loud rattle overhead, followed by a blurred motion.

The brass chandelier had broken loose and was plummeting from the ceiling.

Chapter Three

A tenth of a second later, the chandelier crashed onto the settee. Tipping and swaying, the heavy light fixture balanced for a moment on the cushion, inches from where Sam had been sitting, and then toppled off onto the floor with an ominous thud.

But Laura caught only a brief impression of what was happening. Before the chandelier had stopped swaying, two hundred and twenty pounds of weight forced her back into the pillows of the couch. Jake had twisted around, folded her into his arms and interposed his solid body between her and the falling light fixture. She felt safe there. If you needed a man's protection, Jake Wallace was definitely the one to pick. Then, to her chagrin, she realized she was clinging to the front of his shirt. Unclenching her fingers, she tried to push herself away.

He didn't relax his hold.

"Give it a few seconds, honey. Let's see if anything else besides plaster dust falls out of the ceiling."

For a moment she relaxed against him. When she realized she was enjoying the intimate contact, she twisted around to see what was happening in the rest of the room. Sam had leaped from his seat like a sprinter at the starter's gun. Now he stood shaking and white faced beside the settee. "Jumping Moses!"

Andy rushed to his side, his features an almost comic mixture of incredulity and horror. "Are you all right?"

"Yeah. But I hope you got a guarantee from the people who did your renovation."

"Mercy me!" Martha's brittle exclamation was followed by a squeak. "I believe Emma's fainted."

"I know first aid. I'd better see what I can do," Laura offered.

After another cautious look at the ceiling, Jake released her. Swiftly, she crossed the room to the woman who had slumped forward. With her body bent, the pale skin of her scalp showed through the too-dark hair, making her head look like a large egg covered by a thin bird's nest.

"What—" Emma pushed herself to a sitting position, knocking off one of her gold slippers. When she saw Laura bending over her, fear flickered in her eyes and she cringed.

"It's all right. I only want to help you," Laura murmured.

The older woman blinked.

"Just relax," Laura soothed as she lifted Emma's delicate wrist and took her pulse. Peripherally, she was aware that the attention of everybody in the room was now focused on the two of them. Trying to shut out any distractions, she concentrated on counting pulse beats. But another part of her mind was silently observing the woman she was attending, trying to figure out why Emma had reacted to her so oddly.

Tim started to cough, and Laura's attention, as well as everyone else's, was distracted. Red-faced, he took a gulp from his cup of cold tea. "That's better. Just my corksacking emphysema kicking up."

"It looks like you should have had a doctor on call for this little get-together," Jake said to Andy.

"Folks, I'm so sorry this happened. Believe me, if there are any medical bills associated with this unfortunate incident, ASDC will be glad to cover them.'' Andy checked his watch. "Let's postpone dinner until seven. That will give us a chance to clean up and you a chance to unwind. You might want to take a walk around the grounds, they're lovely this time of year." Then his placid expression became troubled, as if he wished he hadn't made the suggestion. "Just don't wander too far afield. I wouldn't want anyone tumbling into the old ravine."

"I wouldn't think of it." The acerbic remark came from Emma, who had just pushed herself shakily to her feet. Sam took her arm to steady her.

"You all right?" he asked.

"As well as can be expected." She turned to Laura. "Thank you, my dear."

"I didn't do much."

"It's the thought that counts."

Members of the group were still talking about how lucky they'd been that no one was hurt as they filed out of the room. Jake, who had unfinished business in the drawing room, hung back until the room emptied. Most of the other guests opted for a rest.

Laura decided to take Andy up on the suggestion of a walk, particularly since the fresh air might help her think about Emma. In her work, she enjoyed putting bits and pieces of information and testimony together to come up with a complete picture. She was pretty sure she'd never met Emma before. But she had the unshakable feeling there was something about the woman she should know.

The sun had started its descent toward the west, and the air was a bit nippy. Laura walked briskly to keep warm, deep in thought as she followed a path away that led into the woods.

"Hey, I wouldn't go that way if I were you."

She turned to find Jake rapidly closing the distance between them. His walk had looked agile. When he put on a bit of speed, she could tell that his left knee didn't function quite properly. He'd said something about surgery. Maybe he hadn't gotten it, after all. Or it hadn't worked.

For an unguarded instant, she was glad he'd sought her out. Then she was annoyed with her response to him. "What's wrong with this path?" she challenged.

"It leads straight to the ravine Andy was warning everyone about."

"How do you know?"

"I checked out the grounds."

"You seem to have done a lot of exploring." Laura continued in the direction she'd been walking—wishing she weren't so conscious of the man beside her. But why shouldn't she be conscious of him? He took up more than half the path.

"I like to get the lay of the land when I'm in a new situation. That way there are fewer surprises," Jake said, answering her spoken question.

His tone of voice made Laura cock her head to one side as if she'd just come up with an entirely new thread of logic in the middle of a cross-examination. But she didn't say anything.

He slanted her an appraising look. "Something funny is going on around here."

"Oh?"

"I had a look at the chandelier cord. It was cut."

Laura stopped dead in her tracks. "You must be mistaken."

"No mistake. I had a look at it after everybody left the room. Too bad the bulbs weren't lit when we first arrived, then I'd have some idea when it was done."

"It's an old house. It could have happened anytime. Maybe some kids did it for a prank last Halloween," Laura suggested.

"Or someone could have wanted it to fall in the middle of that meeting."

"What are you implying?" Laura asked carefully. Talk about letting your imagination run away with you. Maybe the Gothic mansion looming behind them was having the same effect on him that it was on her.

"I'm not implying anything. I'm just stating facts."

"Suppositions."

"Sam Pendergrast almost got hit," he continued.

"*Almost* is the operative word."

"You sound like a lawyer."

"I *am* a lawyer."

"I won't hold that against you."

"Thanks," Laura returned dryly. "Have you discussed any of your suspicions with Mr. Stapleton?"

"He could have been the one who cut the wire. He was leading Emma to the settee before she said she wanted a straight chair."

"Are you making accusations now?"

"Nope. I'm just being cautious."

"So why have you spilled the beans to me? Maybe I snuck up here yesterday and did it," Laura suggested, wondering if he could fit that into his little scenario.

To her surprise, Jake threw back his head and laughed. "Now you're tryin' to do me one better." Then his expression sobered. "But it's not a joke. I'm serious enough to keep my eyes open and watch my back while I'm up here at this little get-together. I suggest you do the same thing. And since other people could be looking out the window, I also suggest we amble on back to the house as if we've just been getting to know each other better—not discussing attempted murder."

"Murder?" The man must be paranoid. Or trying to scare her.

But what if, somehow, he were right? The chandelier was

pretty heavy. What if it had fallen on Sam or Emma? Or
someone else? Would the victim have survived.

Victim. Murder. Laura shivered and peered into the gathering gloom that suddenly seemed to press in around her.
It wasn't hard to imagine shadowy forms slipping through
the trees. No, it was just a trick of the fading light. While
they'd been talking, the sun had been setting, and if you
let your imagination run wild, you might be able to convince yourself of all sorts of frightening things.

As if sensing her uneasiness, Jake moved in closer and
slung his arm over her shoulder. In her present condition,
it was tempting to burrow into his warmth, to let him protect her the way he had when the chandelier had fallen.

Yet a more rational part of her mind knew he was the
one who had helped maneuver her into her present state.
Besides, she didn't like the way he kept offering protection
and she kept accepting. It was dangerous to depend on anybody except herself. If she'd learned anything in life, she'd
learned that.

Turning her head slightly, she gave him a considering
look. His speculations had made her uneasy, all right. But
suppose he'd had some ulterior motive? He could even
have made the whole thing up to give himself another
chance to get close. She had the feeling the man wasn't
above taking advantage of a favorable situation when it
came to male-female relations.

He saw her watching him and gave her a lazy smile, as
if they really had just come out here to get to know each
other better. When a tiny answering smile flickered on her
lips, he gave her arm a little squeeze.

Aghast that she'd encouraged him, she hastened to set
things straight. "Don't get any ideas, Mr. Wallace."

"What ideas did you have in mind?" he asked inno-
cently. Before Laura could answer—or pull away—they almost bumped into Andy Stapleton, who had rounded the

curve in front of them at something between a walk and a trot.

Jake dropped his hand a proprietary couple of inches lower on Laura's shoulder. "Nice evenin'."

Andy took several panting breaths before answering. "I saw you two wander off down this way a while ago and started to get worried."

"We're fine," Jake replied easily. "Just headin' home to get ready for dinner."

Andy turned and accompanied, or rather, shepherded them back to the house. Laura would have broken away from Jake, but he held her clamped against his side.

"Any ideas on what happened to the chandelier?" he asked in a conversational tone.

"Why—uh—no."

Jake shot Laura a look that said, "He's not being straight with us."

She nodded imperceptibly.

The real-estate promoter didn't follow them up the circular stairs to the second level. Laura was preparing to make a quick getaway to her room when Jake put a restraining hand on her shoulder.

"I think you can drop the act now," she said, in his ear.

"Act? Oh, I think we're being honest with each other. I'm attracted to you. You're attracted to me. Let's see what develops."

"Nothing's going to develop."

"If you say so, honey. But play it cool. I think someone is peeking at us from one of the rooms down the hall."

Laura swung partially around. Following the direction of Jake's gaze, she saw a door ease shut. It was probably Martha, getting a jump start on the Ravenwood gossip. But there was no way to be sure right now. And the best course of action was to make sure there was nothing for her to gossip about. With a curt goodbye, Laura took her leave of Jake Wallace.

A half hour later, Laura stood at the window, looking out as the last pink tinge of the sunset faded from view. Nightfall had intensified her feeling of uneasiness. And in spite of her best efforts, she couldn't get Jake out of her mind. It wasn't just the sexual undercurrent flowing between them—she was perfectly competent to deal with that, she assured herself. It was his attempted murder theory that kept pushing its way back into her mind. Besides, more than just Jake's suggestions had her spooked. There was a brooding atmosphere around this place that gave her the creeps. She had half a mind to sweep her clothes back into her suitcase and head for home. Except that it would be a long, dark ride. And the first part would be down the overgrown, twisting road that led up the mountain. It wouldn't be much fun to negotiate now.

Unwilling to let herself feel trapped, she drew the curtains. There was probably a logical explanation for what had happened to the chandelier. Maybe Andy Stapleton was simply being evasive because he was trying to smooth over the mess. After all, he'd gone to a lot of trouble to arrange the weekend, and things weren't going the way he'd hoped.

LAURA GAVE Jake a cautious look when he took the seat next to her at the oval dining table. He responded with one of his lazy smiles and then began to chat amiably with Martha, who was sitting across the table.

As Laura unfolded her napkin, she watched her dinner partner out of the corner of her eye. His easy conversation almost convinced her that she'd imagined their talk on the path to the ravine. Except that she remembered very distinctly that they'd been discussing murder. Now a person wouldn't know Jake Wallace had a concern in the world, except a good dinner and a little light flirtation. *The man must be an expert at concealing tension when he wanted you to think he was relaxed,* she thought.

Her attention was distracted as Tim, who was now a bit unsteady on his feet, dropped into the vacant seat to her left. After a whiff of his breath as he leaned over to grab the basket of rolls, Laura was certain he'd spent the early evening drinking.

To the discomfort of the group, he began to make a concerted effort to liven up the proceedings with a string of not very funny jokes. At the lukewarm response, he upped the ante. Sober, he'd been almost charming; in his cups, he wasn't very appealing.

"Give a husband enough rope and he'll skip," he quipped in response to a comment about a Maryland politician who'd recently left his wife.

There was silence around the table. Martha shot a knowing look at Emma, who lifted her chin defiantly.

"Don't get your feathers ruffled, Emmie," Sam muttered.

What were they really talking about? Parts of the weekend conversation were so confusing that Laura felt as if she'd come into a play after intermission—and only the senior citizens had been there for the first act.

"Or give him enough rope and he'll say he's tied up at the office," Tim said, trying another variation.

"The office. Yes, tell us what it's like to work at the *Baltimore Sun,*" Sam asked Jake in a pointed attempt to change the subject. Jake obliged with a tale about how the automated interoffice communications system was driving him crazy.

Laura felt some of the tension ease out of her shoulders as she listened. Jake was a good storyteller. And in a few minutes, he had everybody chuckling at his battle with the new five-hundred-page instruction book.

Laura was just taking a sip of wine when she felt a hand

brush her left knee. When she glanced up at Tim, the expression in his bloodshot eyes didn't change. Maybe the familiar touch had simply been an accident. But five minutes later, the caress was repeated.

It would serve the drunk old geezer right if she slapped his hand under the table, Laura thought. But she didn't really want to make a scene. Instead, she turned her back and slid her chair closer to Jake, hoping to convey to Tim that if he was going to keep bothering her, he'd have to deal with the ex-football player.

Jake gave her a warm look. To her disquiet, she felt answering warmth suffuse her nerve endings. Jake Wallace had a way of making her feel more like a woman than she had in a long time. But he probably had the knack for making a woman feel special. That didn't mean getting involved with him was smart. Not when the thought of letting her vulnerabilities show was still so scary.

Still, they continued to stare at each other. To her chagrin, she realized the conversation around the table had stopped and everyone was taking in the exchange.

Then Sam came to her rescue. "So, Jake, what do you think about women reporters in the men's locker room?"

Jake reluctantly pulled his gaze away from Laura. "Women have a right to interview the players. Just so they don't beat me out of a scoop," he quipped.

"Well, I think it's an invasion of privacy," Tim chimed in loudly. "How would you have liked to have to look over your shoulder every time you dropped your towel?"

"It wouldn't be a problem if you set up a special interview room—and make the male and female reporters use it. That would give everyone the same advantage." Jake went on to give a thoughtful analysis of reporter rights versus player privacy.

Laura found herself listening with interest. It would have been easier if she could have dismissed him as a dork-brained former jock who'd weaseled his way into a reporting job. But he was actually quite sharp, with an analytical mind. She found that as appealing as the rugged planes of his face and the way his long lashes framed his dark eyes.

Why was she letting herself think of him this way? She was struggling to change gears mentally when Andy broke into the conversation.

"Well, this is all very interesting," he said, "but shall we have our coffee in the library while we get ready for the presentation?"

"Only if there's no chandelier," Sam remarked soberly.

The developer shot him a quelling look. "I've done a thorough safety check of the room," Andy assured them as he pushed back his chair. The others followed him down the hall and into the book-lined chamber.

Andy had set up a screen and slide projector. After dimming the lights, he went into his act. His voice was smooth. Only the way he rotated his diamond ring with his thumb betrayed any nervousness.

First, there were pictures of the Ravenwood mansion and the surrounding real estate, accompanied by a spiel extolling the virtues of the tract for recreational and vacation-home development. Next came estimates of costs, in stages—starting with zoning approval and perc tests and ending with roads and possible municipal water service.

In a dark corner of the room, Tim was slumped back in his chair, snoring gently.

But Laura found herself listening with heightened attention. Was she understanding Andy correctly, she wondered. She'd thought he wanted to buy the shares in Ravenwood, but that wasn't exactly what he seemed to be saying now.

Around her, she could sense a certain restlessness in the audience. Apparently she wasn't the only one getting the mixed message.

"Would you mind turning on the lights so we could

talk," Sam's voice finally cut through the thickening atmosphere like a blunt knife parting soft cheese.

"If you'll bear with me, I'm almost through with the slides," Andy said.

"I'd rather have some straight talk," Sam persisted. Then in a huffy voice he said, "And for God's sake, turn on the lights so I can see what the hell I'm doing."

At his tone, Laura turned to look at the man. Did Sam suffer from night blindness, she wondered. A man like him, who was so obviously into physical fitness, would probably consider the infirmity a sign of advancing age. And that might make him grouchy.

But he wasn't the only one of the old crowd who was out of sorts. Other voices were raised. Sighing, Andy crossed the room and switched on the lights. For a moment, everybody blinked in the unaccustomed brightness.

"Young man, are you asking each of us to risk additional money in the hopes that this tract of land can be developed?" Emma asked the question that had leaped into Laura's mind.

"I thought you—" Andy looked at her in confusion before abruptly changing tack. "That's a rather blunt way to put it."

"Is it a fair description of the situation?" Emma persisted.

Andy cleared his throat. "In the very early stages of a major project, there are certain minimal costs—"

"Cut the phoney-baloney," Tim advised, as if he'd been paying strict attention to the presentation instead of snoozing. Apparently he'd awakened in time to catch the drift of the protests. Or maybe he was making a lucky guess. "Did you ask us up here to convince us to pour more of our hard-earned money down a rat hole?"

"It's not a rat hole. In today's market, it's a very sound investment decision."

Martha stood up. "If you'll excuse me, I believe I've heard enough."

"Where are you going?" Andy asked the gray-haired woman.

"Up to my room."

Others were standing now. Andy moved rapidly around the room, talking to the investors, but it was clear that he'd lost their confidence. In exasperation, he turned back to Emma, who shrugged. What was going on between them, Laura wondered.

When Jake stood with his hands in his pockets, Laura could see that they were balled into fists. He hadn't joined the protest, but apparently he was angry about having been dragged up here under false pretenses. Had he been counting on making some money from the deal, she wondered.

As the developer approached them, Jake gave him a cold stare and Laura shook her head. Instead of attempting any more argument, he turned away.

Jake muttered something under his breath that Laura was glad she couldn't hear. "I could use a drink," he added. "Our host left a gift-wrapped bottle of bourbon in my room."

"Bourbon. The women got fruit baskets. At least, I did."

"Sometimes there's an advantage in being one of the guys. Care to come up and drown your sorrows?"

"No thanks."

He gave her a boyish smile that she was sure most women would have found irresistible. "Oh, come on. We might as well salvage something from the weekend."

For just a moment, she was tempted to accept the invitation. He was right. They were attracted to each other. Yet she was afraid to take a chance on him. If she ever let another man get close to her, it would be one cautious step at a time. But if she went up to Jake's room, he'd assume she was agreeing to a lot more than a drink.

"I think I'll follow Martha's example and salvage a good night's sleep."

"You sure do blow hot one minute and cold the next."

"I'm sorry," she said before turning away and heading rapidly toward the steps.

She would go to bed early, Laura told herself as she reached her door. That way it wouldn't be hard to get up at the crack of dawn and leave before anything else happened. The locals back at the gas station had been right about her trip to Ravenwood, even if they hadn't known any of the reasons. She should have turned around and gone home as soon as she'd left the pump.

For the past few hours, Laura had erased the disturbing incident from her mind. But now, recalling Ida's word made her remember the fairy cross.

It was for protection, she'd said. How silly. Laura didn't believe in good-luck pieces.

Nevertheless, before she could examine her motives, she hurried to the dresser where she'd left her purse and fumbled inside. She couldn't even remember which compartment she'd shoved the cross into, and several moments passed before she located it. A sense of profound relief washed over her as her fingers closed around the hard, bevelled stone. It was the same way she felt when she thought she'd lost her keys or her wallet and then found where it had dropped. For some unexplained reason, she'd half expected that the little charm would turn up missing. Drawing it out, she held it up to the light the way she'd done in the car, twisting it so that the gold vein winked and twinkled. Then, feeling a bit foolish, she transferred the crystal from her purse to her overnight bag.

Next, she locked her door, listening with satisfaction as the latch clicked. There were worse ways to spend an evening than in her own company.

In the bathroom she began to draw a tub full of water,

profoundly grateful that she didn't have to go down the hall to use the facilities. That was one advantage the ladies had over the gentlemen—even if they hadn't been gifted with a bottle of bourbon to compensate for the disappointing anticlimax of Andy Stapleton's presentation.

The hot bath did wonders for Laura's frayed nerves. Somewhere between the lavender bath oil and scented soap she'd brought, she decided that Jake Wallace was the kind of man who could take care of himself. She also began to construct a philosophical view of the land developer's ploy.

So she wasn't going to make a million dollars on her father's western Maryland investment. Well, she hadn't known until a few years ago that she even had a share in the property, and she certainly didn't need the money. There was no reason not to just sit tight and wait until a better offer came along.

Relaxed, Laura climbed out of the tub, dried off with a fluffy white towel and slipped into her silk pajamas. She may have been having trouble sleeping lately, but it wasn't going to be a problem tonight, she decided after nestling under the wool blanket and soft sheet. She was even too tired to read the book she'd brought along. Ten minutes after she'd turned off the light, she was asleep, unaware of the phantoms hovering in the darkness, ready to seize her when she gave up conscious control of her mind.

JAKE HAD NEVER BEEN the kind of guy who liked to drink alone. Nevertheless, as his solitary evening wore on, he kept glancing up from his Tom Clancy novel and looking at the bottle of bourbon on the dresser.

It was no wonder he couldn't concentrate on Clancy's high-tech toys. The whole trip had been a real fiasco. Because he'd wanted to get his hands on some cash, he'd been dumb enough to get his hopes up about Ravenwood. Then, after the chandelier business, he'd started wondering if the whole weekend was some sort of bizarre setup. Maybe part of a ploy to get a few of the investors to drop out so the rest could strike a new deal and split the increased profits. Or was someone really trying to kill off members of the group? He'd made the suggestion to Laura to see how she'd react, but he wasn't sure things had really gone that far. Or who would be doing it. On the other hand, he did know something for sure: the ASDC land-development deal had gone sour. That had been a major disappointment.

And then there was his near miss with the beautiful lawyer. At dinner, he'd gotten the distinct impression that he and Ms. Roswell were going to get to know each other a lot better after Stapleton's presentation.

Okay, so that hadn't worked out, either. So what? One woman was as good as another. If he was looking for company, there were half a dozen numbers in his black book he could call.

Of course, that argument was a damn lie, he admitted as his large fist clamped around the paperback novel, twisting it permanently out of shape. Unfortunately, one woman wasn't as good as another. For a moment Jake squeezed his eyes shut and pressed his fist against his forehead. His wife's sweet, heart-shaped face shimmered in his inner vision—the way she'd looked on their wedding day. Sometimes, it was hard to remember how pretty she'd been before she'd gotten so sick. Sometimes, all he could recall was the gaunt, haunted face of the last few weeks when it had torn him apart to think about what she was going through.

He'd loved Holly so much. They'd been a matched pair. But he was never going to risk that kind of pain or terror or guilt again. He'd been a basket case after she'd died. And it had taken him a long time to get back to any kind of normal life. Once he had, he'd kept things simple. He liked women. He knew how to show them a good time.

The trick was making sure that the emotions never cut too deep. Because he wasn't willing to risk getting blown away by grief again.

So why was he lying here regretting the near miss with Laura? She was just a pretty blonde who'd crossed his path this weekend. He wanted to believe that. Which meant he'd better not examine his feelings too closely.

What he needed was a good night's sleep before he headed back to Baltimore in the morning. And Andy Stapleton had thoughtfully provided an effective sedative. Getting off the bed, he picked up the bottle of bourbon. He wished he had some ice. Cold water from the bathroom down the hall would have to do.

He'd just climbed back into his jeans and opened his door a crack when he realized someone else was in the hallway. In the dim light, he saw her coming toward him.

It was Laura Roswell. Her long blond hair billowed out behind her as she walked rapidly in his direction. Silky pajamas hugged her shape from the curve of her shoulders down to her gorgeous legs.

Her steps were light, as if her slippered feet were barely touching the floor. As she advanced toward him, he was struck by the odd expression on her pale face. It was intense. Urgent. Obsessed. Not at all the countenance of a woman on her way to a romantic meeting.

"Laura?" he whispered.

He caught the tantalizing scent of lavender as she drew abreast of him. She didn't seem to realize he was there, although that was unlikely, since he'd put down the bottle of bourbon, stepped out in the hall, and was standing almost in her path.

"Laura?" he questioned again.

Again she didn't answer. Now he could see her eyes. They were glazed, flat, unseeing. Yet she moved with unfaltering steps, as if some invisible force were drawing her forward.

Jake felt the hair on his scalp prickle. "What the hell is going on?" he growled.

Laura marched past him in a cloud of silk and lavender. She didn't stop until she was standing in front of the door where he'd found her earlier. When she opened it, the familiar repelling odor wafted out.

The dark cavern beyond was lit only by a few shafts of moonlight from the window at the end of the hall, but Laura's gait didn't falter. Jake's first impulse was to pull her back the way he'd done this afternoon. But he'd had a look around in there after Stapleton had showed him to his room. The floor was safe—at least for fifty feet or so down the hall.

If he stopped her, he wasn't going to find out what she was up to. Instead of interfering, he followed her, repressing a cough as the dead air assaulted his lungs. Laura's steps were purposeful—the steps of a woman who knew exactly where she was going. She halted at the second door on the right, turned the handle and pushed it open. For a second or two, Jake lost her. Speeding up, he gained the doorway and saw her walking across an empty room. When she reached the far wall, she stooped and began prying at one of the floorboards. It came up with a little squeal of protest. Reaching inside, she extracted what looked like a box about the size of a brick. Then she carefully replaced the board, apparently still unaware that Jake was lurking in the shadows.

He took a step forward and the floor groaned under the extra weight of his football player's body.

"Laura, watch out."

It was as if the stuffing had suddenly whooshed out of a giant rag doll. Laura's knees buckled, all the strength deserted her body and she pitched forward, collapsing against him. As he pulled her toward the door, he snatched the box out of her trembling fingers.

Chapter Four

Laura's mind snapped back to some sort of awareness as arms like tree trunks clamped her to an unyielding male body. Shocked, terrified, disoriented, she began to struggle, whipping her head from side to side, balling her hands into fists and raining desperate blows against a broad chest.

Naked arms. A naked chest.

She was trapped in the bedroom. Just like in the dream. Her pursuer had her again. He was going to kill her. She knew that at some gut-wrenching level below conscious thought. Yet even as she opened her mouth to scream, some tiny compartment of her fear-crazed mind realized the cues were all wrong. His body. The wrong size, the wrong shape. His touch. Comforting not rough. It wasn't *him*.

Still, panic bubbled up when a large palm choked off any hope of sound.

"Take it easy, honey. Laura, take it easy. You don't want to bring them all running in here."

The reassuring voice and the hands stroking across her back penetrated the fog in her brain and the hysteria clawing its way up her throat.

"Laura. It's Jake." He trailed a finger against her cheek before lifting his hand away.

"Jake?" His name was a gasp on her lips. "What's happened?'' she asked as she looked up at his face. ''What are you doing in my room? Where's your shirt?''

She heard a deep, masculine chuckle. ''The last thing you need to worry about is my shirt.''

He had unclenched his restraining grip on her shoulders, but he still kept her firmly erect with the pressure of his solid arms around her slender body. It was a good thing. Somehow, she seemed to have lost control of her muscles. They were trembling, and her knees felt too weak to support her weight.

''You're not in your room. You're in the damaged part of the mansion.''

''How did I get here?''

''You walked down the hall and opened the door.''

''That's impossible.''

''You think your room smells like a burned-out mushroom farm?''

She took a breath of the rank air and gagged.

He waited until the spasm passed. ''All right?''

''Yes.''

''Let's get the heck out of here.''

Grasping Laura's ice-cold hand, Jake backed cautiously out of the room, bringing her along with him. At each step, the boards under their feet groaned ominously.

The floor stopped quivering when they reached the relative stability of the hall. At the end of the corridor, Laura could see light shining like a ray of hope from heaven. Jake didn't have to urge her to hurry after him now. When they stepped out into the carpeted corridor, she breathed in a lungful of fresh air. Jake closed the door. Then, before Laura could voice a protest, he opened another door and pulled her inside.

''This is your room!'' she exclaimed.

''Right. Yours is at the other end of the house. Do you want to be seen in the hall with me—dressed like that?''

Laura crossed her arms and grasped her pajama-clad sleeves. At the same time, her gaze riveted to the broad expanse of Jake's naked chest. It was covered with a thick pelt a bit darker than the hair on his head. "No one has to see *us*." She turned and reached for the door handle.

Jake wasn't making any concessions to Miss Manners. He pulled Laura's hand away from the door, dragged her farther into the room and pushed her to a seated position on the bed.

"You're not going anywhere until we have a little talk."

"About what?" She couldn't quite manage to keep her voice steady.

Instead of answering, Jake turned to the double-hung window. Laura followed his gaze to the inky blackness beyond the dimly lit little room. All at once, it was impossible not to feel isolated and vulnerable. Almost as vulnerable as she'd been in the dreams.

As Jake drew the drapes shut with a decisive snap, Laura folded her arms across her chest. When he turned back and began to advance on her, she flattened her shoulders against the headboard. The scream that had come so often to her lips in recent nights hovered in her throat again.

Then with an effort of will, she shook herself out of the fantasy. He wasn't coming for her. He was holding up the box as if it were exhibit A in a courtroom.

As much to avoid his gaze as anything else, Laura carefully examined the exterior. Dull, blackened metal reinforced with brass strips at the corners. A hasp but no lock.

Jake set the chest on the bedside table. When she stroked her finger across the top, she drew a line in soot. This thing had been through the fire.

"Let's see what's inside." Jake pried up the lid using the end of a key as a lever. The top gave a groan of protest but finally yielded.

They were both silent for several seconds as they looked

into the interior. As far as Laura could see, there was nothing here but a pile of charred papers. Jake cursed. "Not your typical buried treasure." He switched his attention back to Laura. "Want to tell me what you were doing sleepwalking in the burned-out part of the house? Or why you knew exactly where this box of trash was hidden under the floorboards." He tapped exhibit A for her inspection.

"I wasn't sleepwalking!"

"What would you call it?"

"I—" Laura's objection had been the automatic denial of a woman who'd never before strayed unaware from her bed in the middle of the night. But it was a fair question and one she couldn't answer. Straining her memory, she cast about for some clue to what had happened. It was no good. The last thing she recalled before regaining consciousness in Jake's arms was snuggling under the bed covers in her room at the other end of the hall.

Blind terror had engulfed her in the moments before she'd realized where she was and who was holding her. And she'd been having trouble holding herself together ever since. Without warning, the terror swept her into its cold embrace once more.

The whole thing was too much. Too much to take. Too much to try to explain, even to herself. Especially to herself.

Laura's muscles began to spasm again, and her teeth started to chatter as if someone had pressed a bowl of ice cubes to the base of her spine.

Just as he'd done when the chandelier had fallen, Jake pulled her close, taking her with him as he leaned back against the headboard. This time, she had no strength to fight him. This time, she knew in some deep, instinctive way that giving solace came naturally to this man.

She might have reached out and anchored herself to the safe harbor of his arms if her muscles had cooperated. In-

stead of clinging, she melted against him, burying her face
in the comforting warmth of his neck.

Her eyelids fluttered closed, and her hands hung limply
at her sides.

"It's all right, honey," he crooned over and over, rock-
ing her tenderly in his arms. Once more, she was struck by
how gently someone so big could handle a woman's body.
Slowly, the words and the solid reassurance he offered
brought her some measure of calm.

"Better?" he asked, sensing the change.

"Some."

Jake gave her a few more minutes. It was strangely
tempting to stay in his embrace again. Perhaps that was
why she pushed herself away.

He gazed at her consideringly. "You still look like you
bumped into Lucifer out there in the corridor. I think you're
going to take me up on that drink I offered you earlier this
evening."

Before she could object, he swung his legs off the bed,
crossed to the dresser and began to open the bottle of bourbon. Laura watched him pour a little of the amber liquid
into two water glasses.

"I don't drink that stuff straight."

"Think of it as medicine—for your nerves." He wrapped
her fingers around one of the glasses.

She didn't take medicine for her nerves. Yet as she
watched him drink, she followed suit—although quite a bit
more cautiously. The bourbon burned her mouth and throat,
and she didn't much like the taste.

Setting his glass on the night stand, Jake leaned back
comfortably against the pillows and put his long legs up
on the spread. He took up more than his share of the double
bed. He also seemed perfectly content with the situation.

Laura was still too unsure of her legs to get up. Wishing
Jake would put on a shirt, wishing he'd opted to sit in the

chair, she lifted up her side of the bedspread and slipped underneath as much from wanting to shield herself from Jake as from the chill. Then she found a tiny corner of the headboard to lean against.

When the man beside her didn't speak, she nervously took several more sips of the bourbon.

Jake drained his drink and began to toy with the glass. She knew he was watching her out of the corner of his eye. "Do you know what happened to you back there?" he finally asked.

She'd been thinking about it. Not just the strange circumstances of waking up and not knowing the wheres and whys. Even more unsettling was the way she'd felt. Afraid. No, terrified with the certain knowledge that some man was going to kill her. Somehow, she knew Jake hadn't triggered the runaway emotion. She also knew she wasn't willing to share the fear with him.

Laura shrugged. "I don't know why I wandered into that part of the house." When Jake continued to stare at her, she swallowed. "Uh—after my father bought into the Ravenwood deal, he used to talk a lot about the place. He'd been up here—to a couple of parties or something. Maybe he told me about the box. Maybe I just don't have any conscious memory of the conversation."

"Maybe." Jake's voice mirrored her own inner doubts.

"How else would I have known where to find it?" she asked.

"Inside information."

Laura sat up straighter, her eyes boring into those of the man on the other side of the bed. "You mean like somebody gave me a tip or something?"

He shrugged.

"Who? Why?"

"I couldn't say."

She gave him a direct look. "All right, maybe there's something we missed in the box."

"Good luck."

Gingerly, she removed the tightly wound bundle of charred newsprint.

"Burned offerings," Jake muttered.

"Baked, actually."

The papers were as brittle and insubstantial as the wasps' nest she'd knocked out from under the eaves last fall.

Hoping some trace of print remained, she held pieces of it up to the light. The words were unreadable, and charred flecks of paper dropped onto the bedspread.

"Well, I'll be damned."

Laura swiveled toward Jake. He wasn't looking at the flaking paper; he was staring into the bed of ash at the bottom of the container.

Following his gaze, Laura saw a glint of buried metal. Jake poked into the ashes and the elongated shape of an ornately carved handle emerged. It stood out clearly against the gray debris.

"What have we here?"

"A knife!" Laura exclaimed as Jake extracted a small, sharp dagger and held it flat across the palm of his hand so they could both get a good look. As Jake turned the weapon, she could see that the hilt was of some red metal, the blade a dull silver. It looked old and valuable—an artifact from another age. Perhaps from some ritual or arcane ceremony.

Laura reached for the dagger, taking it in her own hand and feeling the weight and balance. With the index finger of her other hand, she traced the raised design of vines and leaves that snaked up the grip. Then she looked at the pattern more closely. No, not leaves. Tiny red drops of blood. She shuddered and drew her hand back.

Jake's gaze swung to Laura. His question echoed the

ones in her own mind. Only he expected her to have some answers. "What can you tell me about that thing?"

She put the knife back into the box. "I can't tell you anything about it. I—I—never saw it before in my life."

"You're sure?" He studied her white face and drawn features.

"Of course, I'm sure! I'm just spooked. Anybody would be, finding a wicked looking thing like this."

"Yeah."

Silence filled the room again. As much to distract herself from the evil-looking instrument as for any other reason, she picked up the wad of ruined papers and turned it in her hands. More pieces flaked off.

"Wait a minute," she exclaimed.

"What?"

"I think there's something here in the center." Carefully she began to peel away the damaged exterior and was rewarded when she came to a sheet of paper that was only scorched, not burned beyond legibility.

"Articles from the local newspapers," Jake observed.

Laura handed him some of the sheets. Very delicately, they unfolded the brittle pages and spread them across the bed. Actually, they were from two sources. Besides the county papers, there was also a front page of the *Baltimore Sun.*

The article in the worst shape was a story from the *Garrett County Times Union* about the sale of Ravenwood to a group of investors.

Laura went very still when she realized Jake wasn't looking at the article. He had taken her hand and turned it over.

"Your fingers."

She glanced down and saw that the skin on her fingertips was abraded. It must have happened when she'd pried up the floorboard. But until this moment, they'd both been too preoccupied to notice.

"Do they hurt?"

"No…well, yes. A little."

His fingers delicately stroked her injured flesh as if he could draw away the pain.

She looked up and their eyes met and held.

"You should put some antiseptic on that."

"There's some in my room. I'll take care of it later." Her voice had turned a bit husky. Probably from the bourbon, she told herself.

Somehow, there was more intimacy between them now than when he'd been holding her in his arms. Laura clung to her explanation. She didn't want to consider the possibility that some subtle sexual dynamic had shifted. Yet, now she was very sure the awareness she'd felt when they'd been sipping their drinks hadn't been her imagination.

Well, why not, she asked herself. A man and woman alone in a bedroom in the middle of the night. There were too many cultural signals switched on by the situation— and their clothing—or lack of it.

Sucking in a draft of air, Laura turned back to the article, but she could still feel Jake's eyes on her. To shift the focus away from the two of them, she pointed to a paragraph near the end of the readable portion. "Look here. It talks about my father."

"Yeah." He read the few lines. "And Sam and Emma. But what about Tim and Martha? They were in on the original deal, too."

"Maybe they were mentioned in the burned part."

They both read the rest of the article, but there wasn't much they didn't already know. Laura moved the page aside and turned to an editorial from the same paper. It was a diatribe condemning a series of wild parties at the mansion.

"Looks as if a bunch of carpetbaggers from the city were coming up here and corrupting the morals of the rural area,'' Jake commented dryly. ''I see we've got disorderly conduct, drug-related arrests and a woman from town who was hired as a maid and got beaten up by one of the guests.''

''I guess people in Hazard have long memories,'' Laura murmured.

''What are you talking about?''

''When I stopped for gas back in town, everybody was friendly until I mentioned I was going to Ravenwood.'' She gave him a brief summary of what had happened—except for the part about the fairy cross.

''Maybe they thought you were some kind of party girl.''

Laura scowled in distaste at the idea.

''You get any names?''

''The guy pumping gas was called Cully. I think the old woman was Ida. Why?''

''They might talk to a reporter.''

''You?''

''Yeah.''

''I thought you wrote for the sports section.''

''Maybe the gas jockey is a football fan.'' Jake gave her his most engaging grin.

''Right.'' Laura turned her attention back to the contents of the box. ''Too bad so much is burned. We might have a better idea of why someone was saving this stuff.''

''And whether it's related to anything else that's been going on here today.''

''These articles are over twenty years old. You think that's possible?''

''This whole setup has been weird. Anything's possible. I don't know how many of the current guests have been up here before. Maybe one of them knows about the box.''

''I hadn't thought of that.''

''There's still the front page from the *Baltimore Sun*.''

''Does it have a story about Ravenwood?''

It took several moments before Jake answered. When he did, his voice had turned rough and hard as a piece of corrugated steel. "No. Not a thing about Ravenwood."

Laura glanced up quickly to catch the expression on Jake's face. She couldn't see it because his head was bent toward the paper, but the rigid set of his shoulders matched the voice. Trying to figure out what had caused his sudden change of mood, Laura scanned the headlines. There were articles about a Mafia boss being assassinated, the president's drive against drug addiction and the inadequacy of the state's education budget. At the bottom of the page was the first in a series of articles on environmental-health issues. Across from it was a story on capital punishment. Rounding out the day's top stories were reports about a bomb attack on a Quebec restaurant and a mass murder in Florida.

"Have I missed something?"

He shrugged.

"Something in one of these articles?"

"Nothing that's relevant." He sighed. "Listen, I'm sorry. It's kind of late. I guess I'm getting tired of poring over this stuff and trying to come up with any conclusions."

"I think we're both tired." Laura began to gather up the papers, folding them carefully so as not to inflict any more damage. Setting them back on top of the dagger in the box, she closed the lid.

"What are you doing?"

"As you pointed out, I'm the one who found this stuff. I'm taking it back to my room." She arched an eyebrow, waiting for him to object.

His Adam's apple bobbed, and she wondered if he'd been planning on looking at the papers when she'd left. However, he didn't protest as she tucked the box under her arm.

"Uh, I guess it would be best not to discuss this with anyone else," she ventured.

"Umm-hmm."

She didn't tell him her motive was as much personal as anything else. If she hadn't been able to explain to him how she'd found the box, she doubted she'd do better with anyone else at Ravenwood.

"Thanks for for helping me out."

"Take care of yourself."

Did he think they were going to talk about this again tomorrow? Or was he planning to conduct his own investigation? And was it going to have something to do with one of the front-page articles? She didn't ask and he didn't volunteer.

Getting off the bed, he accompanied her to the door.

She'd just put a foot into the hall when another door opened. Sam Pendergrast looked directly at them, his gaze wide with surprise in the dim light. Instinctively Laura slipped the hand with the box against her thigh.

Jake's instincts were much more dynamic. For a heartbeat, his dark eyes burned a silent message into Laura's blue ones. Then he swept her into his arms and lowered his mouth to hers like a hungry lover who'd just come to the conclusion that he hadn't slaked his desire.

Dumbfounded, Laura went limp. In the next second, she began to struggle but Jake's muscular arms didn't give her much room to maneuver.

"Don't." The command vibrated against her lips. "Make this convincing." Before he finished the sentence, one hand began to tangle greedily in the silky strands of her long hair and the other caressed its way across her back. Earlier, his touch had been meant to comfort. Now it conveyed blatant male sensuality.

Jake Wallace was one hell of an actor. Or maybe he was

simply one hell of a lover. It was hard to believe he was only pretending passion as his lips began to move over hers.

She hardly knew this man, yet she'd sensed the sexual pull between them tightening and twanging all evening, like guitar strings being stretched taut. She'd kept the feelings under control. Until now.

Taken by surprise, taken in his arms, taken by his mouth, she felt her lips open under his, and she gave in to his kiss.

As he sensed her acquiescence, his strong arms enveloped her body, gathering her close. With the kiss she tasted a hint of bourbon. It was far less potent than the essence of the man himself.

Joining the deception, her free hand traveled possessively across his broad shoulders and then up the back of his neck, stroking over the stubble from a recent haircut. One silk-clad leg whispered against rough denim of his jeans.

He was growling deep in his throat when he pulled her back into his room and shut the door. Caught between his hard body and the even harder wall, she arched against him, echoing his response with a little cry of her own. It took several hot, breathless moments before Laura realized no one could see them anymore. She had crossed the line between acting and passion—if there ever had been a line.

He sensed the change in her even as she felt her muscles stiffen. Raising his head, he looked down into the confusion shimmering in her eyes.

"Was that necessary?" she managed.

He chose to answer the more obvious part of the question. "Did you want Sam to know what we've really been doing this evening—what *you've* really been doing?"

She swallowed slowly. "No."

Backing away, he ran unsteady fingers through his hair. At least she had the satisfaction of knowing he'd been as caught up in the dramatization as she.

"I have to leave."

"Not yet. He might be watching."

She stood with her back pressed to the door, staring at Jake, trying to comprehend what had flared so white-hot and so quickly between them. Not just desire. Emotion. She couldn't have responded like that unless she'd felt something for the man. But she didn't want it. Couldn't handle it.

"No."

She didn't care if Sam was still watching. She didn't care if everyone at Ravenwood was watching. All she knew was that the little room had suddenly become too hot and cramped for the two of them. Turning, she threw open the door and fled down the hall to her own room.

Sometimes when her emotions were in turmoil, Laura could make her mind a blank. Tonight, she didn't want to think about any of the things that had happened this evening. She only wanted to escape into the oblivion of sleep. Setting the box on the dresser, she slid into bed and pulled the covers up to her chin. Only a few minutes after she'd rolled onto her side and pulled her knees up against her chest she was asleep.

Angels, or maybe it was ghosts, might have hovered around her in the darkness, offering their protection. At any rate, she slept peacefully through the night, more peacefully than she'd slept in weeks.

"LAURA... LAURA... Wake up, Laura...."

She wasn't sure what roused her in the misty light of morning. A noise? A shout? One moment she was lost in slumber. The next moment she was sitting up in bed and looking around in alarm.

"Who's there?"

No one answered.

Laura's eyes focused on the paneled wall at the other end of the room. The noise seemed to have come from behind it. No, that was just her sleep-drugged mind playing tricks.

For several heartbeats she was enveloped in the early-morning silence. Then she heard a shout, high and thin and frightened. This time she knew it wasn't in her room. It seemed to be floating up from downstairs.

The hair on Laura's scalp prickled as she reached for her robe and swung her legs out of bed.

"Help... Please help me." The plea was followed by a thump from the floor below.

Opening the door, Laura peered into the corridor and saw no one. Thinking she heard scurrying noises somewhere below, she ran down the dimly lit corridor and took the steps two at a time.

"Is anybody there?" she called out. "Is somebody hurt?"

No one answered. In fact, the house seemed deathly quiet. Perhaps it had all been another one of her dreams. She wanted to believe that—except she couldn't.

Her breath rapid and shallow, she tiptoed toward the parlor. As she stepped through the doorway, she saw a figure huddled in the middle of the rug. It was a woman who wore a dressing gown of bright red and orange flowers— and gold slippers. Her too-dark hair was plastered over a white scalp.

"Emma!"

The woman didn't stir, didn't breathe.

"Emma?" Pulse racing, Laura knelt beside her, reached for one of her narrow shoulders and turned her over. For a moment Laura couldn't believe what she was seeing. The flowers of the dressing gown were darkened with blood. And they made an intricate new pattern with the knife she'd found last night. But how could that be? She'd left the weapon in the box in her room under the burned papers. Now it was buried to the hilt in the middle of Emma Litchfield's chest.

Chapter Five

Reflexively, Laura's fingers closed around the handle of the knife. Then she drew her hand back as she realized there was no use pulling it out. That wasn't going to help Emma. The woman was dead.

"Oh God—Oh God!"

Her anguished exclamation echoed in the empty room. Then people were running along the upstairs hall. When she'd needed help, the large house had seemed deserted; now, a crowd pelted down the stairs. Moments later, they clustered in the sitting room.

Andy. Sam. Jake. Tim. And finally, Martha. Most looked as if they'd been wrenched from sleep, the way Laura had been a few minutes earlier. The majority were still wearing night clothes. Only Andy and Jake had pulled on trousers.

Shock, horror, incredulity registered on the faces around her.

"Emma—Emma—called for help," Laura stammered. "That's why I came down here. Didn't anyone else hear her?" The explanations tumbled out. Laura knew her own voice was rising on a tide of panic as she began to realize just how this must look.

"We heard *you*," Tim said.

Others nodded in agreement.

Andy squatted beside the body and touched Emma's

cheek. "She's already cold. She couldn't have called for help. Not in the last few minutes. How long have you been here?"

"I just found her." Laura looked around for support. "I tell you, I heard somebody calling me. I came down to the sitting room and found her like this."

Laura searched the faces of the crowd gathered around her. Some of the Ravenwood guests were giving her speculative glances. Others looked accusing.

No one moved.

Laura's eyes sought Jake's. He was staring at the dagger—the one she'd found last night, the one she'd insisted on taking to her room. Now it was sticking out of Emma's body. Laura held her breath, waiting to see if he was going to blurt out something about the night before. He didn't. In fact, to her profound relief and gratitude, he knelt and put his arm around her shoulder.

"It must have scared you out of your mind—finding her like this," he said.

She nodded wordlessly. The simple statement and the encouraging tone of his voice were like a balm. The others might be staring at her as if she'd jumped out from behind the curtains and assaulted Emma, but Jake was on her side.

Ignoring the knot of spectators, Jake helped Laura to her feet. As she stood, her knees threatened to give way, and he slipped his arm around her waist, supporting her weight against the side of his body.

"You're doin' fine. But let's get out of this room—so you don't have to stare at the body," he suggested. As they moved toward the door, the crowd parted for them.

When they'd turned the corner into the hall, he bent his head toward her ear and spoke rapidly. "We've only got a few minutes to talk. You're a lawyer. You know what you should and shouldn't say."

If she could make her mind·function.

He glanced back over his shoulder to make sure no one had followed them. "We'd better not tell anyone about your finding the knife last night. It could make things worse for you."

Laura felt her chest tighten. A phrase she'd once heard from a police detective had come bouncing into her head. *The person who discovers the body is the chief suspect.* She hated to lie. But she hadn't had a chance to think this through. "Yes," she agreed again in an unsteady voice.

"Was your door locked?"

"I think so."

"It looks as if someone set you up."

"My God, Jake, who?"

"I don't know, but we'd better call the police. The sooner this is cleared up, the better for you...." He hesitated. "Last night, I would have bet I was the only other person who knew the knife was in your room."

Her head whipped up.

"You would have thought of that sooner or later." His gaze didn't waver from hers. "You don't have any reason to trust me. But I hope you do."

Laura nodded uncertainly. She was confused and frightened and unable to give him an answer.

They were walking down the hall toward the room where Andy had made the presentation. Laura stopped abruptly. "If I'm going to talk to the police, I think I'd like to get dressed before the interview."

"Good idea."

They both turned and headed for the stairs.

The first thing Laura did when she reached her room was check the dresser. The box was missing. Not just the knife—the whole box. A sick feeling rose in her throat. Jake was right. It looked as if she'd been a very convenient scapegoat for someone who wanted to kill Emma. But who? And how had the person known about the box? Sam leaped to mind. He'd seen them last night. But she had no way of knowing if he'd spotted the box. And what would he have had against Emma?

Laura felt as if she'd been thrust into the middle of one of those mystery weekends in which everyone goes off to a country house with a bunch of interesting characters, witnesses a pretend murder and then tries to figure out who did it. Only this wasn't an elaborately staged scenario with actors and actresses playing amusing or sinister roles. Emma's lifeless body was lying on the sitting room carpet.

Shuddering, Laura battled the impulse to crawl back into bed and pull the covers over her head like a little kid afraid of the dark. Instead, she began to wash and dress. She knew she should hurry, but speed seemed impossible. She felt as if she were walking around under water, with each movement of her arms and legs held back by the liquid's resistance. By the time she'd slipped into yesterday's knit outfit and put on a little makeup, Andy was rapping at the door to inform her that the chief of police wanted to talk to her.

Laura came back downstairs reluctantly, wondering what to expect. As she stood in the hall, she saw Sam Pendergrast come out of the room in which the real-estate developer had made the presentation the evening before. She tried to catch Sam's eye, but he brushed by her without a word, his muscular shoulders tense, as if he wished he'd left the scene before she arrived. A bad sign, she decided.

However, Sam was swept from her mind as soon as she met Police Chief Hiram Pickett. He was a tall, balding man with sleepy eyes and stooped shoulders. Perhaps to compensate for the thinning hair on the top of his head, he had cultivated a flowing mustache that made him look a little like Wyatt Earp. It appeared to be his only vanity. He wore his uniform as if it had been issued by Goodwill Industries. No tie. Nonstandard shirt so limp, the collar spread wide across the shoulders.

Scuffed hunting boots poked out from under his slate blue pants. On the other hand, a shiny star-shaped badge was pinned to his shirt pocket. And a holstered gun rode prominently on his right hip.

He was standing stiffly with his arms folded across his chest, looking around the room. Laura had the distinct impression that he was holding his emotions as tightly as his body—as if he found being at Ravenwood distasteful and wanted to get things over with as soon as possible. That might work to her advantage, and it might not.

"I hear you found Ms. Litchfield," he began after inviting Laura to take a seat on the couch. The way he sat opposite her, with as little of his body as possible touching the upholstery, confirmed her impression that he wasn't very comfortable here.

His initial questions were about what had happened the first thing in the morning. Why had she come downstairs so early? Why did she think she was the only one who heard the call for help? What did she do when she found Emma? Had she touched the knife?

To her surprise, Laura discovered she honestly didn't know the answer to that question. She'd been so upset that she couldn't remember.

After taking Laura back through her morning, he began to ask about the events of the day before.

Maybe she was going to have to get herself a lawyer—someone who was a lot more savvy than she in criminal law, she thought. No, she'd rather handle this by herself. Besides, even if she was the one who'd found the body, she certainly didn't have a motive.

As she and the police chief talked, Laura tried to gauge his attitude toward her. He wasn't acting friendly, but he was being very polite. Almost too polite, as though the rituals of courtesy and deference put a barrier between them. Was she at the top of his suspect list? There was no way of telling. But he ended the interview with a request that she not return to Baltimore that day.

Tim, apparently the next up to be interviewed, was hanging around the door to the sitting room when she came out. He was clasping and unclasping his hands, and his broad face was pale under the florid complexion. Standing up, he came over to her. Again, his breath was tinged with alcohol. Did he drink all the time? Or was it his way of dealing with tension?

"Laura," he said in a slightly slurred voice, "I'm sorry this happened."

"So am I," she agreed, taking a step back.

"I guess it looks pretty grim for you, darlin', what with the bad feelings between you and Emmie."

"What? What are you talking about?"

"Are you still pretending you don't know she's the one who took your father from your mother?"

Laura's mouth dropped open.

Tim didn't seem to notice her dumbfounded reaction. "Everybody knew about it. We were all wondering if there were going to be fireworks when you two met up."

The fireworks were exploding in Laura's head as she stared at him.

"I just couldn't resist needlin' her at dinner." Tim laughed. "But you were a real good sport about it. Until..." His voice trailed off.

Jake, who had just come into the room must have seen the expression on her face.

"What's wrong?"

"Tim says—I—"

He led her rapidly into the hall and turned her toward him, his large hands gripping her shoulders. "What is it?"

Her answer came in a frightened rush. "Why didn't I figure it out for myself? All that innuendo I didn't understand. Martha watching to see how I'd react when she introduced me to Emma. Emma looking frightened when I tried to help her after the chandelier. And then those jokes at dinner. Tim just told me Emma was the woman who took my father away from my mother. Now Pickett's going to think I was out for revenge.''

The hands on her shoulders became gentle. ''Not after all these years. Why wait until now? Why not do it when you had a lot less chance of getting caught? Killing her this weekend wouldn't make sense.''

''A smart prosecutor would have no trouble coming up with a convincing motive. He'd say I'd been brooding about my father all these years and seeing Emma face-to-face drove me over the edge.''

''No. You're too controlled for that.''

He'd read her pretty accurately. Somehow that was the last straw. ''Jake, I need to be alone. To think this through.'' When he didn't loosen his grasp, she wrenched herself away. She was heading for the stairs when a brusque voice stopped her.

''Just a minute, Ms. Roswell.''

Laura looked up to confront a member of Pickett's staff. While the police chief was questioning the guests, other members of the department must have been photographing the crime scene and collecting physical evidence. Maybe they'd find something that would clear her of suspicion. Her mind glommed on to the possibility even as she knew she was grasping at straws.

''We'd like to get your fingerprints.''

Laura nodded tightly. As she allowed her thumb to be squished against the ink pad, she wondered again if she'd touched the knife that morning. But what did it matter? She'd handled the dagger last night. So had Jake. So had someone else. Unless Jake had stolen the knife after she'd gone to sleep. With a gulp, she admitted she couldn't discount that possibility. He could have taken it and the whole box back to his room. Except that she hadn't heard him unlock her door. She hadn't heard anyone unlock the door.

Finally, Laura was able to escape to her room. But she was too restless to stay in any one place for more than a minute or two. Downstairs, Pickett was interviewing people, gathering information, trying to make a case against her. Probably Sam had already told Pickett about her father and Emma before he'd interviewed her. Tim was probably adding more facts to the story. And Martha.

The realization made her feel trapped. Now, she cursed herself for not having jumped into her car and left when she'd thought about it last night. Even before she'd arrived, she'd had bad feelings about this place. She should have trusted her instincts. As she paced to the window, she pictured herself making a ladder out of her bed linens, sliding down to the ground and speeding off in her car. But then what? Running away clearly wouldn't solve her problem. It would only make her look guilty.

Laura brought her thoughts back to more constructive channels. What she had to do was think logically about the whole thing. There was no doubt that Emma's relationship with her father put her in an awkward position. It would be even more awkward if Pickett found out about what she'd been doing last night. But how could he, unless Jake told him? And they'd both agreed not to talk about that. Suddenly she couldn't help wondering if he'd stick to the bargain. She knew so little about the man, and now her fate seemed inexorably wound up with him. It had been stupid not to talk to him again when he'd given her the chance. She needed to know what had gone on in his interview with Pickett and what he intended to do.

Laura was just heading for the door when someone knocked.

"Who is it?" she called out.

"Jake."

Speak of the devil. When she opened the door, she found him standing in the hall with a tray. It had two cups, a coffeepot and a plate of sandwiches.

"You skipped breakfast and lunch. You need to eat, Laura."

Was it that late already? She stepped aside and let him in, suddenly very glad to see him. And in truth, the smell of coffee and food made her stomach rumble. It was amazing that she could think about eating, she mused as she poured herself a cup of coffee and added milk.

Jake joined her. This time he sat in the easy chair. She perched on the side of the bed. As she watched him take a swallow of coffee, she couldn't help remembering the way the evening before had ended. She wasn't about to bring it up, yet the kiss that had gotten out of control couldn't exactly be ignored, she admitted silently, whether either one of them said anything or not.

He looked around the room. "Are the papers gone too, or just the knife?"

"The whole kit and caboodle."

"I didn't say anything about the box to Pickett."

"Thanks. I guess."

"It's better this way."

"I don't like to lie."

He reached out and pressed his fingers over hers. "Laura, I'm sorry this is happening to you."

"I keep wishing I'd never come up here."

"I can imagine."

She sat stiffly, not responding to the hand over hers. After several heartbeats, he removed it.

Laura took a sip of hot coffee. "I'd be tempted to think I made up the whole thing about the knife and the box—except that you remember it too, don't you?"

"Yes."

"Who do you think could have taken them out of my

room?'' Laura watched Jake's face carefully as she asked the question.

"I don't have a clue.'' He seemed genuinely perplexed.

"What else did Pickett ask you?'' As she listened to his answer, she was thinking about how much she wanted his help and support. But she had to know if she could trust him. When he was finished speaking, she unclenched the fingers that gripped her coffee cup. "Jake, I hardly know anything about you—I mean, how do I really know—'' She spread her hand in a helpless gesture.

"I could give you some character references. Guys from the Broncos. My editor down at the *Sun*. My mother.''

Laura couldn't help smiling. "I'm sure your mother would be very laudatory.''

"She was real strict about the things that counted when I was growing up. Homework first, play later. But she never could get me to keep my room straight. When she visits my apartment, she cleans out the pantry.''

"Why aren't you married?'' Yesterday, she wouldn't have asked such a personal question. But that could be an important clue to his personality. Why was an attractive, eligible man in his early thirties still unattached? Had the football star dumped his high school sweetheart?

"My wife died.''

There was no way to miss the pain that accompanied the simple statement. "I'm sorry.''

"Why aren't you married?'' he countered.

Her chin lifted. "My husband moved on to greener pastures.''

"He must have been stupid—or crazy.''

"I'm doing fine on my own. At least I thought I was until I came here.''

"I get the feeling he destroyed your faith in the male sex.''

"I wouldn't go quite that far." Laura took a bite of ham sandwich and swallowed.

Jake concentrated on his own sandwich for a moment. "Had you met any of the other Ravenwood investors before you came here this weekend?"

"Tim O'Donnell claims he knew me when I was a little girl. I don't remember him."

"And you never met Emma?"

"I don't think so. And I didn't know about her and my father. My mother never talked about the woman who broke up their marriage."

"I believe you."

The simple words meant a lot.

They would have continued with the quick exchange of information, each judging reactions as much as listening to answers, except that the conversation was interrupted by another knock at the door.

"It's Chief Pickett, ma'am."

Laura glanced at Jake. Then, with a hand that wasn't quite steady, she opened the door.

"Laura Roswell, I'm arrestin' you for the murder of Emma Litchfield."

LAURA HEARD A ROARING IN her ears, and the world seemed to contract until all she saw was Pickett's mustache-draped face. She must have heard him wrong. No, he was reading her her rights.

Laura took half a step back and thudded against Jake, who had sprung out of the chair and come up behind her. His arms cradled her shivering body.

"Is this what you do up in Garrett County, railroad innocent bystanders into jail?" Jake bit out.

"In Garrett County, we don't like city slickers comin' up here and tryin' to pull the wool over the eyes of the country bumpkins. We may not be a big-city police department, but we know how to enforce the law.''

Pickett's rejoinder was delivered in a level tone. However, they could both hear the dangerous edge in his reply. Antagonizing the man was probably a bad idea.

"Do you mind telling us on what grounds you're arresting Ms. Roswell,'' Jake asked in a cooler voice.

Pickett stepped into the room. "I don't mind answering a civil question when I'm asked.'' His voice and manner of speaking became more formal, almost as though he were testifying in court. "Just like the law-enforcement agencies in the big city, out here we look at motive, opportunity, evidence and malice. First, there's Ms. Roswell's cockamamie story about hearing someone shout for help this morning. Three people have rooms closer to the stairs than she did, and no one heard any distress call.''

Laura opened her mouth to protest and then closed it again. She couldn't prove she'd heard anything. It was her word against three other people. She was beginning to feel as if she were sinking into quicksand.

"Then there's motive,'' the police chief continued, giving Laura a direct look. "I got an earful about the bad blood between you and the victim.''

"Bad blood! I never met the woman until yesterday.''

"Well, she told Sam Pendergrast last week that she was afraid to come up here because of you. He had to persuade her to change her mind.''

Laura sucked in a deep breath, as if it were the last one she was going to get before the quicksand swallowed her up. There had to be more. Pickett couldn't arrest her on what he'd just said.

"And finally, we have the knife.'' He paused for emphasis. "It has Ms. Roswell's fingerprints on the handle—and only Ms. Roswell's.''

"That's impossible!''

The exclamation came from Jake. Laura whirled around to face him and their eyes locked. They'd both touched the knife. But she had to think through the implications before she admitted anything about last night. Now she shook her head almost imperceptibly.

"How's that?" Pickett asked. "You got some information you've been holding back, Mr. Wallace?"

Jake swallowed. "I mean, that's impossible because she couldn't have done it."

"Well, she'll have her opportunity to try and prove that in court. But right now, I'm going to book her and take her before Judge Ketchum."

"It's going to be all right," Jake whispered, giving Laura's arms a squeeze. "Do you want me to call someone for you?"

"My friend Josephine O'Malley. She's a private detective in Baltimore." Quickly, she gave Jake Jo's home number.

"They have to let you out on bail. You'll be home tonight or tomorrow morning," he reassured her.

"Yes," Laura answered automatically, wondering if they were both mouthing lies.

If the hours since she'd discovered Emma's body had been a bad dream, the remainder of the day degenerated into the surreal landscape of waking nightmare.

It seemed as if everyone at Ravenwood was in the front hall to see her led away in handcuffs, just as they'd all come running to find her kneeling over the body. Laura pressed her lips together and held her head high as Pickett escorted her past eyes that ranged from curious to accusing.

In the back of the police car, she fought to hold on to self-control the way a naked disaster victim clutches a blanket. It only got worse. She'd been in lockups and courthouses before, but never as a prisoner. When she arrived at the jail, her pocketbook and other personal belongings were taken away. She was booked, photographed, searched and left in a cold, damp holding cell until deputies came to bring her before Judge Warren Ketchum.

Well, this was her chance, she told herself, squaring her shoulders and marching out to the courtroom to meet the judge. She'd find out what bail he'd set and make arrangements to be released so she and Jo could start collecting evidence in her defense.

Her first view of Ketchum was daunting. He was a short, barrel-chested man with iron gray hair and colorless eyes that were magnified by rimless glasses. They inspected her from head to toe before spearing her with a look that ripped a hole in her resolve. Still she went ahead with the formalities.

She hadn't reckoned on the judge's attitude toward what he obviously thought of as a criminal onslaught from the city. Apparently his perspective was remarkably similar to that of Police Chief Pickett.

"We will not tolerate being invaded by outsiders who think they can ride roughshod over the residents of our rural area," he began his justification for setting bail. "This is a law-abiding community, not a prime site for felonies."

A prime site for felonies? Did that mean other serious crimes had been committed by visitors to the county? Or more specifically, visitors to Ravenwood. She'd have to check that out.

But all thought of past indiscretions at Ravenwood fled from her mind when she heard the judge's next words.

"In view of the seriousness of the crime and the uncertainty that the defendant will return to the county for trial, bail is set at one million dollars."

Laura's mouth fell open. A million dollars. It might as well have been the interest on the U.S. national debt for all the chance she had of raising that kind of money.

Chapter Six

Jake Wallace sat cooling his heels outside Hiram Pickett's office the next afternoon. He'd tried to see the man after Laura had been taken away. He'd also tried to see Laura. Both attempts had been no go.

Last night, he'd talked to a number of people in town—including Cully, the gas station attendant, who'd clammed up on Laura. Unfortunately, the old woman named Ida was nowhere to be found. Still, it hadn't been difficult to get the locals talking. Although he knew a great deal more about the history of Ravenwood, he hadn't discovered anything that had any bearing on Laura's immediate problem.

Jake looked at his watch again. One-thirty. He'd been here since eight in the morning and had, thus far, been ignored.

He wasn't a man who went around popping off for no good reason. Except in a few dire circumstances his approach to life had been pretty laid back. In the past few hours he'd become intimately acquainted with the meaning of the phrase ''makes your blood boil.''

Laura's friend Jo O'Malley hadn't returned any of the messages he'd left on her home or office answering machines—which must mean she was out of town. Either that or she didn't give a damn about what happened to Laura. That, he simply couldn't believe.

Every time he thought about Laura, he remembered the way she'd looked when Pickett had carted her off to jail. Her hands had been cuffed, but she'd held her head up and walked right by the crowd in the hall as if she were on her way to a meeting with a client. You only saw the vulnerability when you realized how tightly she was clutching her arms against her middle. Had she cracked when she'd found out about the bail? He was willing to bet she hadn't given Judge Warren Ketchum the satisfaction.

Getting up, Jake strode back to the secretary's desk again. Over the course of the past few hours, he'd turned his considerable charm on her. She'd responded with a sort of nervous hesitancy. But she hadn't been willing to go out on a limb by ushering him in to see Pickett.

"I'd sure appreciate it if the chief could fit me into his busy schedule," he tried once more.

"I'm sorry." The woman looked both genuinely perplexed and genuinely regretful. "There's no use buzzing him again. He knows you're out here."

Jake paced to the water cooler, filled a paper cup and swallowed the lukewarm liquid as he glanced once more at the police chief's closed door. A half dozen people had bustled in and out—including the doctor who'd done the autopsy last night. He'd stayed the longest. Almost forty-five minutes. Four or five times during the day, Jake had been on the verge of bursting in and demanding that Pickett give him five minutes of his valuable time, but he knew that was the wrong way to handle things if he wanted to help Laura.

Of course, that didn't make it any easier to explain to himself why he was sitting out here prepared to swear to a lie to save a woman he hardly knew. Not when he'd be a heck of a lot better off heading back to Baltimore. She was in a heap of trouble. And either she wasn't rowing with both oars in the water or she was holding information back.

Jake sighed. He'd tried telling himself he was responding to the appalling predicament in which Laura found herself—and to the strange way the Ravenwood conundrum was tied to his own very personal interests. He knew that was simply too easy an explanation.

This time, he'd decided he wasn't going to run out on a woman who needed his help. At least until he saw her past the crisis point.

Almost as if the police chief had heard Jake's thoughts, Pickett finally opened his door and stepped out into the hall. When his eyes lit on Jake, his jaw muscles tightened.

"What can I do for you, Wallace?"

"I have information that might be important in the Laura Roswell case—something that didn't seem relevant until you arrested her."

"Then I guess you'd better come on in."

Jake kept himself from asking why he was finally being given an audience. Instead, he followed the police chief into his office and dropped into the offered seat. Without appearing to make an inspection, he sized up the opposition. Pickett was wearing the same clothes he'd had on yesterday, which probably meant he hadn't gone to bed. What had kept the man so busy? And why was he looking a bit green around the gills? Just lack of sleep? Or was he worried about the trumped up case he'd tried to build against Laura?

"You say you got important information," the police chief prompted. Last night, he'd been annoyingly polite when he'd interviewed the Ravenwood guests. Now, he'd dropped that pose.

Jake pretended a reluctance to begin. "I'd like to talk to you man to man."

The police chief leaned back in his swivel chair. "Go ahead."

"I can provide Ms. Roswell with an alibi. She couldn't

have killed Emma Litchfield last night because she was in my bed.''

Pickett fixed Jake with a piercing look. ''Why'd you hold that piece of information back when I questioned you yesterday? For that matter, why didn't Ms. Roswell say anything?''

''It was a private matter between the two of us. I was protecting her reputation, and she probably thought our being together didn't have any bearing on the investigation.''

Pickett snorted. ''Actually, Pendergrast saw the two of you smooching—but I didn't think it proved nothin' since he pegged the time at around midnight.''

Jake felt his chest tighten as he watched the play of emotions on the police chief's face. Something was going on here. Something. But what?

Finally, the man sighed. ''You just came here to brag about a sordid little affair.''

''Now wait a minute—''

''And I was hopin' you were going to give me some evidence that would help me hold on to her,'' he added with remarkable candor.

''I'm not going to sit here and listen to you insult the lady.''

''I figure any woman who shows up for a party at Ravenwood ain't no lady.''

Jake's hands grabbed the arms of the chair to keep him from lunging across the desk at the man.

Pickett eyed him coolly. ''You want to be arrested for assaulting a police officer?''

''No,'' Jake ground out.

''Good. Because just remember—in this office, I handle things any damn way I please.''

For a full minute, the two men stared at each other. Then, apparently satisfied that he'd made his point, Pickett leaned back in his chair again. "As a matter of fact, I'm a big enough man to admit when I'm wrong."

Jake hoped he didn't look as if he were gaping.

"I thought I had an open-and-shut case against Roswell, until I talked to the medical examiner this morning. It looks like Litchfield died hours before she was found in the sitting room."

"Thank God."

"But the real killer, so to speak, is that the victim didn't die from the knife wound in her chest—so it don't matter whose fingerprints are on the weapon.

Jake rose half out of his chair. "What?"

"There was a head wound and other contusions. Doc Lawrence thinks she was pushed down the stairs. That's what he's going to put in his autopsy report."

"So if you'd just waited for the report, you wouldn't have arrested Ms. Roswell in the first place."

Pickett glared at Jake. "Yesterday, I didn't think I had to wait for an autopsy report. This morning, it looks like somebody went to a considerable amount of trouble to frame your girlfriend."

"We finally agree on something."

"Yeah. But it's not just her. That same somebody was out to make a fool of me." Pickett's gritty gaze didn't waver from Jake, as if he were evaluating his candidacy for the position of chief suspect in the sting operation.

"Why are you telling me all this?"

"Not because I want to be your best buddy. I've gotten a bunch of reports on you. You've been poking around all over town, stirrin' things up. I'm saving you the bother of stirrin' up any more old dirt. But let me give you a real heartfelt piece of advice, boy." Pickett leaned over his desk toward Jake. "You and Ms. Roswell run on back to Baltimore—before you get in real trouble."

LAURA GLANCED covertly up at Jake as he led the way to the parking lot. When he'd met her at the lockup entrance, he'd wrapped his muscular arms around her and hugged her to him like a man greeting an airplane-crash survivor.

She'd clung to Jake with equal fervor. But the reaction was pretty natural under the circumstances, she told herself. She'd just been through a hellish ordeal—one that she could hardly believe was over. And his was the first friendly face she'd seen since she'd been arrested.

"I'll drive you back to your car," Jake offered.

"Thanks." Laura swallowed. She still felt completely off balance—with Jake and with herself. It was difficult to believe that she was no longer a murder suspect. Except that after the lecture Pickett had delivered before releasing her, she had the feeling that she'd better not show her face in Garrett County again. The police chief had as much as threatened that he'd find a reason to bring her in if she crossed his path a second time.

"How do you feel?" Jake asked as they stepped out of the shade of the building and into warm sunshine.

"Exhausted. Grubby. Relieved. Confused." The last was added in an almost inaudible whisper. She didn't want to think about her feelings. And she didn't want to talk about details like the metal jail bunk with the springs that had dug into her back or the vile graffiti scratched into the wall or the way she'd felt when the bars had clanked shut behind her. Instead, she folded her arms across her middle, the way she'd done when the police chief had taken her away.

Jake didn't press her for the particulars. Perhaps that was why she volunteered a quiet observation. "I didn't like being led off in handcuffs."

"I would have hated it. But the important thing is that you're free now." Jake bent to unlock the door of his 280Z. The low-slung car was a leftover souvenir from his NFL glory days. Only Jake and his mechanic knew how much he'd had to spend to keep it running smoothly.

"I tried last night and this morning to call your friend, Jo O'Malley. I guess she's out of town."

"Really, I don't know how to thank you. You didn't have to stick around like this."

"I wanted to."

Laura glanced over her shoulder at the police building and then waited until they'd closed the car's doors before saying anything else. "I feel so paranoid. You don't think Pickett had your car bugged, do you?"

Jake shrugged. "Not legally."

"I know *that.* I'm just wondering what lengths the man would go to make a real case against me."

"Against *us,* maybe. Let's get the hell out of here and we'll worry about the details later." The car's engine roared to life. Apparently, Jake thought better of tempting the law by speeding down the main street. He tooled out of town at a sedate twenty-five miles per hour and only stepped on the gas when they reached the open road.

Laura was too preoccupied to notice where they were going and wasn't paying attention when Jake turned off onto a gravel road leading into the mountains. But as he pulled off at an overlook that provided a spectacular view of a gold-and-orange valley below, she came out of her reverie.

"What are we doing?" she asked.

"We have to get our stories straight in case Pickett, or someone else, gets back to us."

Laura raised questioning eyebrows.

Before he went on, he rolled down his window. A pine-scented breeze ruffled his hair and played across Laura's face.

"There's no easy way to say this," Jake began. "I guess Pickett did a number on me this morning. I was so damn focused on giving you an alibi that I didn't pick up the right signals from him. He let me give my story and then told me the coroner's report knocked his case against you into a cocked hat.''

Laura hadn't failed to catch the chagrin in his voice. "What exactly *was* your story?''

"I told him we spent the night together.''

"But we didn't! I don't spend the night with men I've just met.''

"I know.''

"Then—''

"It was a calculated risk. I figured I'd only end up an accessory after the fact if Pendergrast opened his door again while you were marching down the hall.''

Laura's muttered response was far from ladylike.

"I couldn't turn my back and leave you in jail!''

"Why not?''

"I—I guess I decided I cared about what happened to you.''

She sat with her arms drawn in to her sides and her knuckles pressed against her lips.

Jake reached out with one of his hands to cover her shoulder. "Is that so hard to take?''

"Yes.''

"Why?''

"Because the only person I want to rely on is me,'' she answered in as steady a voice as she could manage.

"Sometimes you have to open up to other people. If you don't, you lose an important part of yourself.''

Laura rolled down her own window and stared out at the fall splendor, but the valley spread out below them was just a place to focus her eyes. The autumn foliage had lost its appeal some time ago.

"Nothing worth anything is easy,'' Jake persisted.

Before she could answer, he leaned across the console,

took her chin in his hand and turned her face back toward him. Too stunned to move, Laura gazed into his dark eyes. She saw questions there. And also answers.

A little anticipatory shiver zinged through her body. At the last moment, just before his mouth claimed hers, her eyelids fluttered closed.

"Laura, let it happen. Whatever it is."

She wasn't sure if he'd spoken the words or if the advice came from her own head, but she was sure about the kiss. She sensed reassurance. She sensed a challenge. She sensed reined passion as Jake's lips moved over hers.

She didn't want to respond to any of it. Somehow she found herself opening to all of the nuances—to the blend of what he was offering and what he was asking.

Unable to resist the pull, she let her lips part so she could taste him. Then her hands crept up and anchored themselves to his broad shoulders.

As he gathered her closer, her heart began to pound, heat danced over her skin and a sense of rightness unfurled deep in her being.

His lips savored hers. His hands clasped her with tender possessiveness. But he didn't push it any further. Instead, he lifted his head and looked down at her again. This time, there was something warm and confident in his gaze. "I had to know."

"Know what?"

"If last night was only pretend. It wasn't."

"Jake, a kiss doesn't prove anything. Especially not with a woman who feels as if she's about to shatter into a million pieces." She couldn't believe she'd admitted that much.

"I understand."

"No, you don't."

"Better than you know." He swallowed. "I'm scared, too, if you want to know the truth. So I'm not going to push you into anything."

She lifted her eyes and searched his. "You? Scared?"

"When I know you better, maybe I'll explain it to you."

They were both silent for several moments. Part of her wanted to ask what he meant. The part that didn't won.

"There's one more important thing we have to talk about," Jake finally said as he leaned back in his seat again.

"What?"

"The person who murdered Emma. Either he or she intended to frame you, or you were just a convenient scapegoat...." Jake ended the sentence with a little rising inflection, making it more of a question than a statement.

"Why would anyone want to frame me?"

"I don't know."

"Neither do I." Laura tried to swallow and found her mouth was too dry. "Maybe Pickett will figure out what's going on."

"Maybe he needs some help."

"Not from me. At least, not right now. Jake, I just want to go home and stand under a hot shower and scrub off the jailhouse smell."

"I understand."

He reached for the ignition key. "I'll drive you back to Ravenwood so you can get your car."

HE DIDN'T HUG HER GOODBYE. He didn't even tell her he'd be in touch. He didn't have to. She knew he was going to call her soon. But at least she was pretty sure she'd have a few days to marshal her defenses. She was grateful for that because she didn't want to get involved with him, no matter what he thought he was offering right now. She had enough to cope with without the added complication of a man in hot pursuit.

On the way home, Laura turned the radio up loud and listened to rock music. That was better than dwelling on any of her recent experiences.

She had already called Noel Emery from Ravenwood to tell her she was all right. But after she'd dropped her overnight bag in the front hall, she discovered that there were three messages from Jo on her answering machine. They ranged from alarmed to frantic.

"Laura, thank God," Jo answered her office phone on the first ring. "Cam and I were in New York on this spur-of-the-moment trip. A guy named Jake Wallace must have called half a dozen times. He said you were in jail—for murder. Is that true?"

"Not anymore. It's a long story."

"I've got all afternoon."

As briefly and dispassionately as possible, Laura recounted the pertinent details of the weekend.

"Sheez! I've heard about those deals where they give you a set of free knives for listening to a real-estate pitch. But this!"

Taken by surprise, Laura laughed.

"Are you sure Pickett's not going to come up with something else against you?"

"I hope not."

"I guess I'd take his advice and stay away from Ravenwood from now on."

"Exactly what I was thinking," Laura agreed. Just the name of the place gave her a sick feeling in the pit of her stomach.

Changing the subject abruptly, Jo said, "So, what about this Jake Wallace guy? He isn't the one who writes the sports column in the *Morning Sun,* is he?"

"You know him?"

"I read him. He's good in print. Funny. Thoughtful. What's he like in person?"

"He's an ex-football player. Not my type at all."

"He sounded pretty upset about your being in jail."

"Umm," Laura responded noncommittally.

"I guess I'll debrief you when you're in a better mood."

"I'm sorry."

"You've had a pretty rough experience. Why don't you come over for dinner this evening?"

"Jo, I think I'd rather be alone."

"If that's what you want. But just remember, Cam and I are here if you need anything."

"Thanks. I know."

Her shoulders sagging, Laura headed up the stairs to her bedroom. Stripping off the burgundy dress she'd worn since yesterday, she dropped it in a heap on the floor. It had come from an expensive shop at Owings Mills, but she'd never wear it again. Picking up the damaged goods between thumb and forefinger, she dropped the dress into the trash. She suspected that ridding herself of other aftereffects of her ordeal wouldn't be as easy.

The assumption that she wasn't going to be allowed to forget the weekend was confirmed a half hour later. As she stood in front of the bathroom mirror vigorously towel drying her hair, the phone rang. It was Andy Stapleton.

"I just wanted to make sure you were all right." Now that she was no longer the chief suspect, he sounded both solicitous and apologetic.

"I'm fine, Mr. Stapleton."

"If there's anything I can do, let me know."

When hell freezes over, Laura thought, but she was too polite to voice the sentiment.

"I'll be getting back to you soon with a revised Ravenwood proposal," he continued.

Laura stared at the phone. Emma Litchfield had been murdered. Laura had been falsely accused. And Andy Stapleton was still trying to put together a land deal. With very little pretense to politeness, she broke off the conversation.

She wasn't hungry, but she made herself eat a little bit of leftover Tarragon Chicken before crawling into bed.

There'd been no hope of sleeping last night in her jail cell. Not when a guard had come by for an hourly check. Not when every nerve in her body had been quivering with tension. Now, she found herself burrowing down into the comfort of her own scented sheets. Gratefully, she slipped into slumber almost as soon as her head touched the pillow.

For a few hours, she was at peace, until another dark, disturbing dream grabbed her by the throat and almost choked off her breath.

This time, a terrified voice called to her from the darkness. *Help me. Please help me.*

"Emma? Is that you, Emma."

Julie...Julie...my name is Julie.

"Julie?"

Help me. Please. Help me.

The dream. Laura strained her eyes, focusing on a white-robed figure flickering in the blackness. It was a woman with her arms outstretched, as if urging Laura forward. The scent of wildflowers hovered around her.

In the grip of an overwhelming compulsion, Laura began to walk toward the woman. But all at once the image was gone and she was terribly alone in the cold, dark hall at Ravenwood. Frightened, she turned to run. But there was no escape. The man who had pursued her night after night was behind her again. Behind Laura. Behind Julie. Somehow, Laura had become Julie, too.

Again, she ran. She could hear her pursuer's breath rasping in her ears like the scrape of a metal file against sand. Fear almost choked off her breath. Almost stole the strength from her legs, but somehow, she found the power to keep running. She dared not look over her shoulder. But a horrible truth dripped like acid into her brain.

There wasn't just one man after her. There were two. The one who was going to murder her. And the other, a shadow lurking in the background.

One of them caught her, whirled her to face him and fixed her with the blazing red stare of his terrible eyes. Suddenly, they were in a bedroom. In the next moment, he threw her onto a bed. Then his weight came crashing down on top of her, and she knew she was fighting for her life.

For long moments, terror clogged her throat. Then it found release in a scream that filled the darkness of the bedroom.

Laura sat up in bed, her heart threatening to hammer its way through her chest. This time she remembered more of the details than she had before.

The murder. Not Emma's murder. *Her* murder. The way she kept dreaming it over and over. No, *Julie's* murder. A woman named Julie. That was the way it had happened. They'd clamped a hand over her mouth so she couldn't scream, couldn't send them away.

Laura pressed her palms against her eyes, trying to rub away the confusion. The first part was so much like what had really happened at Ravenwood Saturday night. She'd heard a voice call to her in the darkness—just like when she'd gone downstairs and found Emma's body. Maybe she'd transferred it to the dream. That was why it seemed so real. But the rest had been just as vivid. The man who had pursued her night after night had grabbed her and thrown her onto a bed. And now there was a shadowy figure behind him.

Snapping on the bedside light, Laura huddled in the pool of illumination, her arms clasped tightly around her knees. Her eyes searched the framed pictures on the marble washstand as if they held the answers to her questions. They told her nothing. She couldn't shake the nightmare's stranglehold. As her conscious mind replayed the dream scene, she felt her scalp prickle as if ghostly fingers were combing through her hair. She shuddered. It was all so palpable. There was even a strange, lingering smell of perfume hovering around her like the cloying scent of flowers at a funeral.

But that wasn't the most disturbing part. It was the room in which the dream murder had taken place. The bedspread was different and so was the wallpaper. But she recognized ornaments on the dresser and the table, the chair in the corner, the distinctive carving of the paneled wall. It was the room in which she'd slept at Ravenwood.

Was the dream a prediction? Was she going back to Ravenwood? Would somebody murder her?

No. The nightmare was about someone else. A woman named Julie who'd been murdered. Laura was sure of that. As sure as she was of her own name.

For a few moments, Laura was absolutely convinced. Then she clenched her fists in denial. The dream wasn't a glimpse into the past. She was so stressed out from what had happened over the weekend that her mind was playing terrible, unhealthy tricks. No wonder she'd glommed on to that room as the scene of a murder. She'd just slept in it.

That was the logical explanation. Except that the dream was so convincing. As if another woman was reaching out across the years and pleading for her help.

Fiction or reality?

No, just more craziness, Laura told herself.

Chapter Seven

Somehow Laura managed to get back to sleep, probably because her body was simply too exhausted for her to sit up all night clutching her knees. She wasn't sure whether the dream came again. At least she didn't remember it, although she awoke with a vague uneasy feeling that seemed to hang around her in a stale cloud like the perfume from the previous installment.

Determined to put the incident behind her, she climbed out of bed and started to unpack the overnight bag she'd left on the floor the night before. In the bottom of the side pocket, she found the fairy cross, which she'd forgotten all about.

Even stashed away out of the sunlight, it still felt a bit warm, as if the little gold vein running through the center were an electric heating coil. Somehow, the minute Laura's fingers closed around the charm, she felt better. More peaceful. Safer. Maybe the old woman was right. Maybe it did have some sort of protective power.

On her way in to the office, Laura stopped to see Sabrina Berkley, the woman who'd opened a shop off the building's lobby. It sold herbs and condiments as well as a charming assortment of whatever had taken Sabrina's fancy. In fact that's what the shop was called: Sabrina's Fancy.

This morning the proprietor had pulled her untamed red

hair back and fastened it at the nape of her neck with a gold filigreed barrette. The sleeves of her cowl-neck dress were pushed back to the elbows. Bent over an antique East Indian table, she was grinding some fragrant combination of leaves and seeds with a marble mortar and pestle.

"Wouldn't it be easier to throw that stuff into a food processor?" Laura quipped.

Sabrina looked up in horror, as if Laura had suggested throwing her cat in. "No. The potency of the mixture comes as much from adhering to ancient ways as from the ingredients."

"You sound like a white witch."

A whimsical smile flickered on Sabrina's lips. "Sometimes I wonder—" She switched gears in midsentence. "Did you want some more of that scented soap? Or the May Wind tea?"

"No. I wanted some advice about magic amulets." Laura held out the gold-veined charm.

"A fairy cross."

Laura slid it into Sabrina's hand.

"It's beautiful. I guess you must have been up in Appalachian country."

"How do you know?"

"That's where they come from. People find them in certain rock formations. Did you buy this one at a country shop?"

"It was a present." Laura made the explanation as neutral as possible. "I was told it's a good-luck charm."

"I've heard that. You know, crystals can be in tune with a person's natural harmony. Believers say they benefit everything from your digestion to your love life." Sabrina caught Laura's skeptical look. "But if you don't buy any of that, you can just wear it. This one is perfect for your coloring. I think I've got just the right chain." She got up and began poking through one of the drawers in back of her counter. A few moments later she brought out a beautifully worked length of gold links.

Laura hadn't realized she could make the cross into a piece of jewelry. As soon as she heard the suggestion, it sounded exactly right. In fact, the idea took on a certain urgency. She found she was longing to slip the crystal over her head and feel its weight against her chest. "I'd like that," she murmured.

"Leave it with me, and I'll make you a fastening. You can pick it up this afternoon."

"How much is the chain?"

Sabrina named what sounded like a surprisingly modest price.

"That's all?"

"I've had it for a couple of years. I think it was just waiting for the right person."

Sabrina was like that, Laura mused as she headed for the elevator. When she wanted someone to have a particular thing from her shop, she practically gave it away. They'd engaged in a bit of reverse bargaining over the chain. In the end, Laura extracted a promise that Sabrina would make up the difference by asking for legal advice if she needed it.

Upstairs in her office, Laura tried to concentrate on an upcoming child-support hearing. Finally she gave up the effort and snapped the folder closed. Leaning back in her chair, she closed her eyes.

Yesterday she'd told Jake she wasn't interested in helping Police Chief Pickett. All she'd wanted to do was run from the horror and the fear. Now, the reprieved convict in her desperately wanted to go on with her life as if nothing had happened. But the lawyer couldn't be content to count her blessings. Someone had killed a human being. And that same person had tried to pin the murder on her. She wouldn't be serving herself—or justice—if she didn't see this through.

But there was something else going on, too. Something to do with nightmares. And an old murder. Something frightening because it was so outside of normal experience. Ravenwood had affected her in some strange way that she didn't understand. Maybe the effect had started even before she'd gotten there, although she couldn't begin to understand how. But she was afraid to poke into the twisted pathways of her own psyche.

With a shake of her head, Laura turned her attention back to the more concrete problem. She wasn't a criminal lawyer, but she'd studied the basics. Reaching for a pad of paper and a pencil, she wrote down a list of names and tried to fill in some blanks.

Andy Stapleton. He was hiding something about the ASDC deal. Had Emma found out? Would he have murdered her to keep her quiet?

Sam Pendergrast. Maybe he'd lost Emma to her father and taken an opportunity for revenge?

Ditto for Timothy O'Donnell. Or was he working some kind of scam that Emma had uncovered? Laura didn't know much about him, yet he seemed like the kind of man who might have all sorts of shady deals going.

Martha. What if she'd wanted Rex for herself? What if she'd been jealous all these years? But would she have been strong enough to push Emma down the stairs? Perhaps she was less fragile than she looked.

Finally, reluctantly, Laura came to Jake Wallace. He didn't seem to have a motive. But he was the only one who'd seen the knife. Or was he? Maybe Sam had spotted the box she'd been trying to hide. Maybe one of the other guests had known where it was and had planned to pick it up that weekend. Anyone could have seen her walking down the hall and into the burned part of the house. Which would mean they'd seen Jake, too.

Jake. Now that her mind was on him, it wasn't eager to change subjects. He had lied to Pickett to try and get her off. Surely he wouldn't have done that if he'd wanted to frame her. Laura leaned her elbows on the deck and cupped her chin in her hands. Thinking about Jake brought a whole wealth of feelings that she really didn't want to examine.

Just the facts, ma'am, she told herself sternly as she picked up the phone to call Jo O'Malley.

"You aren't free for lunch by any chance?" she asked her friend.

"Actually, I am."

"I'd like to talk to you some more about what happened at Ravenwood."

"I was hoping you'd open up with me."

Over soup and salad at Phillips Harborplace, Laura went into more detail about the weekend.

"I want to figure out what's going on, but I don't want to go back to Garrett County," she concluded.

"Yeah, Pickett and Ketchum both have a real law-and-order reputation." For a moment, Jo looked a little uncomfortable.

Laura raised inquiring eyes to the detective. Then she nodded slowly. "That's right. I forgot. You're from Garrett County."

"Yeah. So both those guys are part of the context of my life. You know," she mused, "you recognize people in a specific role and it's hard seeing them a different way. Pickett was the police officer who came to school and gave the kids safety lectures. And Ketchum—well—most people appreciate his tough approach."

Laura nodded.

"The trouble is, you're one of my best friends and they

were both pretty rotten to you. Not only that, I feel bad that I wasn't here for you over the weekend.''

''Nobody could anticipate what was going to happen.''

Jo ran her fingers up the side of her water glass. ''I've got some slack time this week. Why don't I see what I can dig up about the land deal. I won't be an outsider poking into things.''

Laura took a slow sip of her tea. For a moment, she considered telling Jo about the nightmares. Yet how could nightmares have any bearing on the investigation? ''I'd really appreciate it. But could you also maybe check out Tim O'Donnell? I'll be glad to pay you for the time.''

''Don't be ridiculous,'' Jo shot back.

''At least let me take care of the expenses.'' Laura swallowed, feeling foolish but determined to examine one more possibility. ''Uh—do you think you could also find out where Bill Avery was this weekend?''

''Bill? You don't think he had anything to do with this, do you?''

Laura shrugged. ''I'm not on his list of hundred favorite people.''

''I hope I can put your mind to rest on that one.''

''Jo, I don't know how to thank you. Meanwhile, I'll see what I can find out about Emma and my dad.''

Laura spent that evening and the next going through the things of her mother's that she'd stored in the basement. She stayed late at the task, deliberately tiring herself out, hoping she'd sleep at least until dawn. Monday it worked. But not Tuesday. She woke in a cold sweat, haunted by dream images, dream warnings, even that distinctive dream fragrance. Instead of staying in bed, she got up and went back to the boxes in the basement.

In one of the cartons she opened, she found a box that had once held Russell Stover Candy. Now it was full of letters that her parents had exchanged when her father had been in Korea.

Her fingers unconsciously played with the fairy cross and the gold chain as she read the correspondence. It was obvious that her parents had loved and missed each other. At first, reading the letters gave her a warm feeling about the two people who had brought her into the world. Then her cynicism kicked in. Her father had been far from home, afraid and lonely. No wonder he'd clung to her mother's letters and written to her with such ardor. But he hadn't loved his wife or his daughter enough for the long haul. That was the way it often went with men and women.

When Laura had finished sifting through the letters and other papers in the basement, she tried staying late at the office, doggedly working until she was almost ready to drop. On Thursday, as she was entering some notes on a child-custody case into her computer, she heard Noel talking animatedly to someone. Laura was tempted to get up and join the conversation. Then the talking stopped and the door closed. Laura returned to her work. After a few minutes, she began to feel uneasy. She knew she was alone in the office, but she didn't feel as if she was really alone.

Finally, it was impossible to ignore the prickling sensations that danced across her skin. Sliding out of her chair, she tiptoed to the door and peeked out.

A large male body was planted in the easy chair by the window. At first, Laura didn't register who it was. Jumping back, she gasped.

"Sorry." Jake rose out of the chair. "I didn't think I looked quite so threatening. I had a nice chat with your paralegal, Noel. She said it would be all right to wait for you."

"You're not threatening! I just didn't think Noel would close up shop with someone in the office. Why didn't you let me know you were sitting there?"

He put down the copy of the *New Yorker* he'd been perusing and flexed his left leg. "Noel said you had some stuff to finish up, so I was giving you a few more minutes."

Laura's initial reaction gave way to a quick rush of feeling she didn't want to label. How could she admit that she was soaking up his presence the way a wilted flower soaks up water? Jake looked good even in worn jeans, scuffed Adidas and a baggy crew neck sweater. Apparently, they didn't stand on ceremony down at the *Sun* papers, she decided, trying to bring her feelings back into perspective. She wasn't so much reacting to him as a man, she told herself. She was recalling how he'd been the only one who had stood by her after the murder.

"Aren't you going to ask me why I'm here?"

"I expect you have some information about Ravenwood."

Standing up, he hooked his thumbs through the belt loops of his jeans and rocked back on his heels. "How do you know?"

"I think you'd make sure you had a good reason for getting in touch with me—so I couldn't accuse you of simply making a social call. What do you have to tell me?"

He laughed. "You seem to be feeling a good bit better than the last time we saw each other, counselor."

Actually, she was suddenly feeling better than she had in days. "Well, I'm back on my own turf. And no one is trying to frame me for a murder I didn't commit." She didn't realize that her fingers had gone to the fairy cross hanging around her neck. As always the familiar warmth was comforting. Somehow the thing had turned into a kind of security blanket. She'd worn it every day since Sabrina had attached it to the gold chain.

Jake's eyes followed her hand. "What's that?"

"Just some new jewelry."

"It's pretty. Have I seen it before?"

"I don't think so."

When he came toward her, she realized she wasn't feeling quite so confident. Had the size of her waiting room shrunk, or was he just displacing too many of the air molecules for her to draw a deep breath?

His gaze rose from the cross to her face. "I do have some things to discuss with you."

"What?"

"I'd rather talk over dinner."

That sounded like a better idea than continuing the dialogue in such cramped quarters. "All right. Do you have someplace in mind?"

"Yes. My apartment."

"Jake—"

"Think about it. Where else can we have a really private conversation?"

Laura tried to remember all the reasons why she should say no. Instead she found herself asking, "Did you cook dinner?"

"I picked up carry-out from the Greek place around the corner. They've got great food."

Laura realized he was holding his breath, waiting for her decision.

"I suppose there's no point in wasting great food."

She saw him expel the captive air.

"Why don't I drive," he suggested. "You can pick up your car later."

"Okay. I was planning to come back here and get a little work done afterward."

"Don't you ever quit?"

"I'm taking time off for dinner and a discussion, aren't I?"

"I guess I'd better not push my luck."

It was only a short drive to Jake's apartment, which was in a former men's clothing factory off Paca Street, one of the older industrial buildings in the city that had been converted to residential use. As they rode up to the sixth floor in the elevator, she wondered what Jake's apartment was like.

"Come on in and make yourself at home while I check on dinner," he said as he turned the key in the lock. "Everything except the salad is in the oven."

Jake disappeared into the kitchen, and Laura looked around. Basically, the apartment was one huge room, with areas defined by various groupings of modern furniture. The effect would have been streamlined, except for the piles of books and papers on almost every surface.

Sports magazines and computer reference manuals were stacked on the square table beside the U-shaped sectional sofa and next to the pine shelves crammed with entertainment components and books. The overflow even extended to the stair risers leading to the loft—which must be where Jake slept, unless the sectional opened into a bed. Given the state of his housekeeping, Laura doubted it. Making his bed in the morning didn't appear to be Jake Wallace's style.

Laura drifted over to the outside wall. The warm red brick was set off by a fan-shaped window that looked out over the city.

Jake came up behind her. "What do you think?"

"I love your view."

"I spent a couple of hours straightening up the place."

"What did it look like before?"

"Don't ask."

He was standing so close behind her that she could feel his breath stirring her hair. The sensation sent a little tingle up the back of her neck. If she wanted to, she knew she could let it build into something more sensual. She deliberately pulled her attention back to business.

"What did you want to discuss?"

"Don't you want to eat first?"

"We can talk while we eat."

"Okay."

Jake had set several aluminum-foil pans on hot pads on the dark walnut table. Laura helped herself to *moussaka* and a couple of *spanakopitta*—flaky triangles filled with cheese and spinach—and some Greek salad.

"You're right. This is excellent," she acknowledged after a few bites.

"I may not be much of a cook, but I know how to order out."

Laura could see that he'd piled his plate with a generous helping of everything. "What did you want to tell me?" she prompted.

"I used some contacts down at the *Sun* to get a line on the original Ravenwood deal."

"There was a government restriction on developing the land. That's why the tract wasn't sold years ago and why the original investors were stuck with a dead turkey," Laura filled in before he could continue.

"How do you know that?"

"I asked a detective friend to check into it. She didn't find out much more than that. Except that Andy Stapleton came in like the Wizard of Oz and got the restriction lifted."

Jake took a swallow of the inexpensive white wine he'd poured into both their glasses. "The restriction dates back to the early forties. Andy Stapleton wasn't exactly being straight with us when he made his little presentation."

"Maybe whatever he did to get the land status changed was illegal," Laura suggested. "Maybe he paid someone off and Emma found out about it."

"My speculations were running along those lines, too. Andy could have killed her to shut her up—and decided to pin it on you."

"But the knife, the box—"

"He could have planted them. And taken the knife from your room later. I assume he had a key."

"But how did I know where to look for the stuff in the first place?" That was the question Laura had been subconsciously avoiding while she'd pursued other lines of inquiry. Now it had leaped to her lips.

Jake shrugged. "I don't know. Maybe if you tell me some more details about what happened to you that weekend, we can figure it out." He was staring at her chest. "Like, for example, is that the good-luck charm Ida gave you?"

The unexpected shift of subject and the challenging tone of his voice made her jump. "What?"

"Ida. You know, the old lady who was cleaning the rest room at the gas station."

"How—how do you know about her?"

"When I couldn't get Pickett to talk to me after he'd locked you up, I did some nosing around town. Cully, the guy who pumped your gas, told me about it. Said it's called a fairy cross."

"Why didn't you ask about it back in my office when you were admiring it?"

"I was waiting to see if you'd tell me." He reached for her hand across the table.

She snatched it away. "Why?"

"Because ever since we've started talking that first night at Ravenwood, I've had the feeling you were holding something back. I was hoping you'd decided to trust me enough to come clean with me."

Laura pushed her chair away from the table and stood up. Perhaps because she hadn't satisfied her own doubts about her strange midnight walk, she lashed out at Jake. "You think someone told me where to find that box."

His own chair scraped back and he faced her across the

table. "I didn't say that. We were talking about the fairy cross, not the box."

"The fairy cross. Right. What else have you been digging up about me?"

A guilty look swept across his broad face like a cold front moving over a TV weather map. "I was checking up on your ex-husband."

Laura had thought of the same thing, yet she didn't like finding out that Jake's mind was working along the same lines and that he'd gone ahead and started poking into her private life.

"Somebody killed Emma and framed you," he continued in answer to her scowl. "I want to find out why."

"It isn't your problem and I don't need your help." Laura started for the door.

Jake caught her and spun her around before she had taken two steps. "I think you do. You're going to start by telling me what has you so frightened that you won't even talk about it. Is somebody blackmailing you? Are you getting threatening letters? What?"

"Blackmail. My God. What do you think I've done?"

He took her by the shoulders. "I don't know what to think. Tell me, dammit!"

The air had solidified in her lungs. It was a surprise to discover that she could speak. "Nightmares, Jake. Just nightmares." Laura's voice rose half an octave. Now that she'd started, it was almost a relief to spit it all out. "The kind that make me wake up screaming. I keep seeing this woman who looks a lot like me. Her name is Julie and she's at Ravenwood. She calls out to me, begging me to help her. She's sleeping in the same room where I was sleeping and a man comes in and attacks her. No. Maybe it's two men. One of them kills her. Then he wraps her body in a tablecloth and dumps her into the ravine. You know, the ravine where Andy warned us not to go."

Laura stopped and sucked in a shuddering breath. She hadn't realized she knew so many coherent details. They'd come tumbling out of her mouth as she'd told the story to Jake.

"Laura. Good God."

"That's it. That's all. My deep dark secret." She swallowed. "I guess you think I'm cracking up."

"No."

She knew he'd answered automatically.

"Laura. I'm sorry. I don't know what to say."

Was he responding to her words or the hurt in her eyes?

"Jake, you don't have to say anything. I don't want to talk about it anymore. I'd just like to go back to my office and go to work now. If you don't want to drive me, I'll get a cab."

"I'll drive you."

They didn't talk on the way to 43 Light Street. When Jake pulled up at the front door, he turned to her. "I don't like leaving you like this. I don't like leaving *us* like this."

"Jake, just forget about *us*."

Before he could say anything else, she slid out of the car, shut the door and hurried toward the building.

Chapter Eight

Laura strode briskly across the parking lot, pulled open the glass door and walked into the Monday-morning hush of Macy's. It would have been an ideal time for a leisurely shopping expedition, but she hadn't come out to the department store at Owings Mills to buy anything. Yesterday, she'd gotten a surprise call from Martha Swayzee, the busybody who'd had so much to say about everybody at Ravenwood. They were meeting in the coffee shop adjoining the store's gourmet grocery.

The very idea of seeing Martha again had brought back the murder weekend in all its terrible detail. But Martha was an expert at preventing people from hanging up on her. She'd kept Laura on the phone by claiming to have some important information about the Ravenwood events. Laura was pretty sure Martha's real purpose was to pump her for juicy tidbits about her stay in jail. But she hadn't been able to turn down the opportunity to learn something about the estate and the original investors.

After taking the escalator to the upper level, Laura followed the smell of cinnamon to the small café. There were no other patrons except Martha, who sat at one of the round tables sipping a cup of tea and eating a bun. She was just as Laura remembered her. Gray hair, appraising eyes, brittle smile.

Martha gave her a head-to-toe inspection. "You're looking so well after your untimely incarceration, dear."

"Thank you," Laura answered tightly.

"Did that obnoxious sheriff treat you decently?"

"He wasn't a sheriff, and I'd rather put all that behind me, if you don't mind."

"Of course you would."

"If we're just going to talk about my stay in jail, I might as well say goodbye now."

"I was just offering my condolences before I told you a bit about your mother and father."

Maybe this *was* going to be interesting, Laura reminded herself, if she could sort fact from fiction. But she needed some fortification. "Let me get a cup of coffee first."

"And treat yourself to a cinnamon bun. They're so good here."

Laura was pretty sure she couldn't manage to choke down more than the coffee. When she came back to the table, Martha's dry-as-dust hands were delicately pulling apart the oversized bun and popping little pieces into her mouth.

"So what did you want to tell me about my parents?" Laura prompted.

"Your parents and Emmie."

"I already know Emma was the one who took Dad away from Mom."

"That's only the bare outline of the story. It made me feel so disloyal to say anything while Emmie was alive—or Rex, either."

Disloyal? Laura thought as she took a small sip of coffee. *What a joke.* "And now?"

"Emma was a strange woman. Sometimes she was utterly charming, sometimes ruthlessly calculating." Martha paused for effect. "I think she had some kind of hold over Rex. Something she knew he'd done that he didn't want anyone to find out about. She used whatever it was to get her hooks into him.''

''How do you know?''

''She had this way of gloating about her conquests—of giving you little hints of a story and letting you speculate about the rest.''

Laura wondered how much credulity she could give to the information source, yet she couldn't stop herself from asking the next question. ''What did my father do that was so terrible?''

''I don't know, except that I think it was something to do with Ravenwood.''

''Ravenwood!'' Laura shivered, and Martha smiled smugly at the reaction.

''Maybe you just want to leave the past buried. I only thought you should know that Rex really did love your mother and that he was devastated when she wouldn't take him back. Although I can see her side of the story, too.''

Laura stared unseeing at a display of gourmet jelly jars stacked on shelves in back of Martha.

''Sometimes the wrong relationship can be disastrous,'' the old woman went on. ''I noticed that you and that Jake Wallace were getting kind of cozy.''

At the mention of Jake, Laura's attention focused back on her companion.

''That man is bad news, dear. Maybe even dangerous.''

Laura had just taken a sip of coffee. The hot liquid went down the wrong way and she started to cough.

''Are you all right?'' Martha asked solicitously, reaching out to pat Laura vigorously on the back.

''Yes,'' Laura managed to say. ''What do you mean, 'dangerous'?''

''There's talk that he killed his wife.''

Laura's shock came out as denial. ''I don't believe it!''

Martha shrugged delicately. ''I'm afraid I don't know

any of the details. But I've heard that she was dragging him down just at the peak of his career and he wanted to get rid of her. At any rate, she's dead.''

As she stared at the old woman, Laura felt something inside her twist painfully, like a length of barbed wire unrolling. But she was absolutely determined not to give Martha the satisfaction of letting her strong reaction show. Probably, the woman was also counting on the shock value of her words to cut off further questions. Well, Laura wasn't going to oblige in that respect, either. ''I've never put much faith in gossip,'' she said in a steady voice. ''How did Jake's wife die?''

She had the satisfaction of seeing Martha's cheeks redden. ''You don't have to get so huffy. I was just trying to help you, dear. I believe Holly Wallace died of an overdose of sleeping pills.''

''And you're assuming Jake gave them to her? Why not assume she was depressed?''

''I understand she had inoperable cancer,'' Martha said carefully.

''Then how is Jake to blame for her death?''

''They do say he was the one who filled the prescription.''

''Are you trying to suggest that he went a step farther?'' Laura said carefully.

''Nobody knows what actually happened. I just thought you should have the information so you could make an informed decision about him.''

''Well, thank you so much for taking the time to get in touch with me,'' Laura said coolly as she pushed back her chair.

Martha's expression was uncertain.

''I really do have to be getting back to work,'' Laura continued as she stood and gathered up her purse.

''We'll have to get together for another chat very soon.''

"Mmm."

Laura made a graceful exit. The composed look on her face didn't slip until she was at the door of the coffee shop. But the barbed wire was ripping her insides to shreds.

At the same time, she was mounting a campaign of denial. In court, Martha's testimony would have been slashed to bits. She hadn't come up with a single concrete fact. Just hearsay and speculation.

But cool logic couldn't choke off Laura's pain. Her father being blackmailed? Jake giving his wife an overdose of sleeping pills? Oh, God, poor Jake. What had he been through when his wife was dying? What if she'd begged him to help her escape the torment? What would he have done? Stood by and watched her suffer, or let her persuade him to help her end the ordeal? Laura's chest squeezed painfully as she thought about the horrible choice.

And why had Martha told her about it, she wondered, steering her thoughts back to the old woman. Did Martha want Laura to be afraid of Jake? Morally outraged? Shocked? And why? So she'd stay away from him? That would make sense if Martha was worried that Laura and Jake could find something out about Ravenwood by working together.

Laura almost bumped into a stock boy who'd pushed a cart of fancy canned vegetables across the aisle.

"Are you all right, lady?"

Laura nodded automatically. It took several moments for the cart to be moved out of the way. When she realized her path was no longer blocked, she strode off again, running from her own emotional turmoil as much as from the evil accusations of the old woman back in the coffee shop.

Hardly conscious of where she was going, Laura stepped onto the down escalator. It took her to a different side of the store from the one she'd entered. Momentarily confused, she looked around for the shortest route back to the parking lot. It was over toward the left on the other side of the jewelry and belts. However, as she started into the scarf department, the suggestion of an aroma made her hesitate and then come to a dead stop like a sail boat caught in a sudden calm. Only she was feeling anything but calm as the memory of wildflowers washed over her.

All at once her original intention of leaving was forgotten. As if her feet had developed a will of their own, Laura turned and started moving in the other direction, weaving among displays of gloves and handbags, following the beckoning scent of the flowers. Their fragrance was mixed with other bouquets, yet she was pulled forward by the one haunting scent. Where had she encountered it before?

Her mind had blocked the memory, yet the sweetness of the aroma stood out among the rest like a searchlight on a moonless night. Taken by itself, the fragrance wasn't all that distinctive—sweet and delicate, as much as anything else. Yet it conjured up a whole wealth of lingering associations.

Beauty. Calm. Peace. Mind-numbing fear.

Laura stopped again, her whole body rigid with tension. The dreams. She'd wakened in the middle of the night with this fragrance lingering around her bed like shrouds of mist.

On legs that swayed unsteadily, she wobbled over to one of the perfume counters and leaned against the glass case for support.

"Can I help you?" a chicly dressed young woman asked.

"What is the name of that perfume I smell?"

"Which one?"

"The wildflowers."

"We have several that fit the description. Rambling Rose, Wild Clematis, Spring Meadow—let's see…and Queen Anne's Lace."

Laura had never heard any of the names before, but one pulled some inner cord. "The Spring Meadow."

"It's an older scent, but it's making a comeback. We have it available as cologne, perfume, body lotion and bath beads."

Laura watched in growing agitation as the woman worked the stopper from a small crystal bottle.

When she reached for Laura's wrist, she jumped back as if the sales lady had pulled out a hot poker to brand her flesh. "No! I don't want that on me," she gasped out.

Although the stopper hadn't touched Laura's skin, the scent from the uncapped bottle enveloped her like a cloud of poison gas. In the next instant, the sights, sounds and smells of the department store seemed to shimmer and fade into a white cloud of swirling snow.

She was cold. Icy. Terrified.

Laura clutched at the edge of the counter. Somehow, she kept herself from slipping to the marble floor.

"Miss, are you all right? Miss?" the clerk asked urgently as she recapped the flask.

It was as if an evil genie had been sucked back into a bottle. The world swam into partial focus, real and yet not real. When Laura blinked and tried to draw in a shaky breath, the essence of Spring Meadow seared her lungs.

"I'm sorry." Laura pressed frigid fingers to a brow that was beaded with icy perspiration. "I guess I'm not feeling too well."

"You must be allergic to the perfume. Sometimes that happens," the sales clerk said, but her voice sounded doubtful as she gave Laura an uncertain look.

"Yes. I guess that must be it." Laura was incapable of explaining further, even to herself.

"Do you want me to call a doctor?"

"Oh, no. Please don't go to any bother. I'm fine, really." Laura wanted to turn and bolt from the store, but it took a few moments before she was sure her legs would function properly. Then she began to edge her way out of the perfume department. Wisps of Spring Meadow followed her, almost like fingers clutching at her flesh, trying to pull her back. The light-headedness didn't dissipate until she had stepped out into the October sunshine again. Gratefully, she dragged in a deep lungful of the cold, crisp, uncontaminated air.

Spring Meadow. She could put a name to the scent from her frightening dreams. Up until now, the fragrance was the only pleasant thing she remembered from her nighttime journeys into terror. It wasn't pleasant any longer. Just a whiff had sent her spinning into the twilight zone like a drug addict having a flashback.

Opening the door of her car, Laura slid behind the wheel and sat with her head thrown back against the seat, fighting the sick terror rising in her throat. She'd always thought of herself as the kind of person whose feet were firmly planted on solid ground. And she'd never put much stock in first-person stories of experiences with the occult or extrasensory perception. Even when she'd blurted out the account of her dreams to Jake, she hadn't given her fear a label. But how else could she explain what was happening to her? It was as if some presence—call it a ghost—was hovering around Ravenwood. Somehow, the ghost was invading her dreams, forcing her thoughts into unfamiliar channels, tearing her life into shreds.

She knew that the idea had been creeping up on her slowly, like a prowler tiptoeing stealthily through the dark corridors of her psyche, waiting for the right moment to spring. Now it had thrown open some previously bolted door and leaped into the bright sunlight of the Owings Mills parking lot.

"No. I won't let it happen. It isn't true."

Laura shook her head vehemently, mentally slamming the door shut. She wasn't going to give in to that analysis. She'd been more upset than she'd realized by her discussion with Martha. She'd been susceptible to suggestion when she'd smelled the perfume. She was perfectly all right now.

Starting her car, she pulled out of her parking space and headed for the exit. She'd already taken too much time away from work this morning.

"Right now, you're not going to worry about Ravenwood or Jake or your father or Martha or ghosts," she told herself as she headed downtown. "You're going to attend to some of the clients who are paying you good money to handle their legal business." But the lecture couldn't stop the censured topics from chasing each other around in her mind like buzzards circling Emma Litchfield's dead body.

As she waited for a light to turn green, Laura tapped her foot lightly but impatiently against the accelerator. Briefs, case summaries and appeals were piling up on her desk. But when the signal changed, she turned left instead of continuing toward 43 Light Street. In a few minutes, she had reached the main branch of the Enoch Pratt Free Library.

The knife she'd found in the box had been buried under a pile of newspaper articles. Although they'd disappeared from her room along with the weapon, they were a matter of public record. She didn't have to figure out who had stolen them to read the news stories. All she had to do was get a duplicate.

Once inside the library, she located a public phone. First, she had to check in with Noel.

"Has anything come up this morning that I need to handle personally?" she asked when her paralegal's upbeat voice answered.

"You're in the clear," Noel said. "Until that custody hearing at two."

"Then I'll be at the library doing some research. Don't expect me back until after I finish at the courthouse."

"Okay. But you'd better leave me the number at the library, just in case something comes up."

Laura complied. After hanging up, she stood looking at the receiver. She'd been trying to deny her feelings, but the need to call Jake was like pressure building up inside so that her skin felt tight all over. Suddenly, it was desperately important to hear his voice and get his side of the story Martha had told her.

"Jake?" she asked eagerly when he answered the phone.

However, it was only a recording saying he'd be back later. Before the beep, she hung up. If she tried to leave a message, he'd know by her voice that she was upset. And there was no way she could go into any kind of explanation with a machine.

But she was feeling depressed and cheated as she headed slowly toward the library's reference section, as if she had to resolve everything this morning before it was too late.

She tried to shake off the melodramatic reaction. There was going to be time for the two of them to talk. Maybe not this minute. But later. This evening or tomorrow. Right now, she was playing hooky from work, and she'd better justify her unexcused absence.

At the reference desk, Laura put in a request for the issue of the *Morning Sun* whose front page she and Jake had discovered in the box. Ten minutes later, she received a roll of microfilm that she took to one of the viewer-printers. After locating the issue, she scanned the front-page articles, trying to fit each one into what she already knew. The Mafia boss who'd been assassinated. Did he have something to do with Ravenwood? What about the mass murderer in Florida? Either of them could have used the remote estate for a hideout if they'd had the right connections to the investor-owner.

Drug addiction. That could be related to the wild parties given at the house.

The state education budget. A connection was unlikely. But had that been the article that triggered Jake's obvious interest?

Finally she reached the story in the series on environmental-health issues. Again, that didn't seem like a hot topic with regard to Ravenwood. The estate wasn't near any factories or sources of pollution as far as she knew.

She also dismissed the articles on capital punishment and the Quebec restaurant bombing.

Laura was disappointed. But she wasn't going to give up. What about the material she and Jake hadn't been able to read? The stories that were burned to a crisp. They probably came from the same time period. Still not sure what she was looking for, Laura kept advancing the reel and scanning the headlines.

Whoever invented microfilm must not have been fazed by eye strain. Half an hour later, Laura's head was throbbing, and she was having trouble focusing. She'd leave as soon as she finished this section of the paper, she told herself, as she began to turn the wheel faster.

Just before she reached the end of the tape, half-inch-high letters on one of the inside pages stopped her hand in midspin.

WOMAN DIES AT GARRETT COUNTY ESTATE

The partially clad body of a young woman was discovered in the ravine at Ravenwood, a Garrett County estate, yesterday. Identified as Julie Sutton, the woman was a feature reporter for the *Baltimore News American* who had been vacationing in the area. She had been officially missing since the week before when she failed to return to work.

According to the county medical examiner, Miss

Sutton, 29, died as the result of a fall, possibly while walking along the ravine.

The body was found by the members of Baltimore Boy Scout Troop 10594 who had taken advantage of several days of good weather to hike in the area.

Ida Licotta, a maid employed at the estate, confirmed that Miss Sutton had been a guest at a party there the weekend before and had disappeared under suspicious circumstances. "I cleaned her room Saturday. I weren't mistaken about which one it was 'cause she had that fancy paneling. When I went in there on Sunday, all her things was gone. But we had a devil of a snowstorm that night, and there weren't no car tracks in the driveway. I couldn't figure how she'd left," Mrs. Licotta said.

Rex Roswell, one of the other weekend guests, remembered that Miss Sutton had gone to bed early Saturday evening and had not appeared for breakfast on Sunday. However, a number of other guests also missed the early meal and he simply assumed they were all sleeping late.

Miss Sutton was described as slender, about five foot four, with blue eyes and wavy blond hair. Local authorities are asking area residents for any information.

Police are also in the process of contacting guests who attended the affair.

In the past few years, the Ravenwood estate has acquired a questionable reputation in the community due to a number of incidents related to boisterous parties. Ravenwood owners have also filed a trespassing complaint against the Boy Scout troop members who found Miss Sutton's body.

Laura's skin seemed to have taken on a coat of ice as she read the article. Gasping for air, she tried to push herself away from the microfilm viewer-printer and found her body was shaking too violently.

All this time she'd been terrified that she was going crazy. Now here was evidence in black-and-white that her dreams had at least some basis in reality. She hadn't read this article before. But it confirmed important details from the horrible nightmares that had been plaguing her sleep for months. A woman named Julie—Julie Sutton—had died at Ravenwood and been found in the ravine. She'd been blond and blue eyed. And she'd stayed in the same room that Laura had occupied on her own visit. Laura was willing to bet the woman hadn't died as the result of an accidental fall.

There was always a man in the dream. A man and another shadowy figure with him. The man had killed Julie and carried her to the ravine. That part was so vivid. But there wasn't a hint about it in the article.

Laura's father, Rex, had been at Ravenwood that weekend. Was he the man she kept dreaming about? The murderer? Or his accomplice, the figure in the background? The very thought made her stomach clench. No. Not her father. Not the man who had written those warm, loving letters. Or had he totally changed? Had Emma somehow coerced him into a terrible immoral role? Laura forced her mind to consider other details. What about Ida? It wasn't all that common a name. Was she the old woman from the gas station? Thinking back to their brief talk, it had sounded as if she'd had firsthand knowledge.

How was it all tied together? Did Emma's murder have anything to do with Julie's?

Julie was a reporter. Had she been digging into a story at Ravenwood? Was that why she'd been at the party? Had the Mafia boss been one of the guests?

With a shudder, Laura's mind went back to the dreams.

It was as if Julie had been calling out to her across the years—begging her to set things right. Of course, that didn't make a lot of sense. Unless you believed in ghosts. Unless you believed that Julie's tortured soul was still at Ravenwood—longing for justice, longing to be set free.

Laura printed a copy of the article before returning to the reference desk and requesting microfilm from the next few months. This time, she scanned the headlines, looking for additional articles on Julie.

The follow-up story she found in an issue from about a month later made her draw in a sharp breath, although she'd been half expecting something like it. According to Deputy Chief of Police Hiram Pickett, there were no leads in the case. All the guests at Ravenwood had water-tight alibis, and no one else had ventured onto the premises because of the storm. The deputy police chief had come to the conclusion that the death was an accident. There had been a considerable amount of alcohol in Julie's bloodstream. Maybe she'd simply wandered out into the storm and lost her way and no one had missed her until it was too late. With the goings on at the estate, he wouldn't be surprised.

So, their buddy Pickett had been the investigating officer. Was he covering up a murder? Or had someone pulled the wool over his eyes? Who? Laura's father? One of the other guests? Maybe Martha had been at that party, too. Maybe even Emma.

Laura made several more trips to the reference desk. Next, she requested microfilm from the *Baltimore News American,* from six months before the fatal party. The paper had gone out of business in the late seventies, but the back issues were still on file.

She found a whole slew of material written by Julie Sutton, all from the feature section. Stories about summer fun at Ocean City, Babe Ruth's house, the art show at Druid Hill Park. It didn't look as if Julie had been an investigative reporter. The only thing that seemed remotely pertinent was a piece about vacation property in Garrett County. Maybe she'd been at Ravenwood doing a follow-up on that. Or maybe she'd just been there having a good time with people she'd met on her previous trip and had stumbled into something dangerous.

Deep into the investigation now, Laura would have stayed at the library all day doing more research, except for her custody hearing at two. She left with printed copies of both *Sun* articles and a stack of material Julie had written.

To her relief, the custody hearing went well. Because the husband had been abusive, Laura and her client walked out with sole custody of the woman's daughters and a restraining order against harassment by the father. When her client gave Laura a grateful hug, she felt guilty. Her full attention hadn't been on the proceedings. Luckily, she'd already prepared the groundwork weeks ago.

Back in her office, she inspected the mountain of work that needed her attention. But instead of tackling it, she started in again on the Ravenwood material. First, she read some of the articles by Julie Sutton. They were well researched and often funny and charming. The woman had talent. What a shame she had never been allowed to develop to her full potential. It was hard to tear herself away from Julie's writing, but Laura finally acknowledged that the articles weren't going to shine any light on the Ravenwood murders. She was going to have to take a more direct approach.

At five-thirty, Noel stuck her head in the door.

"Do you need me for anything else?"

"No. And you should have left already. I'll see you in the morning."

"You're sure?"

"You've put in a full day. Go on home before I chase you out. I'm just fooling around with personal stuff."

She couldn't ask for a more loyal assistant than Noel, Laura mused as she turned on her computer and modem. She started by querying data bases, requesting correlations between key words in the *Sun* articles she'd found and Ravenwood or Garrett County. A half hour later, the system had provided bibliographic references to a dozen articles. She looked over the summaries and requested the full text of four. Only one was downloaded, the rest would be sent by fax.

The lone article was about a company named Fairbolt sponsoring an educational program on ecology in the Garrett County schools. Laura scanned the story but couldn't see anything significant tying it into Ravenwood.

While she was waiting for the service to send her the faxes of the off-line articles, Laura realized she hadn't eaten anything since breakfast. Her first thought was to pick up some dinner at the deli next door, until she remembered that it closed at two. She'd have to walk down to one of the food stands at Harborplace.

It was light when she left her office, and a number of suites in her hallway were still occupied. When she returned half an hour later with her hard-shell crab sandwich, the marble lobby was dark and quiet, with only one brass-shaded lamp providing any illumination. The other bulbs must be burned out. Or maybe the cost-conscious owners were cutting corners again. Shadows and silence had never bothered Laura until the past few weeks—until the nightmares had started. Unable to stop herself, she turned and pressed her shoulders against the wall while she waited for the elevator to wheeze down from one of the top floors. She just hoped nobody came out and saw her cowering there like a fool or a criminal.

The hard marble was cold but reassuring against her

back. Just to fill the silence, she began to hum "You've Got a Friend" under her breath.

It was such a long wait that she almost decided to take her sandwich home and forget about finishing up the on-line search until the morning. But that would mean leaving her computer on overnight. And also that she wouldn't have any additional material to study until tomorrow morning. Instead, she hummed all the way up in the elevator and all the way down the hall to her office.

Unlocking the door, Laura stepped into the waiting room, the key still dangling from her fingers. "You've Got a Friend" died on her lips.

Something wasn't right.

She'd been nervous all the way up here. Now she remembered the way she'd reacted last week when Jake had been sitting in the chair by the window and she'd been at her computer. Somehow she'd known she wasn't alone. She felt the same way now. Only this time, she was in the waiting room and someone was hiding in her office. Again, the hair on the back of her neck stirred.

No, she was letting her imagination play nasty tricks. Everything was just the way she'd left it. The desk light and the computer were on; the door was slightly ajar.

Still, she couldn't shake the fear that she wasn't alone. "Jake?" she called, feeling irrational even as she said his name. Had she been sending him extrasensory messages. Had he somehow known how much she wanted to talk to him and come over after work? But how would he have gotten in? And would he want to talk to her after the way she'd left things between them.

Laura reached for the light switch beside the door. Illumination flooded the waiting room, making her instantly more secure. However, in the next moment as she blinked in the light, she caught a blur of motion at the office door.

Gasping, she took a step back. It was too late. A hand thrust through the door. A hand holding a gun.

Laura saw the flash from the muzzle and heard the report reverberate in the small room. A millisecond later, she was knocked backward. Pain exploded in her chest. Doubling over, she sagged to the floor.

Chapter Nine

The story of another death was spread across the bottom of Tuesday *Evening Sun*'s "Maryland" section front page. It was accompanied by a photograph.

LOCAL ATTORNEY KILLED
IN ARMED ROBBERY

A Baltimore attorney, was killed yesterday during a robbery attempt at her office. Laura Roswell, 31, who specialized in women's and children's issues, was working late and apparently surprised an armed intruder when she came back to her office with a carry-out dinner. She was shot once in the chest.

Dr. Kathryn Martin, a tenant in the building at 43 Light Street where Ms. Roswell maintained her law practice, discovered the body in the morning on the way to her own office. Noticing that the door to the third-floor suite was ajar, she stopped to investigate and discovered Ms. Roswell sprawled on the floor.

Building superintendent Lou Rossini speculated that the attacker came in during normal business hours and waited to burglarize one of the offices.

In a bizarre twist, Ms. Roswell herself had been arrested recently in connection with the murder of a houseguest at a Garrett County mansion. Charges were later dropped. Police are investigating to determine if the two incidents are related. According to Detective Evan Hamill, there are no suspects in the robbery-murder.

Other tenants at 43 Light Street expressed shock when they learned of Ms. Roswell's death. "Laura was a wonderful person," said private detective Jo O'Malley. "I don't know who would want to do this to her. She was well liked by everyone in the building." Noel Emery, Ms. Roswell's assistant, expressed similar views. "She was a great person to work for. I keep thinking that if I hadn't let her talk me into going home while she was still working, maybe she'd be alive now."

HEART PUMPING against his ribs like a steam piston, Jake tried to hold the newspaper steady. His hands were shaking too much. With a curse he spread the front page across his computer keyboard. Last night at the Caps game, he'd had to stop himself from finding a pay phone and calling Laura. The conviction that she'd needed him had been so strong.

He'd still been thinking about her the whole time he'd been getting dressed and driving to the office. And now—

Fighting the sick feeling churning in his stomach, Jake scanned the first paragraph again, hoping against hope that his mind was playing terrible tricks, hoping it was all a mistake. But nothing had changed. The harsh black newsprint that swam before his eyes said the same thing.

Laura was dead. Laura Roswell. Not some other attorney with the same name. The woman he'd pulled into his arms that night at Ravenwood thinking they were participating in an Oscar-winning performance. Then he'd found out how wrong he was. And the kiss had only been the beginning.

Now there was an ending. She'd been shot in the office where he'd waited for her last week. His mind still couldn't make any sense of it.

Eyes closed, Jake fought to draw oxygen into his lungs. But his chest felt as if a three-hundred-pound linebacker were stomping on him—with cleated shoes.

Laura. No, not Laura.

He'd been taken by surprise when she'd told him about the nightmares. It had been the last thing he'd expected her to say, and his response hadn't exactly been supportive. But once he'd started thinking about the whole thing, it had fit.

Like the way she'd kept going back to the burned-out part of the house. Or the way she'd looked as if she was in a trance when he'd followed her that night. And then there was her reaction afterward. Her fear. Her reluctance to tell him what she thought was happening. Finally, the pressure of what she'd been going through had been too much and she'd finally spilled it all out. But he hadn't been any help. He'd only acted as if she was a nut case.

Jake leaned his elbows on the desk top and cupped his forehead in his hands, unable to hold back the tears that brimmed in his eyes and began to spill down his face. He could picture Laura lying on the office floor—cold and pale—because he was intimately acquainted with death.

It was still too much to absorb. He needed to hear what had happened—more than just the impersonal newspaper account. Scrabbling through the pieces of paper in his wallet, he found Jo O'Malley's number. She was the friend Laura had asked him to call before Pickett had marched her away, and was quoted in the article. With quick, jabbing motions, he punched her number.

"Jo O'Malley speaking."

"This is Jake Wallace."

"Yes, Jake." Her voice was soft. "I was wondering if

you'd call. I'm sorry I was out of town when you tried to reach me from Garrett County.''

"Yeah, well, Laura wanted me to get in touch with you when she was in jail. A lot of good that does her now.''

"Jake, I know you're shocked. This is pretty bad for me, too. For everybody down at 43 Light Street.''

"Do you know any more than they're sayin' in the papers?''

"Not really." She cleared her throat. "Laura told me about meeting you at Ravenwood.''

"She talked about me?''

"Yes.''

"What did she say?''

"She liked you, Jake. But—she'd been hurt by Bill, her ex-husband. And she was afraid to trust her feelings.''

He swallowed around the baseball-sized lump in his throat. "I know.''

"I'm sorry the two of you didn't have a chance to work things out," she added.

"Do you think we could have?''

"Yes. I think you were good for her.''

It was cold comfort, but he clutched it to his breast. "I— Jo—thanks.''

"I'll call you when we know about the funeral.''

"I'd appreciate that.''

He hung up quickly before his voice got any thicker. Then he sat hunched in his chair with his eyes squeezed shut and his fists clenched against his chin.

A messenger came into the tiny cubicle, left a stack of photo copies Jake had ordered from the library last night and backed away. Jake didn't acknowledge the intrusion.

"Laura, I'm sorry," he whispered when he was alone again.

He'd failed her. Just the way he'd failed Holly. No, this was different. Holly's haunted gaze had followed him around the room until he could hardly bear to make eye contact. Laura had been in one hell of a mess. But she hadn't asked for anything until the last time he'd seen her. And then he'd blown it. He'd let her down. The way her father had. And her husband.

Now he felt a strange mixture of self-disgust and grief. It had almost happened again. He'd almost let himself care too much. Only this time, fate had stepped in a little more quickly. But somehow, that didn't make it hurt any less.

"I'M SORRY, JAKE," LAURA murmured as she stared unseeing out the bedroom window at Kathryn Martin's Ellicott City garden. She'd gone to sleep thinking about Jake, and he'd been the first thing on her mind when she woke up. She knew how much this charade would hurt him. But the police hadn't given her any other choice.

Everyone who'd been at Ravenwood during the investors' weekend was a murder suspect—and not just in the Emma Litchfield case. Now they were conducting the Laura Roswell attempted-murder investigation, as well.

With tentative fingers, Laura touched the center of her chest. It still felt as though she'd been sandblasted. The only reason she wasn't in the hospital for observation after her close brush with death was that Dr. Martin had volunteered to keep an eye on her.

"Laura, are you awake?" The low-voiced question was followed by a light knock at the door.

It was five in the afternoon. Laura hadn't gotten to bed until eight that morning because there'd been so many details to take care of once she'd realized that playing dead was the best way to stay alive.

"Come on in."

A couple of years older than Laura, with sparkling blue eyes and wavy brown hair, Katie was subletting Abby Franklin's office while the psychologist was on a six-month tour of India with her husband. Now she stepped into the bedroom carrying a tray with a cup of coffee and an English muffin. She also had a stethoscope hanging around her neck and a medical bag tucked under her arm. They were a bit incongruous with her faded jeans and plaid flannel shirt.

"How's our patient doing?"

"You didn't have to bring me breakfast—dinner—whatever it is—in bed."

"You're supposed to be taking it easy. And while I'm here, let me listen to your heart and lungs again." The physician made quick work of the examination and then changed Laura's bandages. "You're doing fine."

"And damn lucky to be alive." Once more Laura gingerly moved her fingers against her chest, still half expecting to find a hole gushing blood. The police were amazed that the crystal cross she'd worn around her neck had stopped the bullet. So was Laura. Was it possible the talisman had supernatural powers? What else could explain it? She had debated whether to share her speculations with the police, then decided to keep her mouth shut and let them simply think she'd been lucky. Maybe she had. Her worst complaint was that brittle shards of crystal had shredded the fabric of her blouse and left needle-sharp slivers in her flesh. None of the wounds was too deep, so Katie had simply removed the fragments and bandaged the wounds.

But that was just the beginning of an incredible twenty-two hours.

Katie hadn't discovered Laura in the morning as the newspaper article had reported. That was part of the fabrication they'd worked out. Lou Rossini, the building's superintendent—who'd been making his evening rounds—had heard the shot and rushed into the office to investigate. He'd known Katie was still upstairs working and had called her when he'd found Laura sprawled on the floor.

Things had really gotten interesting when the police arrived twenty minutes later. The detective who had walked in the door was Evan Hamill, the same man who'd helped the task force when Jo O'Malley had been abducted by a psychopathic killer the year before. Laura, Lou and the black detective had gotten to know each other during the search for Jo.

"Can you identify the man who shot you?" Hamill had asked.

"I'm afraid I only saw an arm and hand with a gun and then his legs when I was lying on the floor."

"Did he take anything?"

Laura began to open file and desk drawers. "I don't think so. No—wait. The newspaper articles I got from the library this afternoon are gone." She pressed some buttons on her keyboard. "And the computer queries I was making are wiped out."

"What's important about the articles and the computer stuff?" Hamill demanded.

Swallowing her reluctance, Laura told him and Katie about Ravenwood, Emma's death and the murder charge against her. She also speculated about the Julie Sutton connection. "But why didn't they leave the newspaper articles?" she asked the detective. "As soon as I saw they were missing, I started thinking that the break-in must be connected."

"You weren't going to see they were missing. You were going to be dead," the detective replied evenly. "And no one else would have known you had the material."

The unimpeachable logic made Laura's scalp crawl.

"Maybe when you beat the murder rap up in Garrett County, whoever killed Emma decided to follow you to Baltimore and finish the job. Too bad he can't go on thinkin' he did."

"But why can't he?" Laura asked in a quiet voice. "The

guy shot me from ten feet away and didn't stay around to take my pulse. As far as he's concerned, I'm history.''

Hamill pursed his lips. ''If he doesn't find out otherwise, that would sure be the safest thing for you.''

''But wouldn't he check the TV and newspaper to make certain he really put you away?'' Katie asked.

''Yeah. He'd have to be certain it was true, all right. And I'm not sure the department would go along with pulling a fast one like that. They're not exactly *Miami Vice*,'' Hamill added. Yet there was a gleam in his eye that told Laura his agile mind had begun to turn over the idea.

''I was just thinking out loud,'' Laura interjected before they all got too carried away. ''Actually, I'm not sure I could go for it, either. What happens to my clients if they think I'm dead?''

''What happens to them if the guy who shot you comes back to finish the job?'' Katie asked.

''You've got a point.''

''Let's talk about it,'' Hamill suggested.

As they hashed over the idea, studying the pros and cons and enumerating what needed to be done, the impossible scheme began to look as if it could work. With the help of the police department and Jo O'Malley, and with the okay of the District Attorney's Office, Operation Opossum went into effect.

Now sitting in Katie's bedroom, Laura clasped her hands together and pressed them against her lips.

It wasn't just Jake who'd be hurt by her deception. She'd gotten so involved in some of her clients' lives. Now she felt conscience-stricken about running out on them, even after Jo had promised to arrange for another attorney to take over the most pressing cases.

Laura might have been worried about her clients, but her mind kept coming back to Jake. What if her premonition at the library had been right? If she hadn't been wearing the fairy cross, there never would have been a second chance to talk to Jake. But what if there never was going to be a second chance? What if he felt so hurt and betrayed once the truth could be told that he could never trust her again? Guilt and loss gnawed at her. She drove the hurt away the only way she could—with another question. Had Jake really been honest with her?

"You look pale. Do you want to go back to sleep?" Katie asked.

"No, I want to get up and get dressed."

"If you take it real easy."

Laura climbed out of bed and stood holding on to her friend for a moment.

"How do you feel?"

"A little shaky. But a shower would feel great."

"Make it a bath. And don't get your chest wet."

"Okay," Laura agreed.

"Leave the door ajar—in case you need help."

Laura sat down on the edge of the tub while she opened the taps. As far as Hamill was concerned, the plan was for her to stay in hiding at Katie's while the police tracked down the killer. She hadn't told anyone that staying in seclusion was impossible. She was involved in this mess the way no one else was. At first she'd been afraid that her dreams were a symptom of mental illness, but the newspaper articles about Julie Sutton had changed everything.

Perhaps the police would dig something up. But they didn't have the advantage—or maybe it was a curse—that she'd been given.

Every time she put the theory into words, it still sounded like the ravings of a lunatic. Julie Sutton's spirit—or ghost or whatever it was—had reached out to her across the years and provided her with special information. She didn't understand why she'd been picked. Maybe it had something to do with looking like Julie. Or maybe it was because of her father. What if she were being called upon to atone for his past mistakes?

She could wait for another one of the dreams she dreaded. Or she could go back to Ravenwood where the vibrations—or whatever they were—were strongest. While she was there, she'd do some exploring. She didn't consciously admit that somewhere along the line, the need to return to the Garrett County estate had turned into a compulsion that she couldn't fight.

The next morning, when Katie went out to get some groceries, Laura put on the disguise Jo had provided in case she had to go down to police headquarters and wrote Katie a note explaining she'd gone to Ravenwood and would call that evening. She also apologized for taking Katie's car, even though the physician had another.

As Laura drove toward western Maryland, she slipped a finger under the edge of her brunette wig and scratched her temple. The damn thing itched. Or maybe the problem was having to jam it down on top of her pinned up blond hair.

Glancing in the rearview mirror, she was amazed at the transformation in her appearance. It was weird how big a difference could be made by darkening eyebrows and using different makeup. Of course, Katie's jeans and flannel shirt didn't hurt. They were the right size, but they definitely weren't Laura's normal style or color. And neither were the huge sunglasses she'd purchased at the drug store. She'd wear them if she got out of the car.

Her altered appearance gave Laura some sense of security, although she certainly didn't plan on buying any gas from Cully. Still, she'd have to be crazy not to be anxious about what she was doing. The chief of police had as much as promised he'd arrest her if he saw her in the area.

Laura was suddenly unable to hold back a wild little laugh. There was one gigantic factor that kept slipping her mind because it was such a bizarre concept. No one would be looking for her. No one would be expecting her at Ravenwood or anywhere else in Garrett County. No one would be giving a thought to Laura Roswell because she was supposed to be dead. There were newspaper articles and TV reports to prove it.

Still, the closer she got to her destination, the tighter her hands gripped the wheel. Dead or not, she hadn't lost her reflexes.

It was early in the afternoon when Laura turned in at the Ravenwood gateposts. This time, she was grateful for the underbrush pressing in on either side of the rutted drive because she knew it would hide her car. Instead of following the winding tract all the way to the house, she turned onto an almost invisible side road she hadn't even noticed on her first visit. It was about an eighth of a mile away from the house, but somehow, it seemed prudent to walk the rest of the way. Climbing out of the car, she reached for the knapsack that she'd brought along and hoisted it over one shoulder.

At the edge of the woods, Laura stood still and regarded the looming mansion. It was just what she remembered, a gigantic fortress of gray stone. Except that now it looked abandoned. There were no lights in the windows and no cars in the parking area. Over the past two weeks, dry leaves had blown across the front lawn and drifted against the foundations. Nothing moved but the wind, gently stirring the leaves and swaying the branches of the trees. Up here, the wind was cold, and Laura was glad she'd borrowed Katie's woodsman jacket.

For several minutes, Laura cowered in the shadows of the oaks and maples, eyes and ears straining as she focused on the house. She knew she was marshaling her courage to approach it. Maybe no Garrett County residents were on the property. But Julie Sutton was in there somewhere. Not her body. Her restless spirit.

The sun was hidden behind a cloud as Laura made her way toward the mansion. Pulling up the collar of the borrowed coat, she hunched her shoulders against the wind and shoved her hands into her pockets.

As she walked across the parking area, her sneaker-clad feet crunching on the fallen leaves, she wondered how she was going to get into the house. She'd brought a screwdriver, a rope and a hammer in her pack, but she wasn't sure what she was going to do with them. She might have been accused of murder, but she had never been on the wrong side of a breaking-and-entering charge.

Deciding on a less invasive option, she tried the front door. It was locked. But the window next to it was unlatched. It yielded when she gave the sash a hard upward push.

Until now, she still hadn't broken any laws, except maybe trespassing—like those Boy Scouts in the ravine. As she hoisted herself up and climbed through the window, she was conscious of taking a step into unknown territory.

When Laura's feet hit the floor, her first thought was that it felt good to get in out of the wind and chill. Her second was that it was eerie to be in this place where she told herself she'd never return. She wanted to flip on a light to dispel the shadows lurking in the corners, but that wouldn't be a good idea. Instead, she pulled out the flashlight she'd stuck in her backpack and trained it on the stairs.

On the drive up, she'd planned her course of action. Eventually, she'd have to explore the burned-out portion of the house. But she also needed to search the room in which she'd slept. Someone had taken the box from the night table and then awakened her when everyone else was asleep. Either the intruder had had a key or there was some way to get into the room besides the door. At the very least, she needed to see if there was a ledge outside the window. And she also wanted to look for evidence. Maybe the intruder had left something behind.

An almost palpable silence followed her up the stairs and down the long hall. As she tiptoed down the corridor, she couldn't shake the conviction that she was being watched, even though all the doors were closed.

"Julie?" she whispered, feeling a little frisson of fear skitter up her spine. It was one thing to acknowledge the existence of a Ravenwood ghost when you were in the parking lot of Owings Mills Mall. It was quite another to contemplate the prospect from this close a vantage point.

A patch of light knifed across the hall in front of her. It was coming from her room, she realized. The only one to which the door stood ajar. Why?

As she tiptoed up to it, Laura could feel her heart start to gallop. Inching the door open, she peered inside. To her profound relief, the room was empty. Yet the tension didn't lessen.

"Julie?" she questioned again. There was still no response.

The bed had been stripped, and the mattress was covered with clear plastic, but the knickknacks she remembered were still on the tables and the shelf along the paneled wall.

First she checked the window. It was at the back of the house and three stories above the ground with no balconies or ledges. No one had climbed up there unless he'd had an extension ladder.

Next she searched the closet. There were no telltale pieces of physical evidence. And the walls seemed to be solid. Laura was disappointed. She'd been so sure she would find something.

"Now what, Julie?" she whispered.

You haven't finished with the room. The answer echoed in her head. But it could just as well have come from her own mind as from the supernatural. Once you started expecting ghostly communications, you were more likely to receive them, Laura thought wryly.

Still, it was startling to turn back to the bedroom and find that the light had changed completely, as though someone had flipped the switch. But the illumination wasn't coming from inside. The sun was no longer blocked by a cloud, and warm rays streamed through the window, shining directly on the paneled wall.

The illumination brought out the rich color of the wood and highlighted the carved design—particularly a row of circular flowers about five feet from the floor. The center of each one was deeply indented—but two right in the middle caught the light in a different way from the others. With an odd, shivery feeling, Laura crossed the room and poked one of the dissimilar flowers with her finger. When the finger went right through the wall, she gasped and pulled her hand back.

A mixture of trepidation and excitement churning in her chest, Laura began to tap lightly on the paneling. It was solid, except for a three-foot section in the middle. Just the right size for a hidden door. In fact, now that she knew what to look for, she could see the seam. But how did it open? And did it lead to secret storage or a secret passage?

Laura had read about this sort of thing in books on old houses. Hidden passages had a number of purposes. Sometimes, the owner of the property had wanted to spy on his guests. Sometimes, he'd been preparing for midnight assignations—or to make a quick getaway from the law. Sometimes he'd simply been eccentric.

Laura began to run her fingers along the wall, checking for pressure points or concealed latches that might spring the mechanism open. Finally, when her fingers hit one of the flowers on the left side of the wall, it slid up, revealing a circle with a button in the center. It looked like an old-fashioned buzzer.

For a moment Laura hesitated. Maybe this thing was a booby trap and the light fixture or something worse would come crashing down on her head. Or maybe it was an alarm. With her teeth clenched, she pressed the button. For a moment, she thought that nothing had happened. There was no sound of wheels moving or gears grinding. As if the tracks had been oiled that morning, the panel slid to the side and she was staring into a dark, musty tunnel wreathed with spider webs.

She'd found a secret passage, all right. And in the room where she'd slept. But where was the other end of the tunnel, she wondered as she peered inside. It looked about as inviting as the burned part of the house, but she was going to have to investigate.

She had just taken a tentative step inside when she stopped dead in her tracks. The house had been blanketed in brooding silence. Now she could hear something.

Footsteps. Coming toward her from the lightless, gaping hole into which she'd stepped.

Heavy footsteps. Unmistakably moving in her direction. Around a bend, she saw the beam of a flashlight.

Laura ducked back into the room, knocking off her wig as it brushed the opening. She didn't even notice as she jabbed at the button that controlled the panel. It didn't respond. Could she outrun whoever was about to turn the corner? Probably not. And he had a big advantage. In a moment, he'd be able to spot her standing there in the room, and she wouldn't be able to see him in the dark passage.

Jumping to the side, she looked wildly around for a weapon and grabbed for the statue of Cupid and Psyche. It wasn't much, but it was all she had.

Laura's blood roared in her ears. Her whole body tensed. Then a large man ducked his head to step through the opening, and she brought the statue down in a sweeping arc.

Chapter Ten

Laura gasped as a man in a navy windbreaker and faded jeans crumpled to the bedroom floor. It was Jake.

"Jake! Oh, my God, Jake." The heavy ornament she'd used as a club slipped from her fingers and smashed against the floorboards, landing beside the wig. She didn't spare either one a glance. Dropping to her knees beside Jake, she gently felt for the place where she'd hit him on the head. There was a lump, but the skin wasn't broken. At the last moment, when she'd recognized who he was, she'd pulled back on her swing, striking him with less force than she'd originally intended. Still, the blow had been hard enough to knock him unconscious.

Cradling his head in her lap, she smoothed her fingers across his brow. His eyes were still closed, but his breath accelerated in response to her touch.

"Don't—don't go. Don't leave me." His voice was slurred but urgent.

"Jake. I'm here. It's all right. I'm sorry."

He didn't seem to be paying attention because he kept muttering over her words of reassurance. "Need you."

Jake's cheek moved against her lap, and he groaned in pain. As one of his large hands flailed up to touch the back of his head, it hit her in the ribs. She grabbed his hand and knit her fingers with his, trying to keep him still.

"I'm right here."

"Holly. Oh, God, Holly. Don't..."

"Jake, please. It's Laura. I'm sorry. I didn't know it was you."

"Laura's dead, too." His lids were squeezed shut now as if he were fighting his return to reality.

"No, I'm not."

All at once, Jake was staring up at her like a diver coming up from the dark depths of a turbulent ocean. As if he didn't trust his own senses, he extended a shaky arm and lightly touched his fingers to her face. They began to move over her eyebrows and cheeks. When they reached her mouth, Laura pressed a tiny kiss to his fingertips.

"It's me," she whispered.

"Lord God almighty. You really are alive!" As he uttered the exclamation, he was dragging her down to the floor, wrapping his corded arms around her and clasping her body against his as though he thought she would vanish if he let her go. His lips moved over her face, just as his fingers had done earlier. Laura clung to him with the same intensity, until she felt him begin to shake.

"You'd better take it easy."

"I'm okay."

But he wasn't. Holding himself very still, he closed his eyes again. Sweat had broken out on his brow, and Laura knew he was fighting against shock—both physical and mental.

Half sprawled on top of his large body, she stroked her cheek against his. "Please forgive me, Jake."

It was several moments before he answered. "My God, Laura, what happened?"

"I hit you with the statue. I'm so sorry. I didn't know it was you coming up the tunnel."

"I mean, what happened to you? The paper—the story said you'd been shot by a burglar. It was on the news, too."

"Someone was hiding in my office and tried to kill me. We decided it would be safer for me if he thought he'd succeeded."

Jake pulled them to a sitting position. The effort left him breathing raggedly. Leaning his head carefully against the wall, he stared at Laura. "You should have told me. I saw that story and just about went crazy. Does your friend Jo think you're dead, too? Or is she one hell of an actress?"

"She knows."

"But you couldn't tell me." His hand had been gripping her shoulder. Now it dropped to his side.

"Jake, Detective Hamill said the fewer people who knew, the better." The excuse stuck in her throat.

"You mean after I lied to Pickett because I thought it would get you out of jail, you still didn't trust me?"

"Trust you! My father did a whole bunch of things that made me trust *him*. And what did it get me?" The words exploded from her lips. "He told me I was his best girl. He took me out to the park or a museum or a movie every Saturday. He used to read me stories at night in bed to help me fall asleep. Then one day while I was at school, he packed up his clothes and left. He didn't even say goodbye to me." Realizing how much she'd just revealed about her own insecurities, Laura stopped short. At the moment, she couldn't face Jake. Standing up, she walked toward the knapsack lying on the floor. "I brought aspirin. Do you want some?" she asked with her face slightly averted.

"Yeah. That would be good."

"I—uh—hope I didn't give you a concussion."

"Every football player knows the symptoms. I'll tell you if I start seeing double."

Laura fished out the small first-aid kid she'd brought, handed over two tablets and went to get a glass of water from the bathroom. Letting the cold water run, she looked back to where Jake was slumped against the wall. He was sitting quietly, and his eyes were closed. She thought of how he'd hugged and kissed her so fiercely when he'd first found out she wasn't dead.

It was so hard to say anything personal now—after her little outburst about her father. But she had to give him something to try and make up for her gigantic lie of omission.

Kneeling, she handed him the glass of water and the analgesic, watching his Adam's apple bob as he swallowed.

"I guess I was afraid to trust you," she said in a low voice. "I trust you now."

He nodded tightly and she knew he was still smarting. Not just from the bump on his head. For several moments, he seemed to be brooding.

Then he sat up straighter. "So, if you're supposed to be running a scam on the guy who shot you, what the hell are you doing here instead of laying low and letting the police handle things?"

"That's what I was supposed to do. But I couldn't, not when the answer's in this house."

"To Julie Sutton's murder?"

Her mouth dropped open.

"I guess we've been doubling up on our research again. When I haven't been scraping through my assignments, I've been buried in the morgue at the *Sun*. It didn't take a genius to find out what happened at Ravenwood twenty years ago."

"And I've been haunting the library." She stopped abruptly. "Jake—"

Maybe it was the tone of her voice that made his eyes lock with hers. "What?"

"Remember when we found the box with the articles. Something on that front page upset you. But you wouldn't talk about it. Will you tell me now?"

He ran shaky fingers through his hair, encountered the

bump on the back of his head and winced. "It was the story on environmental toxins."

"What does that have to do with Ravenwood?"

The lines around his mouth tightened. When he spoke, his voice was raw. "I don't know. But I'd been thinkin' for a long time that it had something to do with Holly's death."

"Your wife?"

He swallowed painfully. "It's not easy for me to talk about this. For a year, I couldn't deal with it at all."

Laura knelt beside him and slipped her arm around him, silently lending him her support. For long moments, he leaned against her. "Holly was only twenty-eight when she died," he finally said. "She had a kind of cancer that has a very low statistical occurrence in women her age. But in Danville, Ohio, where she was raised, there's been a hell of a lot of cases. Like her cousin, for example. And two other women on her street. Pretty suspicious, don't you think?"

Laura turned so she could press her cheek against his shoulder. His arms came up to stroke across her back as if he needed the contact.

"Are you talking about something like Love Canal?" she asked.

"Not that blatant, unless the EPA is keeping it under wraps. I had to dig like a mole to get anything at all. But I've found out that the army had a secret chemical-weapons plant outside of her town during World War II. I've been trying to find out what they were producing and if anyone's done any environmental toxicity studies. I'm going to write a book about it. An exposé. At least then maybe her death will mean something."

Laura nodded. "Jake, I'm so sorry about Holly."

"Yeah, it's tough when someone you love gets ground up in the gears of government bureaucracy."

Her arms went around him, cradling his large body as best she could. He seemed to be drawing strength from her, and the knowledge made her heart swell. Yet his next words made her realize that he still didn't want to share all of the pain that he'd sealed inside himself.

"Too bad I couldn't give you a lead on the Ravenwood problem."

The easy thing would be to let him withdraw. She was past being able to take the easy way. "Martha asked me to meet her for breakfast yesterday. She acted like she wanted to be helpful."

"I get the feeling Martha enjoys stirring up trouble. Do you put much stock in what she says?"

"I don't know. After she got through with my father and Emma, she warned me to stay away from you." Laura felt his body tense.

"What does she have on me?"

"She told me you killed your wife."

Jake swore. "Funny how nasty rumors make the rounds."

"Tell me what happened."

He swallowed convulsively. "It's not a very nice story."

Her own tension matched his. "I want to hear it."

His voice was harsh and self-accusing. "Okay. The big football-star husband had enough pull to get his wife in at the top clinics in the country. But there was nothing the specialists could do for her. Laura, she was in a lot of pain, and we both knew it was only going to get worse. At home, she had a bottle of sleeping pills in the drawer beside her bed. I could have hidden them. I didn't. And I let her talk me into going down to Annapolis for the Army-Navy Game because I needed to get away from the pressure of watching her suffer." He stopped and gulped in air. "I didn't know that she told her nurse not to come in that weekend because

I was going to be home. When I got back Sunday night, it was all over.''

Imagining all those heartbreaking months and then the terrible ending, Laura ached for him. No wonder his emotions were still raw. Her marriage had ended in disillusionment. His had ended in tragedy. And she knew that what he'd suffered had been far worse than her own loss. She turned and wrapped her arms around him again, feeling his body shake as the memories assaulted him.

"You didn't know what she was going to do. It sounds as if she thought it out pretty well."

"Yeah. Sometimes I can convince myself it was better the way it happened. Other times I can't live with the knowledge that I wasn't there when she needed me. Or that she died alone, with no one to hold her."

"Jake, her illness—her death—they were both terrible things to have to cope with. You did the best you could."

"I wish I could be sure of that."

Laura continued to hold him, continued to offer comfort with the gentle stroking of her hands across his back and shoulders. "You wouldn't feel so guilty if you didn't have a strong sense of morality. That's getting rarer and rarer these days."

"A lot of good that does me."

"It counts for a lot with me."

Jake raised his head and his eyes searched her. "Why?"

"In my practice, I meet too many men who leave wives and children destitute and don't have a milligram of remorse."

"The way your husband left you?"

"Sort of." Laura broke the eye contact. Even after what he'd told her, it was still so hard to talk about herself. "Except that I wasn't destitute. I had an established law practice and no one else to support...." She stopped short. She was so used to letting people see only what she wanted them to see that it had become an automatic response. She wasn't going to do that to Jake now. But how could she tell him that when Bill had left, it had made her question herself as a woman? How could she talk about the way she'd lain awake at night wondering what deficiencies of hers had sent her husband into the arms of someone else? She'd told herself she didn't need another man. Perhaps the truth was that she was afraid to take the risk again.

"Maybe I drove Bill away," she said in a barely audible voice.

"Maybe he was an insensitive clod."

She laughed. "I've heard that from some of my clients, too." Thinking about her practice made a shadow cross her face.

"What?"

"You aren't the only one who thinks I'm dead. There are women who need my help, and I can't give it to them until we get to the bottom of all this."

"Then let's get on with it." Jake pushed himself up and stood with his back against the wall, breathing in deep lungfuls of air.

"What do you think you're doing?"

"I'm going to go exploring—like I planned when I came up here."

"You can't—you've got a lump on your head."

"I've had worse and carried a ball for a forty-yard touchdown. Come on."

"Wait. We don't want anyone to know we were in the house. See if you can make the secret panel close. The button's right here." She showed him the mechanism hidden in the carved design.

While he fiddled with the wall, Laura began gathering the pieces of the broken statue into a pile. Mixed with the debris was a small metal disk slashed with a lightning-bolt symbol. Apparently, it had been embedded in the bottom

of the ornament, because there was a corresponding inden-
tation in the broken ceramic.

"Got it. The mechanism must have been stuck."

Laura glanced up to see that the wall had silently slid
closed again. Jake was staring at the metal disk in her hand,
his brow furrowed.

"Where did you get that?"

"It was in the base of the statue—like a nameplate. Only
it's just got this symbol."

"I've seen—" He stopped and shook his head.

"You've seen it before?"

He shrugged and rubbed the back of his head. "Can't
remember. Maybe it will come to me."

Laura wrapped up the pieces of the statue in a T-shirt
she'd brought along and stuffed them into her knapsack
along with Katie's jacket and the wig.

When she finished, she found that Jake was looking at
her expectantly. "Where to?" Reaching out, he helped her
to her feet.

"I'm not sure."

He didn't let go of her hand. "That first night we were
here, you sniffed out that box under the floorboards like a
bird dog makin' a beeline for a pheasant."

Laura nodded. "I think I was in some kind of trance. I
went to sleep, and the next thing I remember, we were in
that room. I don't recall getting out of bed or walking down
the hall." She watched Jake, trying to sense his reaction to
the admission.

"I want to try and understand what happened."

"At least you've got an open mind."

"I did some reading on ghosts and extrasensory perception. Stuff like that. You took me by surprise when you
sprang that dream stuff on me. I didn't know what to think
at first."

Laura smiled at him shyly, touched that he'd taken the

trouble. "I guess I took myself by surprise. I'm a very logical, down-to-earth person. Having my sleep invaded by something I didn't understand was disturbing. I didn't want to talk about it with anyone—and then it just sort of came out when you started asking me questions." She laughed. "And it sounded just as bizarre as I thought it would."

Jake's grip tightened on her hand. "You're not crazy."

"That means a lot coming from a man I assaulted with a deadly weapon."

He grinned. "So now that we've gotten that out of the way, have you picked up any strange vibrations since you've been back in the house?"

"The whole place makes me feel strange."

"Yeah."

"I keep turning around expecting to see someone looking over my shoulder. And before you came up the tunnel, I had this fantasy that Julie was trying to tell me something. But I'm pretty sure it was just my overactive imagination."

"So you don't have any, uh, extrasensory idea where we ought to look?"

"I don't know. Give me a minute," Laura answered slowly. She closed her eyes, hoping some special inspiration would waft into her brain. It didn't. "Maybe there's nothing else left to find at Ravenwood," she mused. "Except, if that's true, why are the dreams still getting worse? Why did I feel compelled to come back?"

"Maybe the ghost can only speak to you at night or when you're asleep. Do you ever remember it happening while you were awake?"

"No." Laura wrapped her arms around her shoulders. "I didn't think of that. But I'm not sure I'm up to spending the night here."

"Who would be, after what's happened? I guess I'd feel like I was in the middle of a haunted house story. The kind kids tell to spook each other around the campfire."

Laura laughed uneasily. They both glanced toward the window. There were still a few hours of daylight left, but not many.

"Okay, if you don't have any better ideas, let's go back to the part of the house where you found the box," Jake suggested.

"Sounds logical. You first."

It wasn't the need to have Jake run interference that made Laura ask him to go first. As they made their way out of the room and down the hall, she watched him carefully. He seemed to be steady on his feet, but he wasn't moving anywhere near fast enough to run for a forty-yard touchdown.

This time the door to the unused wing of the house was locked, and they had to pause while Jake pulled a set of compact tools out of one of the pockets in his windbreaker.

"You came equipped to burgle the place," Laura accused.

"I just came prepared—for whatever I was going to find."

"Did you bring a gun?" she asked, half jokingly.

Jake reached into the waistband at the side of his slacks and brought out a snub-nosed .32.

Laura stared at the weapon, which had been hidden by his windbreaker.

"My dad started taking me to the practice range when I was ten. I know how to use a gun. I know gun safety. And I assume that whoever thought he'd killed you shot first and didn't stick around to ask questions. I also assume it's not a ghost."

"Yes," Laura agreed on a breathy sigh.

"Do you know how to use this thing?"

"My husband dragged me to a firing range a couple of times—when he was on a home-safety kick."

"Home safety! Do you know how many home-safety

nuts end up shooting members of their own family by mistake?''

"I'm not sure I could shoot anything besides a paper target.''

"I hope you don't have to.''

Laura swallowed. Jake worked on the lock. After a few moments, it clicked. The familiar musty, charred odor assaulted them as he opened the door. They both switched on their flashlights and trained the twin beams down the hall.

"Stay close to me,'' Jake warned.

"Don't worry. I'm glad I'm not trying this alone.''

He reached back to squeeze her arm. "Me, too.''

They moved cautiously down the hall, listening to the creak of the old wooden boards. When they reached the room in which Laura had found the box, Jake hesitated. "I'm not sure I'd advise going in there again. The floor wasn't too stable. Let's see what's in the next room.''

"Okay.''

Jake took several more steps. Laura hung back and glanced nervously over her shoulder. The same strange feeling that had hovered around her earlier had started to coalesce in the dank atmosphere of the passage. All at once, it was hard to breathe and hard to put one foot in front of the other.

"Jake, wait!''

"What's wrong?''

"I'm not sure.''

In the next second, they both found out. With a sickening groan, the burned boards under Jake's feet gave way, and he plunged through the floor.

Chapter Eleven

It seemed to happen in slow motion. Laura watched in horror as first Jake's legs, then his hips and finally his chest disappeared into the chasm that had opened in the hallway. Debris rained on the ground below. Sooty dust rose in a fine black cloud, choking Laura and obscuring her vision.

"Jake. Oh, Lord, Jake."

A millennium passed before the surface stopped creaking and splintering.

"Jake?"

"It's okay." He coughed several times. "I'm still hangin' in."

The observation was literally true. To her relief, Laura could see the upper part of his body a few yards in front of her. He looked like a man hanging through a hole in the ice of a frozen pond. Only the margin of the opening was black and charred.

"Thank God," she breathed. Now they just had to get him back on solid ground. Instinctively, she started to move forward.

"No. Stay back," he choked out. "The damn floor's not stable."

Before he finished issuing the warning, the surface was tipping like the deck of a ship caught in an ocean storm. Laura shrieked as she found herself rolling downhill toward the hole. If she crashed into Jake, they were both going to go through.

She bent and twisted her body, desperately trying to stop her forward motion. Then her shoulder brushed the door of the room Jake had just passed, and she grabbed for the frame. For a terrifying moment, her fingers slipped. Finally, they held. Panting, Laura clung to the swaying door. When her body had stopped shaking, she gritted her teeth and began to pull herself slowly back to safety.

"The whole thing's likely to go," Jake warned. "You get the hell out of here."

"I will not."

They were both breathing hard. And Laura's chest, where it had scraped along the floor, felt as if it had been dragged across the Sahara.

Feeling helpless, she watched as Jake tried to heave himself up. His face turned red with the effort, but he didn't move more than a few inches. "I can't get enough leverage."

The floor creaked and shifted again from his efforts. Was he right? Was the whole hallway going to collapse, Laura wondered. Then she remembered the rope she'd stuffed into her pack.

Jake's grim expression brightened when he saw her pull the coiled hemp from her knapsack.

Casting around for an anchor, Laura gave a tug on the doorknob. It seemed solid.

After securing one end of the lifeline to the knob, she tossed the other end toward Jake. It wasn't quite long enough. Her exclamation of dismay would have been right at home in a marine barracks.

"It's okay," Jake said in a voice that hovered between reassurance and frustration. "We just need to make it longer."

Laura looked frantically around for something she could

use. There was nothing suitable—except the clothes on her back. Unbuttoning the flannel shirt, Laura slipped out of the garment. She was shivering in the cold, damp air as she tied one sleeve to the end of the rope and tested the knot. It was only after she'd tossed the lengthened rope back to Jake that she realized how she must appear conducting a rescue operation in her bra—with bandages across her chest.

Jake shot her a turbulent look but didn't waste any breath on a comment. Wrapping his powerful hands around the fabric of the shirt, he began to pull himself out of the hole. As Laura's gaze fixed on the place where the shirt and rope were connected, she prayed the knot would hold. Grabbing her end of the rope, she began to tug. He was heavy, and the strain of pulling made her shoulders ache.

"Come on, Jake. You can do it."

He grunted and speeded up his hand-over-hand progress. When a section of the hallway under him gave way, she gasped. He had slipped back several inches. She tugged harder.

Precious seconds stretched into minutes, but finally, he was flopping onto the relatively solid section of the floor where she'd made her stand.

"Move," he barked. They could both feel the boards vibrating ominously under them.

Laura snagged her knapsack and scrambled back toward the door through which they'd entered. Jake followed.

Not until they had reached the corridor in the renovated section of the house did they sink to the floor, both breathing heavily.

"Are you okay?" Jake asked.

"Yes."

He peered at her critically. "You look like you've been through a black-and-white snowstorm."

"What do you think you look like, Wallace?"

"Damn glad to be on solid ground. Damn glad you are, too."

"Jake, I was so scared. I thought you were going to get killed."

When he pulled her into his arms, she clung. His broad hands swept across her bare back and shoulders, rubbing the goose bumps from her chilled skin, warming her from the inside as well as the outside.

When she tipped her face up, he pinned her with a fierce, dark look that stole the breath from her lungs.

"That was too blasted close."

No, this is. She was too close to him, too sensitive to what he'd suffered, too glad that he was safe and sound and in her arms.

She stopped trying to make sense of her emotions when his mouth came down hard against hers. The kiss was hot and possessive, the kiss of a man telling a woman exactly where things stood between them.

The woman responded. Opening to him, welcoming him.

He sensed the answer to his unspoken question. His lips were no less greedy as they slanted over hers. But they were gentle now, seductive instead of insistent.

She made a low sound in her throat as her body shifted, fitting itself more intimately to his.

He murmured her name as his hands lifted her hair and kneaded the muscles of her shoulders. His lips trained kisses down her neck. When he reached the bandage on her chest, he stopped. "God almighty—what am I thinkin' about? You're hurt. Are you all right?"

Laura's eyes snapped back into focus. Her mind followed several seconds later, and she nodded. "The bullet shattered the fairy cross. It saved my life, but there were a few pieces of crystal in my skin."

"And you've been running around like a deck hand on the *Titanic.*"

"You haven't been doing too badly yourself."

He pulled Laura to her feet. "We have to get out of here. I don't suppose you have another shirt in your bag of tricks."

"My friend's jacket." She extracted it from the knapsack and was stuffing her arms into the sleeves when there was a loud crash behind them.

Jake took her hand and tugged her toward the door. "Let's go."

"I guess the whole wing of the house must have been weakened by the fire," she said as she followed him down the hall.

"Not just the fire. While I was hanging in that hole, I had an up-close-and-personal look at the floor. It didn't break at random. Parts were cut."

"Cut?"

"As in booby-trapped. You know like the chandelier cord."

"My God, Jake you've been right all along."

"And whoever set the trap may be on his way here to see what he's caught."

Bypassing the front of the house, they climbed out the back window through which Jake had entered. As they made their way along the edge of the woods, Laura could see that Jake's teeth were clenched and that he was limping.

"You hurt your leg when you fell."

"I've got a bum knee from my football days. I gave it a good whack when I went through the floor."

Laura slowed her pace.

"We gotta put some distance between us and that house. I'll be okay."

The reassurance didn't match the expression on his face as they hurried away from the house.

"Where's your car?" Laura asked.

"At the tourist cabins about three miles down the highway. I hiked up through the woods."

"Lucky I didn't think of anything so tricky. My friend's Chrysler is just down the drive, hidden on a side road. Let's hope it makes out better than her shirt."

Before getting into the car, Laura tried to brush some of the soot and plaster off her pants and out of her hair. Then she slid behind the wheel. Jake climbed in the passenger door. Moving the bucket seat back as far as it would go, he leaned against the head rest and winced as he stretched out his leg.

"What's the name of the place we're going?" she asked as she cautiously backed up to the main drive.

"Slumbering Pines."

Nosing the car down the drive as fast as she dared, Laura gripped the wheel with white knuckles, half-expecting to round a curve and come face-to-face with another car roaring toward her. The most persistent image she had was of a police cruiser driven by her good friend Hiram Pickett. But she and Jake seemed to be alone on the Ravenwood property.

When they came to the highway, she let out the uneasy breath she'd been holding.

"Turn left," Jake directed, wearily settling back into the seat. "Look for a dented green sign with gold lettering."

If he'd glanced behind them, he might have seen a car pull out of the side road just beyond Ravenwood and trail them down the highway at a discreet distance. Unfortunately, Laura wasn't thinking about being followed, either. She was still too off balance from their narrow escape.

When she slowed to pull in at the tourist court, Jake leaned forward and pointed toward the left.

"My cabin's up that way. It's got two double beds—and a shower."

Laura contemplated her options. She couldn't exactly

walk into the office and register, and it was safer being
with Jake if someone came after them, anyway. On the
other hand, there was nothing about his kiss that had made
her feel safe. But there was another factor she had to consider. She'd thumped him pretty hard over the head. Even
if he was too macho to admit he needed watching, he probably shouldn't be alone.

"Which one?"

"Number 11. It's around back and up the hill."

Instead of Jake's 280Z, a beige Ford Tempo was parked
in front.

"Where's your car?"

"I rented something that wouldn't stick out up here."

After pulling up beside the Ford, Laura reached into the
back seat and grabbed her overnight bag.

The sun was disappearing behind the mountains, streak-
ing the sky with soft orange and pink as Jake unlocked the
door. The light helped soften the cabin's rather stark effect.

It was nothing fancy. The promised two beds both had
metal frames. The pine dresser was scarred with rings from
a legion of cold soda bottles. And the upholstery on the
one chair had faded to bilious yellow.

Jake noted her reaction. "I was lookin' for close, not
fancy."

"I'm not complaining. Just give me first dibs on the
shower." Laura shouldered her bag, disappeared into the
bathroom and locked the door.

She hadn't taken anything but a cautious bath since the
shooting. And Katie had told her not to get the bandages
wet. Stripping them off, she gave her wounds a critical
inspection in the mirror. They seemed to be healing all
right. Maybe she could just skip the dressing.

Ten minutes under a hot, needle-sharp spray restored her
sense of well-being. Until she heard Jake pacing around the
bedroom on the other side of the locked door. After dress-

ing quickly, she slipped back into the bedroom and busied herself with towel drying her hair while Jake took his shower.

He emerged wearing a clean pair of jeans and a dark-green-and-white rugby pullover that made him look as buttoned up as a preacher. Except that few preachers had the physical presence of six-foot-two, two-hundred-pound Jake Wallace. Few were as ruggedly masculine. And none of them made her pulse start to pound with a mere look. Laura wiped her damp palms on the legs of her jeans as she eyed him uncertainly.

Since she'd hit him over the head with the statue, they'd been coping with one crisis after another. Now, they were in the eye of the storm, and the undisturbed tranquility wasn't having a soothing effect.

Laura expelled a tattered wisp of air from her lungs. Alone in a tourist cabin, she and Jake were perfectly capable of creating their own tension. Sexual tension. And something else, as well. A new intimacy. A new awareness of each other.

Trying to find neutral territory for her gaze, Laura found herself focusing on Jake's shirt. In response, he brushed a nonexistent speck of lint off the cuff.

So Jake was nervous, too. That was a totally new phenomenon.

"I—uh—brought some food so I wouldn't have to go out for dinner. We could have an indoor picnic."

"Yes. Right. I am hungry."

They'd found a safe subject for the moment. Safer than talking about the way they were feeling. "It's just sandwiches and beer." He swung a cooler out of the closet and hoisted it onto one of the beds. Sitting down, he began to take out several wrapped packages. "Roast beef on whole wheat, turkey and ham on rye, bologna on white."

"This is dinner for one?" she teased.

"And maybe breakfast."

"You eat cold-cut sandwiches for breakfast?" Laura inquired.

"When there isn't any leftover pizza."

"Maybe there's a muffin shop in town."

There were several moments of silence. Apparently, they had run out of scintillating conversation. Jake unwrapped one of the sandwiches and began to eat. When Laura realized she was watching him again, she quickly reached for her own dinner. But as she eyed the sandwich in her hand, she licked her suddenly dry lips. There was no hope of washing down bread and roast beef without a drink.

"I guess I'll get myself a Coke."

"Planning on makin' an appearance as the second ghost in the area?"

Laura didn't miss a beat when she answered. "I brought a disguise." She retrieved her dark wig from the knapsack, shoved her hair underneath and turned back to Jake. "What do you think?"

"I think blondes have more fun."

"I didn't come up here for fun."

"Too bad," Jake commented as he tried to move his leg into a more comfortable position.

Laura didn't miss the grimace on his features. "Will an ice pack help?"

"For my head or my leg?"

She smiled. "Your choice."

"I'm willing to give it a try."

"I'll be back in a few minutes." Making a quick exit, Laura closed the door. As she drew in a deep lungful of the cold mountain air, she tried to reach for some inner reserve of composure. She'd gotten to know Jake pretty well by now. Nothing was going to happen between them tonight that she didn't invite. The problem was, now that they were alone together, she wasn't sure what she wanted.

Not with all her insecurities about men and women churning in her chest. Not when she was so conscious that the first step toward intimacy could be the first step toward disaster.

When she saw the telephone next to the Coke machine, she remembered Katie.

Fishing out more change, she called Ellicott City.

The phone was answered on the first ring.

"Sorry I forgot about you," Laura apologized.

"Forgot!"

"I've been kind of busy. And I, uh, lost one of your shirts." Laura sketched an account of her adventures.

"Don't worry about the shirt. Are you sure you're going to be all right?" the physician asked.

"I'm with Jake."

"Well, that answers the question."

"I'll be at your place late tomorrow. Or I'll call again."

Before coming back to the cabin, Laura also filled a bucket with ice. When she returned, Jake was sitting on one of the beds, propped against the headboard. But his body was far from relaxed, and the sandwich in his hand was barely eaten.

"I was just getting ready to send out a search party."

"I forgot I'd promised my friend Katie I'd call."

As Laura finished the sentence, she tugged off the itchy wig. Turning toward the mirror, she began to run her fingers through her hair and fluff out the curls. The absence of motion on the bed behind her drew her attention. Jake had put down the sandwich and was watching her. His eyes had changed from brown to ebony. The way they followed the motions of her hands made her stomach flutter. She hadn't intended to be provocative. Now, her hands dropped away from her hair.

She scooped some of the ice into a plastic bag and wrapped the bag in a towel.

"Which will it be your knee or your head?"

He laughed. "My head's not too bad. I can never be sure about the knee."

"This should cool you off." The observation was barely audible, but she was pretty sure he'd heard. He closed his eyes for a moment as she adjusted the makeshift ice pack.

"How's that?"

"It feels good."

Laura took in the smouldering look in Jake's eyes and the husky tone of his voice and knew she had to put some distance between them. She picked up her soda and settled herself on the other bed.

"I was thinking about the implications of what happened this afternoon."

"Oh yeah?"

"I mean, the floor was probably cut by whoever stole the box from my room," she clarified. "Saturday night, he must have come in through the tunnel behind the panel. Where does it lead?"

"There's a door behind the drapes in the sitting room— where the body was found."

"I'll bet that as soon as I left my room to run to Emma's rescue, whoever was on the other side of the wall stepped through and exited that way. Then he could have woken everyone up with a shout in the hall and come downstairs with the rest of the crowd."

"That's probably the way it happened. I wish I could remember whose voice woke me up. But I vote for Andy. He's the one who tried to seat Emma under the chandelier."

"That's just circumstantial evidence."

"You don't have to be a stickler for legal technicalities."

As she finished the sentence, Jake had put his finger to his lips. He had turned to stare at the closed curtains. Laura followed his gaze, eyes and ears straining. She couldn't see anything through the curtains. But after a moment, she picked up a faint crunch of gravel outside. Someone or something was right on the other side of the window trying to be quiet. She was willing to bet it wasn't a mountain lion.

"It's been a long day," Jake said loudly. Easing off the bed, he walked around the cabin, turning off lamps until the room was illuminated only by a shaft of light from the bathroom.

Laura watched him reach into his overnight bag. When he took out the gun, she sucked in a sharp breath. Flipping off the safety, he laid the weapon on the bed beside her. "Sit tight," he whispered.

She was afraid to answer as he glided toward the door. In the next moment, he threw it open and disappeared into the night. Laura sat perfectly still on the bed, her pulse pounding, her eyes flicking from the gun to the door.

There were no shouts, no verbal challenges in the darkness. But the gravel outside the window seemed to boil up as if it had been hit by a tornado. Then the sounds of two sets of running feet tore off across the parking lot and faded into the distance.

Laura hardly dared to breathe as she waited in the darkened room. Jake should have taken the gun. But he had left it to protect her.

It was only a few minutes later when one set of footsteps returned. Laura's heart skipped a beat, but she reached out a surprisingly steady hand toward the pistol. Her fingers had closed around the cold metal of the grip when she heard the hobbling step.

"Jake?"

"I couldn't keep up with the sonofagun."

"Your knee…"

He responded with a string of curses. "I'm a pretty sorry bodyguard."

Matter-of-factly, she set the weapon on the bedside table and slid the safety into place. Then she crossed the space between the two beds, picked up the ice pack and put it back on Jake's leg. "I didn't hire a bodyguard. I came up here with some half-baked idea of communicating with the ghost and spying around Ravenwood, and I'm pretty sure I would have gotten into a lot more trouble without you."

"Yeah, well, you would have had better luck chasing that guy than I did."

"But what would I have done when I caught up with him?"

Jake couldn't stifle a wry laugh. "There's that."

"Who was it?"

"Couldn't tell in the dark. He had a wool cap pulled down low and some kind of funny-looking goggles that hid the rest of his face. And he's got great reflexes. He ran like the devil was after him as soon as he saw me hit the door." Jake sighed and began to smack his fist against his palm. "I made a bad judgment call on that one. I thought I could move fast enough to tackle whoever was out there listenin'. I didn't think it was going to turn into a hundred-yard dash."

"Didn't your knee hurt when you got up?"

"I've learned to ignore pain when I have to."

The bleak statement made her chin lift. She suspected he wanted to look away. Her gaze didn't give him permission. "You did the best you could under the circumstances."

"Sometimes that's not good enough, is it?"

Laura understood the hidden meaning in that remark. "Don't. Jake, you did the best you could for Holly."

"Don't make assumptions about the way I feel."

"Then tell me."

He swallowed hard but didn't turn away from her. "After Holly died, I couldn't do much more than sit and stare out the window for six months. When I finally got my head screwed on halfway straight, I promised myself I was going to nail the SOBs who were responsible—expose them so the whole world would know. It gave me a reason to get up every morning. It's still important. It just doesn't rule my life anymore.''

"Jake—"

"Let me finish. I may not be saying this in a very direct way, but I'm getting to it. Once something like that happens to you, you never go back to the way you were. Holly and I were pretty damn close. But for the past three years, I've stayed away from any kind of relationship with women that wasn't based on the mutual pursuit of fun and games. That's what I was looking for with you at first. A quick fling. Then these warm, kind of protective feelings ambushed me. I wasn't sure how to cope with them. When I opened the newspaper and read that you were dead, I thought I wasn't going to get the chance to try.''

Laura didn't know that her eyes had filled with tears until they spilled over and trickled down her cheeks.

"I told the *Sun* there'd been a death in my family and that I needed to take some time off. Then I came up here to snoop around. It was as good a place as any to start looking for the animal who shot you. When I found him, I was going to beat the bejesus out of him. Then I was going to turn him over to the police.''

"Oh, Jake." She took his face between her hands and kissed him very gently on the lips. Words she had been afraid to say suddenly spilled out. "I don't think I can give you what you want. I don't think I can give it to anybody. Once I was naive enough to assume that if you loved someone, he'd love you back, and the two of you would live happily ever after. I found out how stupid that was.''

An unprotected expression flashed across Jake's face before he got control of his features. Then he reached up to gently stroke a finger across her trembling lips. "I wish I could spin you stories about happily ever after. But I'm as confused as you are. I still don't know what kind of relationship I can handle. I just know what I need tonight.''

Perhaps his total honesty was her undoing. She didn't have to worry about a string of broken promises because he wasn't making any. No. She forced herself to be honest. There was a lot more to the way she was feeling than that. All evening she'd been afraid of the emotions tugging her toward him. She'd been worrying about herself. Worrying about what she had to lose if she let herself open up to intimacy. Now she knew Jake needed her. And suddenly, it seemed more important to give than to receive.

He sat as still as the dark shapes of the mountains looming behind the cabin. A moment ago, his breath had been warm against her face. Now she didn't feel it and knew that the air had stopped moving in and out of his lungs while he waited for her reply.

Jake didn't realize he was holding his breath until Laura's lips moved against his. At first the kiss was as soft as a drop of dew sliding down the velvet petal of a flower. It deepened by slow degrees.

Her lips parted on a sigh. When his tongue made an expedition into the inviting warmth of her mouth, he tasted the sweetness of nectar. And then her tongue was moving caressingly against his, sending his senses spinning.

The kiss went from sweetness to blatant hunger in the space of a heartbeat, a man and a woman communicating with each other on a primitive level.

Remembering her bandages, he had gathered up handfuls of the chenille bedspread to keep from dragging her against him. Now the need to touch her made his whole body shake.

''Your cuts. I don't want to hurt you,'' he whispered hoarsely.

''It's all right.'' She lifted his hands and cupped them

over her breasts. He sucked in a shuddering breath. Her nipples were like hard, plump berries against his palms—and there was nothing between his hands and her flesh except a thin layer of flannel. "You're not wearing a bra."

Her body swayed. Murmurs of pleasure welled up from deep in her throat. "It's—hanging—up—to—dry—" She managed the explanation between nibbled attacks on his lips.

She had finally let down the barriers and opened herself to the joy of being with Jake.

Hard, frantic kisses punctuated his shaky movements as he slid open the buttons of her shirt and pushed it off her shoulders.

When he'd bared the upper part of her body, he gently touched the healing skin in the center of her chest.

"I'm all right."

Reassured by her words, he bent so his mouth could find her nipples. The pleasure of it ignited the pool of heat that had coalesced in her center. Suddenly, it wasn't enough to have his hot, arousing hands and mouth sliding over her skin. Urgently, she tugged at the hem of his shirt. He tore it over his head and tossed it onto the floor.

With a glad little exclamation, she burrowed her face into the crinkly hair that fanned across his chest, drinking in the warm male scent of his skin.

She liked the way he felt. Liked the rumble of excitement deep in his chest when she caressed him.

She'd thought she might be shy the first time after so long. But she was too eager to be in Jake's arms, kissing and being kissed. Touching him. Feeling his touch. Feeling his naked body pressed to hers.

His needs were the same as hers. He murmured fierce, sexy words as his hands and lips learned all her womanly secrets.

When she felt him hesitate, she lifted her head. "What is it?"

"Just a little problem with my knee."

"Not to worry."

Laura found there was something very sexy about getting to be in charge. With a seductive, feminine smile, she moved on top of him, straddling his body, bringing him inside her. Then she began to move, and nothing existed in the world besides the two of them delighting in the discovery of each other.

It was hot. Perfect.

Beyond the fantasies he had conjured up.

Beyond what experience had taught her a woman could expect.

As she moved in sensual rhythm, his strong hands stoked her passion with sweet, languid caresses. The heat built, consumed her, fed their mutual ecstasy until she tightened around him, gasping his name as they both exploded in shimmering, incandescent release.

Chapter Twelve

Bright morning light danced at the edge of the curtains as Jake eased down onto the edge of the bed. Laura shifted in her sleep and smiled.

He was glad she was smiling now. Near dawn, she'd gone into one of her nightmares. But he'd woken her up as soon as he'd felt her thrashing around next to him. Then he'd held her and stroked her until she told him she was all right again. Somehow, comforting her in bed in the darkness of the night had brought him a profound sense of peace.

Probably because tenderness had been missing from his life for such a long time. So had caring, for that matter. He'd convinced himself he was getting along fine without them. He'd been wrong about that—and a lot of other stuff.

Unfortunately that didn't make things simple when it came to him and Laura. She'd said she didn't know whether she could trust any man enough to give him her love. Well, he still didn't know whether he could give her what she needed, either.

With any other woman, he could take it one step at a time. See how the relationship developed. But Laura was different. If things went too far, he could end up hurting her terribly. And that was the last thing in the world he wanted to do.

The part of him that was still afraid said that backing off was the easy way out. Then neither one of them would be at risk. But he couldn't just do that, either, because he wasn't going to make the same mistake he'd made with Holly. If he understood anything at all, he understood that Laura needed his strength and his protection right now. And if he didn't have the guts to see her through this ordeal, he wouldn't be able to look himself in the eye.

Suddenly needing to touch her, he brushed a lock of tangled hair from her forehead.

"Jake?"

"I don't want you to wake up and wonder where I am. I'm gonna look for those muffins you wanted. And some coffee. You want cream and sugar?"

"Mm-hmm. How's your leg?" she murmured.

"A little stiff. But I'm not complaining."

She reached for his hand and the covers slid away from her bare shoulders, making her shiver in the cold mountain air.

He squeezed her fingers and pulled up the blanket again. "How are you?"

"Fine."

"The nightmares—are they like that every night?"

"Just about. Thank you for waking me up before it got bad."

He answered with a soft kiss on her cheek. "I'll turn on the heat and it'll be nice and toasty in here by the time I get back. You catch a couple more minutes of sleep."

"Mmm." She was already snuggling back under the covers.

It only took twenty minutes to get the muffins and the coffee because he was lucky enough to find a convenience store at the next crossroads.

The moment Jake pushed open the door of the cabin again, he knew something was terribly wrong. Choking fumes made him start to cough. Gas. The whole room was full of gas. Eyes watering, he dropped the bag of food and dashed toward the bed.

"Laura!"

She was lying on her stomach, her blond head barely visible at the top of the covers. She didn't move. If she was breathing, he couldn't tell.

"Laura!"

He had to get her out of there. Fast.

Still coughing, he scooped her limp body up in the bed-clothes and tore outside. Slamming the door with his foot, he laid her on the porch and peeled back the covers.

The heater. He'd turned it on before he left. Had it been pouring gas into the small room the whole time?

He'd taken a couple of first-aid courses in Boy Scouts and later when he'd been a camp counselor. His mind scrambled for the facts he knew about asphyxiation. Once the victim was unconscious and in respiratory failure, the heart kept beating for a few minutes.

He found a weak pulse at her neck. How long had Laura been unconscious? Knowing that every precious second counted, he tilted her head back to clear the airway, inhaled a deep gulp of air and started mouth-to-mouth resuscitation.

His own pulse was ragged and his lungs ached as he tried to force life-saving oxygen into her system. In between breaths, he checked to see if she was breathing on her own.

Not yet. He refused to stop believing he could bring her around.

Time narrowed to the mechanics of inhaling and exhaling—his life force desperately trying to reawaken hers. Somewhere deep in his mind, a scream of anguish welled up. He was going to lose her again. And this time, it was for real. He couldn't afford to give the terror voice. Not when Laura's life depended on staying calm and steady.

Finally, she started to cough. Then she was gasping in cold mountain air.

"Laura. Thank God!"

Her eyes fluttered. "Jake?" Another coughing spasm took her and her eyes watered. "What happened?"

"The heater. It was pouring gas into the cabin." He threw a glance back at the closed door. "I guess it still is."

She began to shiver and he tucked the covers more closely around her. "I think you're going to be okay. But I want to take you to a hospital."

"No!"

"Laura—"

"You can't. They're going to want identification—and information on insurance coverage. And I'm supposed to be dead, remember?"

"The hell with that." But even as he denied her protest, he was evaluating the risks. Maybe no one had turned on the heater since last season. Maybe the damn thing had simply malfunctioned. But that would sure be a hell of a coincidence. He'd put his bet on sabotage—carried out by the creep who'd been sneaking around the cabin last night. Had the intruder known Laura was there? Or had he been the target?

He lifted his head and looked around at the stand of trees screening the cabin from the others in the tourist court, trying to pierce the shadows. Someone could be watching to see how things turned out. Or maybe the assailant had done his dirty work in the middle of the night and decided it was too dangerous to stick around.

If nobody had spotted Laura, then she was right. She was a lot safer playing dead. But in any case, the sooner they got out of there, the better.

"Okay," Jake finally said. "I'll take you back to your friend Katie. You said she's a doctor, didn't you?"

Laura nodded.

"I've got to go in and get our stuff."

"Jake—don't." Her fingers clamped around his hand with surprising strength as her gaze shot to the closed door.

He stroked his thumb across her palm. "Not to worry. I'll be careful." Taking a deep breath, he opened the door just wide enough to enter. First he shut off the heater and pushed open the window, then he grabbed their overnight bags and Laura's knapsack. It took two more very brief trips to clear everything out.

Laura had pushed herself erect and sat with her back against the cabin wall.

Jake eyed her critically. "How do you feel now?"

"Okay." She shook her head, remembering the experience. "It's strange. The gas made me feel kind of peaceful. I could have just drifted off to sleep and never woken up."

He sat beside her and slung an arm around her shoulder, holding her against his side, but keeping his eyes on the woods. "Oxygen deprivation does funny things to your brain."

"I guess so." She watched Jake eye the two vehicles in front of the porch.

"You'll be more comfortable lying down in the back of your friend's car."

"What about the Ford?"

"I can tell the rental company the keys got locked inside and they're gonna have to pick it up."

"But they're not."

"They will be. As soon as you make sure Katie's are in your purse."

Laura fumbled around for the keys, surprised at how groggy she still felt and hoping Jake didn't notice. After unlocking the car, he tossed most of their stuff into the trunk.

"Am I going to ride back to Ellicott City in my nightgown?"

"You're not going into that cabin. Can you change in the back seat?"

"More or less."

He reached for her hand, helped her up and swung her into his arms. For a long moment, he simply held her, nuzzling his lips in her hair.

"Jake, I think I forgot to say thanks for getting me out of there."

"No charge."

After carrying her to the car and settling her in the back seat, he waited with his hips propped against the car door, his gaze sweeping the vicinity, as she slipped into last night's jeans and shirt.

"I'd feel better if you lie down in the back under the blanket while I stop at the office."

"Okay."

He drove to the manager's cabin and parked out front. "Back as soon as I can."

"I'll be right here."

Still not entirely happy with the arrangement, Jake turned so that he could watch the Chrysler out of the corner of his eye while he told the manager of the cabins about the heater and the car. The manager was so upset that he wouldn't accept any payment.

"Nothing like this has ever happened to me," he kept repeating as he walked Jake to the car.

"Did you have the heater checked at the beginning of the season?"

The man flushed. "I do that every other year. That's been good enough until now."

Jake wasn't going to take the time to give the man a lecture, not when his primary mission was getting Laura back to her doctor friend. But he did ask one more question. "Did you see anyone suspicious around here last night?"

"Suspicious?"

"A guy with a hat pulled down over his face and goggles. He was outside our cabin earlier in the evening."

"Didn't see nobody like that."

"Well, get the heater checked out before you rent the room to anyone else." Turning, he headed back toward the car.

"Are you still feeling okay?" he asked Laura again after he pulled out onto the highway.

"Can I sit up?"

"Wait till we get out of town."

Jake kept glancing in the rearview mirror as they made their way toward the interstate. No one seemed to be following. But he waited until he'd put twenty-five miles between them and the tourist court before stopping at a gas station so Laura could wash up. When she came out, she insisted on sitting in the front seat—with the back reclined. Twenty minutes later, her eyes drifted closed. Ten minutes after that, she began to thrash around and moan.

Was she having a convulsion? An after-effect of the gas?

"Laura?"

"Don't hurt me. Please, I won't tell anyone—" She gasped and cringed back into her seat.

It was one of the nightmares. And this time it was happening in broad daylight. Jake's knuckles whitened as he clenched the wheel. Was a dream going to ambush her every time she fell asleep now? He reached out to shake her awake, then he pulled his hand back. They were coming up to a rest area; it was safer to wait until he could stop the car. Watching her grimace and shiver made his stomach churn. But if she woke up now, she might flail out at him. Somehow, he brought the vehicle to a slow, smooth stop, under some trees at the edge of the parking lot.

"Please—oh, God—no—I won't tell—" Laura gasped, her eyes still tightly shut. She folded her arms protectively across her chest. Beads of sweat glistened on her forehead.

Jake was reaching out to gently stroke her cheek. Before his fingers contacted her flesh, he resisted. If the terrible nightmares were really a pipeline to the truth, maybe he'd be doing both of them a favor by letting her ride this one through a little longer.

To keep from touching Laura, he clenched his fists at his sides. "What is it?" he whispered. "What's happening to you?"

"One of them has a mask!" The exclamation was a strangled sob. "They—they're going to—rape me."

His whole body tensed. "Rape you? Who?"

"Dorian," she sobbed out.

Now every protective instinct screamed at him to wake her up and end the torture. But he had to try for more information. "Dorian who?"

"Dorian. Just Dorian." A whimper of pain followed the words and Jake couldn't take it any more. Grasping Laura by the shoulders, he shook her. For a few seconds, the dream held her in its thrall, and she thrashed frantically against him as if her life depended on escape from her attacker.

"Laura, it's Jake," he repeated over and over. "I'm not going to hurt you."

Laura's eyes snapped open. They were dull with terror as she cringed away from the large male form leaning over her.

"It's all right, honey. It's me. You're safe with me."

She sucked in a trembling breath. "Jake. Oh, God, Jake. It was so horrible."

Her teeth began to chatter and he held her close. "It's okay. It was just a nightmare."

"No. It happened. To Julie." She pushed her hands against his chest so she could find his eyes with hers. "It's too real to be just a nightmare. They raped her. Both of them. While everybody was out of control at the party."

"Are you sure?"

"Things got pretty wild and Julie was frightened by the way people were acting. So she went upstairs and locked herself in her room. But they didn't need a key. They knew about the secret passage. That's how they got in." She stared wide-eyed at Jake. "The two men. They came up the passage, found her and raped her." Laura's hands dug into Jake's shoulders. Her mouth quivered, making her voice rise and fall. "It was horrible. She was so frightened and they—they—"

"It's a dream." Jake stopped her. "You don't know—"

"It's not just a dream." Laura's voice thinned as she struggled to get the terrible words out. "They gagged her. Then they took turns holding her down on the bed."

"Who? Do you know who it was?"

"One of them had a mask. That's why I could never see his face.

"Dorian?"

Her whole body convulsed as if she'd touched a live wire. "Dorian!"

"Who is he?"

Laura closed her eyes for a moment, concentrating. "That's what they called him. That's all I know."

"Someone who isn't on the suspect list?"

"I guess so. But the other one looked familiar."

"One of the guests at Ravenwood?"

"I don't think so. But the murder was years ago. He must be older now."

"What else do you know about Dorian?"

She shuddered. "He waited until his friend left. Then he—he—killed Julie."

Jake's fingers knit with hers. "With the dagger?"

"No. He wanted it to look like an accident, so he hit her on the head with—" she moaned "—with the same—statue…" Her voice trailed off.

Jake pulled her against the protective wall of his chest, feeling the frantic pounding of her heart. He rocked her in his arms, willing the fear away. "Jake, that was the worst dream yet." Her voice cracked. "It isn't even safe to fall asleep in the car."

He offered what comfort he could. "Maybe it had something to do with the gas from the heater."

But her face turned chalky. "Or maybe I'm never going to be able to sleep without waking up in a cold sweat."

"Yes, you will. We're going to figure out what Julie was investigating. Then the nightmares will stop."

"God, I hope so!"

The tension was slowly seeping out of her body when she went rigid again.

"What is it, honey?"

She gulped. "The one in the mask. The one in charge. You don't think it was my father, do you?"

"No." The reassurance was automatic. Jake had no way of proving things either way, or of even knowing the dream was the truth. Yet her terror and anguish were terribly real. "Do you really think your father was capable of something like that?"

"How much can a child tell? I loved him. I think we had a good relationship until he left. But I was only eight. My mother was so bitter, she made him sound like a monster. After a while, I got so confused, I didn't know what to think."

"Don't jump to conclusions about your father. We don't know about my uncle, either."

"Your uncle! I forgot he left you his shares." Laura looked relieved and then guilty. "I feel terrible hoping it's him."

"That's all right. I hardly knew the man, but I'm sure gonna start checking up on him. I should have done it before now."

"There may have been other investors we don't even know about. But I bet Andy Stapleton does. I guess you're right. Even if he's not the one who killed Emma, paying him a visit is next on our agenda when we get home." Laura raised her head and looked around, aware of her surroundings for the first time. "Where are we anyway?"

"West of Cumberland."

"It'll be so good to get back to Katie's."

He reached for the ignition key and then hesitated.

"What is it?"

"I hate bringing any of the nightmare back again, but while it's fresh in your mind I have to ask you one more question. There's something you said while you were still dreaming. That you wouldn't tell—some secret, I guess. Do you remember what it was?"

Laura's brow wrinkled. "A secret…Jake, I'm sorry, I just don't know."

"Keep it in the back of your mind. Maybe something will come to you."

After Jake pulled out of the parking area, Laura closed her eyes and leaned back against the seat. He knew she wasn't sleeping—that she wouldn't dare sleep in the car now. But he sensed that she wanted to be alone with her thoughts, so he didn't ask any more questions.

Two and a half hours later, they arrived at Katie's.

After quickly introducing himself, Jake got right to business. "I want you to check Laura over."

"What happened to her?" the physician demanded, sweeping a worried gaze toward her friend.

"When I came back with breakfast, I found her unconscious in our cabin, with gas pouring out of the heater. She didn't want to go to a hospital, so I compromised on coming straight here. On the way back, she had another nightmare. A bad one."

Katie took her houseguest to the bedroom, and Jake sat

in the living room, trying to concentrate on a copy of *The New England Journal of Medicine*. When Katie came back without Laura, he threw down the periodical and stood up.

"How is she?"

"In amazingly good shape for what she's been through."

"That's the best news I've heard since I found out she wasn't dead." There was a hollow ring to the quip.

Katie took a seat on the couch and leaned forward, her fingers clasped together in her lap. "Jake, Laura felt terrible about leaving her clients in the lurch. But not being able to let you know what was going on was the worst part of that whole performance for her."

Jake swallowed. "It looks like they're still trying to kill her. Or maybe they were just after me and she got in the way."

Katie glanced at the window. "Is this place still safe?"

"I don't think we were followed, if that's what you mean."

"Do you need a place to stay, too?" Katie asked.

"To tell you the truth, I'd feel better not letting Laura out of my sight."

As if on cue, he looked up to see her standing in the doorway. Fresh from the shower, she was wearing a terry robe, her hair wrapped in a towel.

Jake gave her a quick inspection. The color had returned to her face, and she seemed both more animated and more composed. She also looked a bit unsure as her eyes flicked to him. He wanted to cross the room and put his arm around her shoulder. Instead, he wrapped his hands around his knee.

Katie looked toward her friend. "I've only heard the high points of your adventures. I was about to ask for a full account. But maybe I should feed you first. Have you eaten?"

"No. I wanted to get Laura back to you as soon as I could," Jake answered.

Katie nodded at Laura. "You finished getting dressed, and Jake and I will get lunch on the table. When I'm nervous, I cook. And I've been nervous since I got home yesterday and found you'd flown the coop."

"Sorry."

"You did what you had to. Now, you have a choice between Chicken Cacciatore, Beef Bourguignon and homemade cheese ravioli. Unless you want meat ravioli."

Jake laughed. "Quite a lineup. But don't you have any dessert?"

"Scones, apple pie, Black Forest cake."

When Laura returned, the table was loaded with half a dozen different dishes and Jake was already filling his plate.

Katie had a little of the beef. Laura nibbled on the ravioli. To Katie's delight, Jake took man-sized helpings of everything and was lavish in his praise of her culinary accomplishments.

While they ate, Jake and Laura recounted the events of the past thirty hours. The narrative was liberally punctuated by questions and exclamations from their hostess.

"If that's a sample of life in the fast lane, I think I'll stick to my quiet little genetic studies," Katie murmured as she twirled a slender finger around one of her dark ringlets.

"I'll pass next time around, too," Laura assured her, getting up to clear the table.

Katie also stood and began reaching for serving dishes. "Let me do it. You can go get that broken ornament. I want to have a look at it."

A few minutes later, Laura set the knapsack on the living room table and pulled out the T-shirt-wrapped chunks. "If my dream was right, then we've got the weapon he used to murder Julie,'' she said in a low voice. ''Although I'm not sure what good it's going to do us in pieces like this.''

Katie knelt beside the table and examined the fragments. ''I'm afraid there's not much we can tell from these now.''

Laura threw Jake a guilty glance. ''I wish I hadn't hit you over the head with it.''

''It's my fault. I should have been whistling the Buckeye fight song on my way up the tunnel.''

Katie picked up the metal disk and fingered the lightning-bolt symbol. Then she fitted the disk into the matching depression in the base. ''What does this thing have to do with Fairbolt?''

''I don't know,'' Jake said.

''The lightning bolt is their corporate logo.''

''Fairbolt—never heard of it,'' Laura mused. ''No, wait a minute. I remember it from one of my data searches when I was trying to find out which of the newspaper articles had anything to do with Ravenwood. Fairbolt funded some school co-op projects in Garrett County. Maybe they were giving the statues away, too.''

''I don't know about statues,'' Katie said, ''but they're big into working with schools. That's why I know them. When I was in college, they had an arrangement to supply the chemistry department with reagents at cost.''

''They're a chemical company?'' Jake asked.

''That and a bunch of other stuff. Like everybody else, I guess they've diversified over the past few years.''

Jake stroked his chin. ''I've never heard the name, but there's something about the symbol that rings a bell. I just can't make the connection.''

''Maybe you saw an ad somewhere.''

He shrugged, but while the conversation continued, he sat with his chin propped on his hands.

''Jake?'' Laura finally asked.

"Sorry." He ran his fingers through his hair. "Listen, I don't like leavin' you, but I have to go home and check my notes. That symbol has something to do with the research I did on Holly's death. I want to know the connection."

Fear flashed in Laura's eyes. "Jake, if you were the target of the heater gas leak, it could be dangerous for you to go home. Someone could be waiting for you to show up."

"I know. But I need to get a look at those notes."

"Jake—"

"Don't worry, honey. I'll be real careful."

"How long are you going to be?" She struggled to keep the panic out of her voice. It only made things worse for him.

"Two or three hours."

"Call me when you get to your apartment, so I know everything's all right."

"I don't think I should. What if someone's bugged my phone?"

"I didn't think of that." Would the man who'd been lurking under the cabin window go to such elaborate lengths? Laura didn't know. Jake was right. Why take a chance? Jake pulled her into his arms and for just a few seconds, she felt warm and safe the way she always did when he held her. However, the embrace was over before she could bind him to her.

He was halfway out the door before he turned and gave the women a sheepish look. "I don't have a car."

"Take the Chrysler," Katie offered.

When he'd left, Laura stood in the middle of the rug, biting her lip, wanting to call him back, yet knowing he needed to go—for his own peace of mind, if nothing else.

Chapter Thirteen

Laura stood at the window until the car disappeared around a bend in the street.

Katie came over and laid a hand on her sagging shoulder. "You look tired. Why don't you get some sleep while he's gone?"

"No!" Laura answered before she had a chance to consider how the exclamation must have sounded.

"You're afraid of the dreams."

"I can't help it."

"I could give you a strong sedative."

"Maybe tonight." Laura stared out the window in the direction in which the car had gone. "I want to be awake when Jake comes back."

"I think you need to take your mind off your problems." Katie's voice was warm and encouraging. "Let's go out in the garden."

"I probably shouldn't be outside."

"The backyard is very well screened, and you can't see it from the street. Come on, it's nice and warm out there in the afternoon."

Katie led her to a sunny patio protected by the back of the house, the garage wall and a stand of miniature hollies. Laura stretched out on one of the comfortable chaises.

"I'll be right back. Do you want tea or something cold?"

"Tea is fine."

Laura looked around at the herbs and fall mums planted in U-shaped beds at the edge of the open space. What a nice place to relax. If she could relax.

Closing her eyes, she listened to the soothing gurgle of the little shell-shaped fountain. Ever since she'd been arrested by Hiram Pickett, she'd felt as if she were bouncing from one tense, perilous moment to the next. In between were periods of strained waiting. She wasn't sure which was worse. Now her stomach was in knots because Jake was putting himself in danger again. It was hard to keep herself from calling to make sure he'd gotten to his apartment and everything was all right. She knew that could cause trouble for both of them.

The depth of her anxiety was surprising—and alarming. It seemed as if Jake Wallace had become important to her very quickly. But there was no way to rely on what she was feeling. Or what he was.

Obviously, he was still emotionally tangled up in his memories of Holly and still driven by his need to avenge her death. Or why else would he have rushed off like that to go over his notes? Laura told herself she understood. Even as she tried to convince herself it wasn't true, her stomach clenched again. This time she knew it was from jealousy. Jake had turned to her last night. Yet she didn't have any claims on him. So why was she so upset that he was still in love with another woman? Because irrational as it was, despite all her fears about involvement, she had started imagining what a future with Jake might be like.

Footsteps on the patio made Laura's eyes open.

Katie was holding two mugs of tea.

Laura sat up straighter, grateful for the interruption. Looking around the garden, she tried to dredge up some sort of normal conversation. "This is so pretty. Maybe I'll put in something like it in the spring."

"You can have a garden just like it, if you want. Sabrina did the planting. She even keeps it weeded and pruned for me. All I have to do is enjoy it."

"I didn't know she did landscaping."

"Mostly herb gardens. But I don't really think you want to talk about gardens."

Did she want to talk about Jake? No. That was too dangerous. "I've been wondering about my father," Laura said instead.

"You've been letting yourself worry about whether your father was a rapist and a murderer."

Laura nodded tightly and set down her mug.

"What was your father's name?"

"Rex Roswell."

"Not Dorian."

"That could have been a code name the conspirators were using. Or a nickname."

"Have you ever heard anyone refer to your father as Dorian? What about your mother when she was angry with him?"

"I guess not."

"What about that investors' weekend at Ravenwood? Did anybody talk about him?" Katie persisted.

"Yes."

"What did they call him?"

"Rex."

Katie's next question seemed to come out of the blue. "What conspirators?"

Laura looked puzzled.

"You used the word just now. Do you think there's some kind of conspiracy involving Ravenwood?"

Laura hadn't put her thoughts into exactly those words until she'd made the offhand statement. Now she hesitated for a moment before answering. "Yes. And even if my father wasn't the man who murdered Julie, he could still be in on it. He and Emma.''

Katie looked at her friend's drawn features. "I was trying to make you feel better—not worse.''

"I know.''

The two women sat in the sun, drinking their tea in silence. But as the afternoon lengthened, the air began to cool, and they decided they'd be more comfortable in the house.

Katie went into the kitchen and began browning bony pieces of meat in a large kettle. "For Ox-tail soup,'' she explained to Laura.

"We've already got enough food for an army!''

"Jake can put some in his freezer. You start chopping the onions and the leeks. And when you finish with them, do the carrots, celery and parsnips.'' She got out a recipe book, opened it to a page near the middle and set the book on the counter.

There *was* something sort of soothing about cooking, Laura decided as the cutting board filled up with vegetable slivers. And it kept her from glancing at the clock. Jake had said he'd be back in two or three hours. It was past the deadline now.

Katie was just dumping the onions into the pot with the oxtails when the doorbell rang. Laura's knife clattered to the cutting board. "I'll get it.''

"Look out the window before you open the door.''

Jake was standing on the porch, a thick expanding file holder under his arm.

Relief flooded through Laura. He was back—safe and sound. Throwing open the door, she launched herself at him. He caught her and held her tightly for long moments, as if he'd been worried about her as she had about him.

"I'm glad you're back,'' she murmured.

"So am I. And wait till you see what I found.''

"Something important?" she asked, making an effort to match his mood.

"Yeah. But I'm not sure what it all means." He strode inside, set the expanding file on the coffee table and extracted a spiral-bound notebook. "These are my original interviews from residents who lived in Danville, Ohio."

Katie had come in from the kitchen wiping her hands on her apron.

As they watched, Jake flipped through the book and folded open one of the pages. "Look at this." It was a crude sketch of a lightning bolt inscribed in a circle.

Laura pulled the disk out of her knapsack and laid it on the paper. They were a good match if you allowed for the artist's inexpert rendering.

"Where did the drawing come from?" she asked.

"A farmer. He said it was painted on the side of some trucks coming to the weapon's plant. We both assumed it was the emblem of an army division. But when I tried to trace it through army records, I didn't find anything that matched."

He slapped his hand against the page. "Now it looks like Fairbolt was involved in the army project."

"That opens up a whole new line of investigation," Laura murmured.

"Yes. But what does it have to do with Ravenwood?" Katie asked.

Neither Jake nor Laura could answer.

"Well, what exactly was Fairbolt supposed to be doing in Garrett County?" Katie said attacking the question from another angle.

"An environmental educational project." Laura struggled to remember the details of the article she'd skimmed. "I think it included free health screenings."

"Nice of them to go to so much expense—unless they

had their own agenda." Katie thought for a moment. "For example, health screenings are a good way to collect data."

"What kind of data?"

"Perhaps to assess long-term health risks and epidemiological factors. Sometimes, rural populations are used as control groups."

Jake raised questioning eyebrows.

"Like the Framingham, Massachusetts study where healthy men are being followed for several decades to see how their life styles affect their incidence of heart disease. There are lots of others. Some are concerned with very narrow risk factors, like the relationship of sun exposure to skin cancer or the correlation of coffee drinking to heart disease. Others are very broad."

"Are they ever done by private companies?"

"Sure. Cigarette manufacturers used to run them all the time. They're still claiming that the link between smoking and lung cancer hasn't been proven."

"I still don't see why Fairbolt would want to test a large population of kids in Garrett County. Could they have been doing something else in the area, too?" Jake wondered aloud.

"That's just speculation," Laura countered. "The trouble is, we still don't know what we're looking for."

"How about a chemical-weapons plant? Apparently they had one in Danville, Ohio," Jake suggested in a strangely quiet voice. "One that released all sorts of toxic chemicals into the environment."

The hair on the back of Laura's neck stood on end.

"Maybe that's what Julie was investigating!"

"I think one quick way to get some information is to sneak a look at Andy Stapelton's files," Jake went on. "If he got the government restriction on the sale of the land lifted, he probably had some idea why it was issued in the first place."

"Sneak a look at his files—as in breaking and entering?" Laura asked.

"Let me worry about that."

"If you're going, so am I."

"You had a rather bad experience this morning."

"And I'm fine now." For the past few moments, they'd been ignoring Katie. Now Laura glanced at her for confirmation. "Ask my doctor."

"Your doctor thinks you're both crazy," Katie shot back, but she couldn't change Jake's mind—or Laura's. The best she could do was point out that they'd be better off waiting until dark.

At eight o'clock, they started for the office park near Baltimore-Washington International Airport where the ASDC offices were located. First, they checked out the building. It was three stories of red brick and glass with a guard desk in the lobby to control evening and weekend access. After circling the structure, Jake suggested a plan for getting in.

Laura, who had donned her disguise again, would go in and say her car wouldn't start. When the guard came out to have a look, Jake would slip into the lobby. Then he'd hide in the rear of the building and open the back door for Laura.

"What am I supposed to claim is wrong with the car when it starts right up?"

"That you've been having carburetor trouble and it must have flooded. Be sweet and thank him for taking the trouble to help you. Men always go for that."

"I haven't had much experience in playing games with men." She gave Jake a direct look. When he didn't comment, she added, "But I'll give it a try."

Laura left the car in the parking lot around the corner and headed up the sidewalk to the front entrance. Jake stayed in the shadows until the guard had been lured away from his post. Then he crept inside with as much invisibility as a man his size could manage.

By the time Laura had driven out of sight and circled back to the other side of the building, he was waiting by the exit.

"I already checked. ASDC is on the second floor," he whispered.

Laura was feeling strangely calm. This was her second breaking and entering in two days. Maybe once you got into a life of crime, it became second nature. "I hope we didn't set off an alarm," she murmured.

"I don't think there is one."

"What about the guard?"

"Either we're out of here before he makes his rounds again or we hide behind the desk."

The second-floor corridor was dark and quiet with only a few hall lights glowing dimly. Jake had brought along his burglar tools again, but not his gun. If they got caught, they didn't want to get pinned with armed robbery. But they weren't going to get caught, she reminded herself. And she wasn't going to make the same mistake she'd made with the knife at Ravenwood. This time they were both wearing gloves.

The outer door of the ASDC offices yielded with the same facility as the lock at Ravenwood. After they stepped into the waiting room, Jake quietly closed the door. Laura stuffed her wig back into her pocketbook, and they got out their flashlights.

Everything was sleek, tasteful and expensive.

"It looks like this ASDC operation is either making big money or they're putting up a good front," Jake muttered.

He stopped at the secretary's file cabinet. It wasn't locked.

"The good stuff is probably in there." Laura jerked her arm toward a glass door with Andy Stapleton's name on it.

"Yeah, but you take a quick look in these files anyway. Maybe he uses the hide-in-plain-sight system. I'll start on his personal stuff."

Laura was just about to pull a file drawer open when she heard a muffled exclamation from the inner office.

"Jake? What is it?" Somewhere along the line, her calm had begun to unravel. With her pulse pounding in her ears, she hurried toward Andy Stapleton's office. The moment her feet crossed the threshold, she knew something was terribly wrong.

A slash of light from the parking lot illuminated a limp male form slumped over the wide rosewood desk. The hand with the diamond ring Laura remembered was clamped around the handle of an ugly little revolver. Andy Stapleton! A dark stain spread across the blotter under his head. It wasn't ink.

Laura felt an icy chill sweep over her skin. "My God."

Jake drew her close. This time, his warmth couldn't stop the shivers racing up and down her arms.

"Another death." Her voice quavered as she said the words.

"Yeah."

"Jake, when is it going to end?"

"When we figure out what's really going on." His voice was hard.

Somehow, his harsh response helped her mind start functioning again. Sucking in a steadying breath, Laura looked around the office, glad they were both wearing gloves.

"We've got to get out of here." She tried to tug Jake toward the door.

"Not yet."

"Jake, we can't let anyone find us!"

Ignoring her words, Jake took a quick look out the window and then crossed to the files.

Laura glanced back toward the door. Somewhere down

the hall, she thought she heard a noise. "Jake, we've got to get out of here."

"Not until we've gotten what we came for."

"Jake!"

"Give me just a minute."

Opening a file drawer, he began riffling through folders. There was one on Ravenwood. It was empty. Jake cursed and began looking through other folders.

She could either stand with her back to the wall, or join the search, Laura decided. Maybe if she found something, she could pry Jake loose.

Gloved hands pressed to her hips, she edged closer to the body. As she rounded the corner of the desk, she spotted a piece of paper half off the edge. It looked as if it had whooshed out of place when Andy had fallen forward.

"I've found a suicide note," she whispered as she scanned the words. "He says he killed Emma and can't live with himself."

"That nails it down pretty tight," Jake muttered, but the didn't slow his search of the filing cabinet.

Just then, the door of a nearby office opened, and Laura's body went rigid. She realized she'd heard the same sound before—only farther down the hall.

"The guard's making his rounds!"

"Yeah. I heard him."

He'd known and he'd coolly kept searching!

Laura glanced back toward the silent outer office. Did the guard just check out front or did he come into the back? They'd talked about hiding behind the desk. They couldn't take the chance now. "He can't catch us here!"

Jake crossed to the casement window and began rapidly turning the crank. "There's a roof on the next level. It's only a one-story drop. I think we can make it out that way."

"Sounds better than the alternative."

When the window was open, he helped Laura onto the sill. Then he leaned over and lowered her as far as their outreached arms could stretch. Bracing for the impact, she let go.

Laura hit the gravel roof, lost her balance and fell to her seat. However, only her dignity seemed to be injured. Brushing off loose bits of gravel, she stood and looked up, expecting to see Jake's legs dangling from the window-frame. Instead, he had disappeared from view.

''Jake!'' she called.

There was no answer.

Chapter Fourteen

Laura's heart stopped and then threatened to thump its way through the wall of her chest.

"Jake!" she tried again in a hoarse whisper. Nobody answered.

Frantically, she looked up at the long expanse of wall above her. There were no projections suitable for climbing. The window through which she'd escaped might as well have been at the top of the Washington Monument for all the chance she had of getting back in again.

What was happening in the office? Had Jake deliberately lowered her to safety to get her out of danger while he kept searching? Or had the guard come in and discovered what looked like a murder-robbery in progress? Was he holding Jake at gunpoint while he called the police? Laura couldn't stop her imagination from running wild.

Seconds ticked by. Or was it centuries?

Finally, a muscular arm reached out the window. "Here, catch."

"Jake. Thank God."

Like a perfect touchdown pass, a bulky manila envelope sailed through the air. Laura snagged it with considerably less style. It was sealed like a Christmas present with several silvery lengths of duct tape crisscrossing at right angles.

Jake's arm withdrew and Laura suffered another panic attack. In the next moment, she realized he was only trying to figure out how to wiggle through the opening. As he twisted and turned, maneuvering first one shoulder and then the other out the window, she unconsciously imitated his gyrations—while clutching the envelope to her chest.

When he dropped to the gravel beside her, she wanted to throw her arms around him with relief. He didn't give her a chance. Grabbing her shoulder, he urged her toward the roof's edge. "I'm tired of feelin' like a fish in a barrel."

"I guess the guard didn't see you."

"No. He only stuck his head in the front door. He must just do a spot check on a couple of offices each time he makes his rounds. Maybe he won't investigate Stapleton's inner sanctum tonight."

"Where did you find the envelope?"

"Stuck to the bottom of the center desk drawer. My guess is it's a duplicate Ravenwood file."

When they reached the edge of the roof, Jake repeated the process of lowering Laura to the ground before joining her.

"You're limping again," she said between puffs of air as they trotted to the car.

"So what's new?"

The words were clipped. From pain or tension, Laura wondered. She wasn't sure what response he wanted from her. So she held her tongue until they were back on Route 195, heading toward Katie's house. Then her anxiety came bursting out. "Jake, that was a pretty stupid stunt."

"Which? Breaking into Stapleton's office or staying behind to look for evidence?"

"Both."

"You came along for the break-in."

"I wasn't going to let you do it alone. But I didn't know Andy was going to be slumped over his desk—dead."

"Sometimes when you make an end run, you don't have any idea how it's going to come out."

The tone of his voice made her head jerk up. "What do you mean?"

"This Ravenwood deal is tied to Fairbolt, which is tied to Holly's death. I'm going to find out how."

"Is it worth getting charged with murder?"

"He killed himself. He had the gun in his hand. You found the note."

"I'm starting to wonder if it's a little bit too convenient. Besides, however it went down, if the police find any evidence that we were in that office, we're in big trouble."

"Come on, Laura, we can't have it both ways. It was either murder or suicide."

Laura didn't see any point in continuing the argument. Tension seemed to fill the car like humid air, making it hard to draw in a satisfying breath. It wasn't all generated by their narrow escape. She kept throwing Jake covert glances, although she couldn't see his face in the darkness. But as she imagined his grim features, her fingers curled over the edge of the seat.

Why were they so on edge with each other? From the scene in Andy's office? Or was Jake sorry about last night? Was he wishing he'd never gotten so deeply involved with her?

It was a relief to get back to Katie's, to another person who could act as a buffer between them.

"Why haven't I heard anything from the police? They're supposed to keep you informed of developments," was the physician's first question after they'd told her about Stapleton.

"We didn't call them." Laura's voice was carefully neutral.

"They're going to find out about it soon enough," Jake

added. "When ASDC opens for business tomorrow morning."

"But—"

"I've been trained to respect the law," Laura said, cutting her friend off. "Keeping quiet about a dead body makes me feel as if I'm teetering at the edge of a cliff. But it would be pretty risky to have to explain what we were doing breaking into Stapleton's office tonight. Besides, now that I'm thinking a little more clearly, I realize we could make a mess of things for Detective Hamill. He laid his job on the line setting it up so I could go underground. If his superiors find out that I haven't been hiding out like I'm supposed to, he'll be in big trouble."

"I didn't think about him," Jake admitted.

"That's because you haven't met him. But I owe him a lot. And I hope I haven't let him down."

The conversation had been taking place with the three of them huddled just inside the door. Now, Jake shifted his weight and Laura saw a grimace flash across his features.

"Maybe we ought to sit down," she said.

"What am I thinking about, keeping you standing here in the dark?" Katie reached for the light switch.

"Better close the curtains first," Jake warned. "Just in case we have another busybody outside." He was already easing onto the sofa.

Both women looked at him critically. "What's wrong with your leg?" Katie asked.

"An old football injury."

"Aggravated by jumping down from two roofs," Laura added.

"Want me to have a look at it?"

"No, I just need some ice."

"And a painkiller," Katie added.

"I won't argue with that. I guess it's convenient to be hiding out with a doctor."

As their hostess began bustling around dispensing the medication and the ice, Laura was struck with a new pang of guilt. "We're getting you into a lot more than you bargained for," she murmured.

Katie paused and looked at Laura. "I signed on for the duration. I'm not going to quit when the going gets rough."

Laura nodded and ducked her head. If the going got much rougher, she'd figure out a way to get her friend off the hook. But she wasn't about to start a debate about it in the middle of the night. Especially when Jake needed to take care of his leg.

"Can I get anyone a drink?" Katie asked.

Jake eyed the brandy on the sideboard. "I suppose that stuff doesn't go too well with whatever you just gave me."

"Sorry. That's a combination I wouldn't recommend."

"Then how about coffee. I have the feeling we're going to be up pretty late." He was already pulling the papers from the envelope as Katie went to get the coffee.

Dropping down beside him on the couch, Laura tried to read along with him. She was so wired that the script on the ancient deed of sale wasn't making any sense.

Without thinking about it, she let her head drop to Jake's shoulder.

He touched her hand lightly. "I guess I was kind of sharp with you back in the car." His voice was gruff. "You doin' okay now?"

"No."

He turned, giving her his full attention.

She sat up straight again. "I'm no worse off than you are, I guess."

Just then, Katie stepped into the room with a tray of mugs and a coffeepot. For a few minutes, they were all busy pouring and stirring coffee.

Then they began to read the deed. Apparently, the Ravenwood tract of land had been purchased from the state of Maryland by a Colonel Miles Ravener in 1849 for what sounded like a ridiculously small amount of money.

"Looks like it wasn't worth much back then, either." Jake punctuated the remark with a long pull on the coffee mug.

Under the deed was an annotated list of Ravener's descendents.

Laura studied it thoughtfully. "I think it was typed on an old electric machine," she observed.

"Why?" Katie asked.

"The print's pretty even. But the typeface reminds me of my dad's old Remington portable."

"But it's not the same machine," Jake clarified.

"His was manual. When anybody typed on it, the q's and z's were always faint."

They went back to the list. Ravener had had two sons, one of whom had been killed in the Civil War. A daughter had died in her early twenties without having any children. Her husband had remarried soon after and had made no subsequent claim on the property.

The remaining son had moved to Baltimore and had never married. Ravenwood had been inherited from him by a cousin named Stewart Middleton, an Illinois resident.

"This information wasn't all in one place. Somebody went to a lot of trouble to dig it up and put it together." Laura set down her coffee mug and ran her finger along the page.

"They must have had a pretty strong interest in the property."

"Or maybe they were looking for land that met certain requirements, and this happened to be one of the candidates," Katie suggested.

Below the list was a letter written in 1950 to Stewart Middleton on official stationery from the Defense Department. It began with a patriotic appeal, a reminder of every citizen's duty to support the country's fight against Communist aggression in any way possible. It ended with a request to buy eight hundred thirty-two acres of Garrett County, Maryland, property owned by Middleton. Located as it was in the Allegheny foothills, the land had little commercial value. But its isolation would make it perfect for the training of U.S. troops being sent on sensitive missions.

"Troop training?" Katie wondered aloud.

"Nobody in Hazard mentioned anything like that when I was asking questions," Jake told her. "In a small town, you'd think a concentration of troops would have been a big deal."

"If it was supposed to be a secret training camp, maybe they didn't know about it," Laura suggested.

"Or maybe the request was deliberately misleading. The Defense Department had to give Middleton some reason why they wanted the land," Laura offered.

Apparently, the owner's patriotic spirit had been stirred by the appeal. Or perhaps he'd seen the request as a way to unload seemingly worthless land on which he was paying property taxes year after year. At any rate, a copy of the new deed of sale was attached to the letter.

"I don't know a lot about land prices back then. But I think the army got Ravenwood dirt cheap," Jake observed.

Laura wasn't listening. Instead, she was staring at the deed, her face bloodless.

Jake sensed the sudden stillness of her body. "What is it?"

"Look at the signature of the clerk who recorded the sale."

Everyone's eyes went to the bottom of the yellowed paper. Written in precise black script was the name Warren Ketchum.

"Warren Ketchum. Judge Ketchum," Laura breathed. "The last time we met was in his courtroom when I was arraigned for Emma's murder. He's the man who set my bail at a million dollars because he couldn't be sure that I'd return to the county for trial if he let me out of his sight.''

"I thought he was doing a law-and-order number. Now you have to wonder how he really fits into all this.''

"I'd like to know exactly what he's been up to.''

Jake began to shuffle rapidly through the rest of the papers. "Here he is again in 1951, authorizing the building of a county road to the property. And what do you know. He graduated from clerk to head of the planning commission.''

"Wasn't he awfully young for a position like that?'' Katie interjected.

"Yeah. And why wasn't he off in the army himself?''

"Either he was 4F or he had some kind of special status.''

"Is there anything personal on him?''

"Give me a minute.'' Jake shuffled through more papers. "There doesn't seem to be any private stuff. All the material in the envelope is related to the history of Ravenwood.''

Laura gave a disappointed sigh.

"But here's a new deed for the property in 1960, selling the tract to the Ravenwood Limited Partnership,'' Jake continued. "That must be the group of investors that included Martha and Sam.''

"And my father and your uncle.''

"And Warren Ketchum.''

"What?''

"We wanted to know who else had invested. Well, his name is here on a list along with the rest of them.''

"Warren Ketchum is one of the investors?'' Laura clarified.

"Yes.''

"But nobody ever mentioned him. Not Andy Stapleton. Not the other partners."

"Maybe only a few of them knew—and they were keeping quiet about it. This isn't his signature. It's just a typed list. Maybe it was a payoff for services rendered. Or maybe he was some kind of silent partner."

Laura took the stack of papers off the coffee table and shuffled back to the first typed sheet they'd found, the one with the names of the Ravener descendents. "It's the same typewriter," she said.

"Let me see." Jake held the two pages side by side, comparing individual letters. If it wasn't the identical machine, it was a twin.

"Of course, none of this proves Judge Ketchum did anything illegal. There's nothing criminal about recording a land sale. Or authorizing a county road project. Or joining a group of investors. Or typing a list of names."

"No," Laura said slowly, her eyes unfocused as she stared across the room in the direction of a Renoir print that hung over the fireplace. But the lush flower garden in the picture was just a blur before her eyes. Her inner vision was focused on a far less peaceful scene. "I'd like to see a picture of the judge when he was younger," she said slowly.

Jake looked at her inquiringly.

She fought to keep her voice steady. "Do you remember when I had that dream in the car—the one where the two men raped Julie Sutton?"

"Yeah."

"I told you I thought one of them looked familiar, but I wasn't sure where I'd seen him."

"Was it Ketchum?"

"Now that I think about his face, it could have been him. But the man I saw was thinner, and there wasn't any gray in his hair."

"You mean you wouldn't want to swear to it in a court of law."

"I'm afraid it's the kind of evidence that would be laughed out of court."

"Yeah." Jake thumped his fist against his palm. "But if we're sure it's him, we can go after better evidence. Ketchum's a public figure. I'll bet his picture has been in at least a couple of newspaper articles."

Laura nodded hesitantly. She'd thought they knew what they were looking for. Now a new piece had been thrown down on the table with the rest of the puzzle and she couldn't quite fit it in.

Katie, who had hardly joined the conversation over the past forty-five minutes, sat up straighter and stretched. "I vote we get a good night's sleep and start again in the morning."

Laura hadn't realized how wiped out she was until her friend spoke. Now, her body sagged back against the cushions.

Jake's gaze took in her whipped appearence. "Sorry. I got so caught up in this that I just wasn't thinkin'," he muttered. "You started off the day in a gas-filled room."

"It seems so long ago."

They all stood up a bit uncertainly.

"As I said before, you're welcome to stay here," Katie told Jake.

"Thanks. When I went home to go through my notes, I stashed some clean clothes in my duffel bag. It's still in the car."

Laura cast a quick glance up at him and then dropped her gaze. They'd made love last night—and slept in the same bed. What happened now?

It was Katie who made the decision for her. "I think the couch is long enough for you," she told Jake. "And I'll get you a blanket and a pillow."

"Appreciate it."

When their hostess had departed, Jake and Laura stood awkwardly in the center of the rug.

Jake cleared his throat. "Laura...I thought I could handle this by not saying anything—by putting the personal stuff on hold until this crisis was over. I guess that's not going to work."

She nodded tightly.

"But I can't lie to you, either."

"My God, Jake. I don't want lies. That's the last thing I want."

"I know that, honey. And I care about you a lot. More than I ever thought I'd care again. But I lost so much the last time." His eyes were very bright, and he had to stop speaking for a moment. When he started again, his voice was thick. "I want you. I want to take the risk of loving you. But there's this part inside of me. This tight, closed part that's afraid to open up. Do you understand what I'm trying to tell you?"

"Yes. And I appreciate the honesty. More than you know." She gave him a quick, hard kiss on the lips, a kiss that was over almost before it had started. Then she was running down the hall to her room before he could see the tears in her eyes. She knew how he felt because she'd felt that way herself. After what Bill had done to her, she'd been afraid to love again. She'd told herself she wasn't going to let anyone hurt her like that again. Only she didn't have the iron control of Jake Wallace. She simply hadn't been able to help herself. She loved him and there wasn't a damn thing she could do about it.

Chapter Fifteen

The morning after they'd made love, Laura had awakened to the feel of Jake's fingers stroking back her hair. She awoke that way now. For a moment she thought she was simply dreaming about wanting him to be there. Then she looked up and saw him gazing down at her with a tenderness that made her breath stop. If he could look at her like that... No, she wouldn't try to convince herself it meant any more than what he'd told her last night. He cared about her. But he didn't know if it could go any further than that.

"Honey, I'm sorry I have to get you up." There were dark circles under his lower lashes, and his face was haggard.

"Didn't you get to bed last night?"

"I had stuff to do."

"What?"

"I'll tell you about it in a minute. But there are some things you need to know. Your friend Hamill called this morning to fill you in on the Stapleton development."

Laura felt tension bloom in her chest. "What did you say?"

"Katie answered the phone, so she didn't have to pretend she hadn't been there and seen the body for herself."

Laura winced. "Do the police think it's murder or suicide?"

"You know how it is. They don't broadcast information until they have a suspect nailed down." He hesitated for a moment. "But she could read between the lines. Hamill was worried about you. So she put me on the line and I had to tell him about our trip to Ravenwood—and the heater."

"Jake, why?" The question was a protest against the way events were overtaking her. She'd gone into hiding to avoid being staked. Now everything was closing in on her again.

"If whoever killed Stapleton has figured out you're alive, then you're in danger. He thought he got you once. Next time he's going to make sure."

Laura swallowed past the grit clogging her throat.

Jake slipped his arms around her and pulled her against the shelter of his body. As always, she felt as if she'd found a haven. "I'm not going to let anything happen."

"You're a good man to have in my corner."

"Yeah." She felt him swallow. "And I brought some pictures for you to look at."

"Okay." Laura stayed with him for just a moment longer. Then she sat up in bed and plumped the pillows behind her. Jake took a manila folder off the bedside table and laid it across her lap. Inside, there were several newspaper photographs and some black-and-white glossies.

"Where are these from?"

"The morgue at the *Sun*. After I finished going through the Ravenwood file, I couldn't sleep, so I figured I might as well drive back downtown."

Laura hefted the pile. "You must have spent half the night in the file room."

Jake shrugged. "Once I got into searching, I just kept going." He gestured toward the pictures. "These aren't all of the same man. I thought it would be a good idea to give you some choices."

"Kind of like a police lineup."

"Right."

Laura studied the first photograph. Jake had started with faces from the investors' weekend. On the top of the stack was what looked like a twenty-five-year-old picture of Sam Pendergrast taken at a black-tie dinner.

"From that celebrity photo section the paper runs on Sundays," Jake told her. "Everybody gets his fifteen minutes of fame."

Her laugh was brittle as she began to spread out the rest of the pictures.

Under the photo of Sam was one of a much younger Tim O'Donnell, caught tossing a ball at what appeared to be a bush-league baseball game. He'd been quite a handsome man in his early years, Laura decided. And a lot healthier looking, too.

The next photo made her hands tingle. "My father."

"Uh-huh."

"I guess this was taken a couple of years after he moved out."

"But you don't get any kind of vibrations from the picture?"

"Nothing to do with the dream. It just makes me remember him not being at home with us." Laura was anxious to go to the next exhibit. When she did, the tingling feeling danced all the way up her arm and triggered an erratic pounding of her heart. The photograph showed a dark-haired man dressed in a conservative business suit. He was smiling as he handed a check to a solid-looking matron.

"Ketchum," she breathed. "Years ago."

All at once, the atmosphere in the room was like the last moments before a thunderstorm breaks.

"It was him." The sentence came out as a little gasp.

"Take your time and be sure," Jake whispered.

"I don't need to take any more time. He's the man in the dream. I told you. That's why I thought he looked familiar." She closed her eyes for a moment. "I mean, he's one of the men who raped Julie Sutton. The one whose face I could see."

"Not the one who killed her? Not Dorian?"

"Not Dorian."

"Even if he didn't kill her, he's guilty of rape!"

Laura shook her head. "No jury is going to convict him on evidence from a murder suspect's dream."

"Former murder suspect," Jake corrected.

"And no one is going to accept the secondhand testimony of a ghost," she continued, sitting up straighter. "Besides, we don't really know anything for sure." She sensed that Jake was going to speak, and she shook her head. "Let's be logical for a moment. I've been caught in the grip of a terrible, overwhelming feeling that my nightmares are somehow being broadcast to me by a woman who was raped and murdered twenty years ago because she was investigating a conspiracy. It's flattering that you believe me."

He covered her hand where it still gripped the edge of the photograph. "I'm with you all the way."

"But it's not very realistic that anyone else will be." She swallowed. "And I *could* be dreadfully wrong, you know."

"Okay, so forget about the dreams if you want. There's all the evidence we found in Stapleton's file."

"Evidence we illegally obtained by breaking and entering—at the scene of a suicide or murder. No good, Jake."

"But there's no reason I can't duplicate at least some of the stuff with material from the newspapers. I can even go up to Garrett County and get a copy of the deed at the county courthouse. And Ketchum's on record as the head of the planning commission, too."

"Which doesn't prove any wrongdoing," Laura pointed out. "So what if his name keeps coming up in connection with Ravenwood? It's all got perfectly logical explanations. Anyway, his being involved in the land deal could be a coincidence."

"Why are you playing devil's advocate like this?"

"It's the way I was trained. You always try to come up with the objections the other side is going to make. But in the final analysis, it doesn't matter what we think," Laura added. "Evidence obtained without proper search warrant isn't admissible in court."

"Couldn't you plant it somewhere and let an—uh—third party discover it?" a voice asked from the doorway. It was Katie.

Laura and Jake laughed, glad the tension had been broken for a moment.

"I think you've been watching too much TV," Laura observed.

"Okay, so that won't work. But we're going to figure out what will. And we've got a lot of extra brain power." At Laura's puzzled look, Katie explained. "I remembered Jo was from Garrett County, told her about what we'd discovered last night and asked if she could come over. Not only is she here but she brought Cam."

"Yes, it's good to have a genius inventor on our side," Laura murmured.

Katie and Jake went to join the others while Laura quickly got dressed. When she stepped into the living room, the first thing she saw was the strained look on her friend Jo's face.

"What did I miss?" Laura asked.

"Nothing. I've just been hearing how Judge Ketchum is mixed up in all this. It's sort of a shock for me," Jo said.

"That's right. You know him, don't you?"

"Actually, my aunt has been cleaning his house since

before I was born. I can't say I knew him well, but sometimes, Aunt Pauline would have me come up to his place to pick up stuff he was getting rid of—clothes my brothers could wear or furniture he didn't want. Things like that. And while I was there, the judge would ask me to do a small job for him—like weed his flower garden—and then pay more than the chore was worth." She cleared her throat. "You've got to understand how it is in a small community. People live in each other's pockets. Everybody knew that my family was dirt poor after my father died and that we needed help."

"Jo—" Cam said softly, reaching for his wife's hand.

"It's okay. Being poor is something we couldn't help. I'm just trying to make a point. Everybody in town admires Warren Ketchum. It's a folk legend how he went off to college when he was fifteen and how he suddenly had a lot of money. People used to wonder about where it came from."

The implications of what Jo was saying began to sink in.

"Everybody wondered but nobody did anything?" Jake asked.

"What should they have done? Launched an investigation? He was a respected member of the community. A lawyer and a judge. Besides that, he contributed a lot to charity, so his wealth benefited people who were less well off. Another thing, he was a strong moral influence in the county, and a local celebrity. People talked about the way he dressed, the food he bought, the addition to his house, his Christmas parties for poor kids." She looked at Laura. "I'm sorry. When you told me he was the judge at your arraignment, I just thought 'Well, that's the kind of thing you'd expect with Judge Ketchum.' But I should have started making other connections."

"Jo, you had no reason to make any other connections,"

Laura said softly. "Anyway, I wasn't telling you the whole story when I asked you to do some investigating for me. I still couldn't talk to you about the dreams I was having. Even if I had told you about them, I hadn't dreamed about Ketchum yet."

"The important thing is to go on from here and find out what we've got," Jake cut in. "So now we have more of a circumstantial case against the judge. He's been getting large sums of money from somewhere. Maybe they were payoffs from Fairbolt."

"We could ask for an audit," Jo mused. "But they might have found a way to hide the transactions. Maybe there's no way to make the links we need. Or even if we could, it might take months. Laura doesn't have that kind of time."

"What if you can get the judge to confess? That would solve a whole lot of problems." The suggestion was tossed off by Cam.

"Sure." Katie couldn't keep the sarcasm out of her voice.

"No. I guess I sounded flip, but I really mean it," Cam insisted. "Guilt makes people do strange things. Maybe he's been contributing to charity all these years because he's been feeling as if he needed to atone for his sins."

Laura looked doubtful. "He was pretty self-righteous when he set bail."

Jo's face had taken on a flush of excitement. "Wait. Don't make assumptions the way I did. Suppose coming down hard on other people is one of the ways he copes with his guilt?"

"Where does that get us?" Jake asked.

"Keep an open mind," Laura said catching Cam's enthusiasm, too. She turned to Jo. "Okay, what else can you tell us about the judge? Personal stuff. Something he wouldn't want people to know. Something we could use against him."

"I don't know what you can use against him. Unless you want to spill the beans about his collection of lucky charms."

"Don't tell me he wears a fairy cross around his neck!" Laura exclaimed.

"If he wears one, it's under his shirt. But he's got some in a case in his living room. He's also got rabbit's feet. Four-leaf clovers encased in lucite. Hex signs. He's got stuff like that all over his house. When I was a kid, I used to love looking at all of it."

As her friend spoke, Laura felt her excitement mount. "So we know the judge is superstitious. How do you think Judge Ketchum feels about ghosts—or evil spirits?"

"You mean, does he believe in them?"

"That. And is he afraid of them?"

"If you'd seen all the stuff in his collection, you'd make that assumption. It's a pretty odd hobby."

"Where is all this getting us?" Jake asked.

Laura had unconsciously flattened her hand against her chest where the fairy cross had shattered. Now she turned excited eyes to Jake. "I've got an idea. Maybe it's too dangerous. And I'm not even sure if it will work." She glanced over at Cam. "But I'm going to need your help if there's a chance of pulling it off."

"Of course."

"Let's hear about the dangerous part," Jake said.

"I'm going to need you, too. If you don't mind," she told him in a low voice.

"Honey, you've got everything I have to give."

Everything, Laura asked herself. Or everything short of the one thing she wanted? For a moment she closed her eyes as if she were gathering her thoughts. Then she began to tell the group about her plan.

TUESDAY AFTERNOON, JAKE pushed himself back from one of the computer terminals Cam had provided, rubbed his bloodshot eyes and shook his head. Over the past two days, he and Laura had been correlating material from sources as disparate as the EPA, the Defense Department, the Maryland Extension Service, the *New York Times* Data Base, the National Cancer Institute and the Center for Disease Control.

"It's amazing what you can deduce when you can put together enough facts. The trouble is, this stuff is so convoluted, I'm not sure we'd be able to prove it to anyone else."

Laura laced her hands behind her neck and stretched tired muscles. Standing up, she went over to Jake and began to knead his shoulders. He leaned into her hands. "That feels great."

She wanted to brush her lips against his hair. But she didn't. In a few days, he might disappear from her life, and she didn't want him to think she was trying to hold him. Yet, while they were together, she wasn't going to deny herself everything. Not the pleasure of touching him, for example.

And there was something she could give him. Information. Falling back on the pattern that had served them so well when things got too personal, she began to talk about the work they'd been doing.

"I've just come up with another site and put the data on one of those worksheets we designed. Spruce Valley, Tennessee. It's set up like Ravenwood, purchased through the army but really under the complete control of Fairbolt. I've used the Center for Disease Control data to correlate with clusters of cancer deaths and miscarriages."

"You've come up with more places than I have."

"My analytical mind, I guess."

"Well, with your stuff and mine, we've got correlations for plants and chemical dumping sites around the country.

Pine Grove, Georgia. Centerville, Illinois. Layton, Nebraska. Hazard, Maryland. And none of the communities knew.''

"They will now. Like for example, Fairbolt was dumping every thing from trichloroethylene to ethylene oxide and dioxin in the Ravenwood ravine. No wonder they were studying schoolchildren to find out if there were long-term effects.''

Jake stood up and paced to the window. "You know how it is when the line of a song keeps running through your head?"

"Yes."

"I keep thinkin' about the phrase 'heartland of America.' You know an idyllic little town where all the kids are cute, none of the dogs bite and you can leave your door unlocked.''

"The great American myth.''

"Yeah. Except that was the kind of place where Holly grew up. A picture-postcard community. She had a great childhood. Teachers who cared. Ice-cream socials. Summers at the swimming hole. And all the time, the sod on the playground was laid over a chemical field. And the cows in the nearby meadows were munching on the stuff. And it had leached into the water supply."

Laura could feel her eyes sting. "I know. It's such a damn cheat. But your book is going to blow the lid off the whole thing. Not just in Danville and Hazard."

"Finally Holly's death is going to make a difference. And I don't think I could have put the research together without you. I guess I haven't said thanks yet."

"You could have done it yourself. It just might have taken longer."

"But your help means a lot to me."

Laura pressed her lips together and nodded. She'd wanted—needed—to help. But had she been hoping all along that nailing the company whose chemicals had killed Holly would free Jake from the bonds of the past? She was too tired and confused to be sure of her own motivation anymore.

Jake broke into her thoughts. "The question is, if Ketchum knew about the dumping, why did he stay in Hazard?"

"I checked that out with Jo. His house was way out on the east edge of town. That's not exactly in the danger zone. And thank God she was in a pretty safe place too.

"Yeah." Jake nodded. Then his mind returned to the Ravenwood puzzle. "I keep wondering if anybody else was being paid to keep their mouths shut? Any one of the other investors could be involved. Did Tim look like he was in the money? Or Martha? What about your father?"

"Tim was trying to look prosperous. He had a rented Cadillac El Dorado for the weekend. But Sam Pendergrast is the one who's pretty well off."

"Yes. But I checked his financial rating. His car dealerships are doing just fine."

"What about Emma?"

"Either she was in on the cover-up from the beginning or she stumbled on to something. Or maybe she just found out how Andy Stapleton got the development restrictions lifted."

Their speculations were broken off by the ringing of the telephone. It was Cam, who'd finished testing the equipment they'd ordered.

"Everything's ready," he announced over the speaker phone. "So anytime you want to leave for Ravenwood, I'll bring the van and we can go over the instructions."

"Are we ready?" Jake asked Laura.

There were still pieces they hadn't fitted into the picture. But she was pretty sure they had enough information to convince Ketchum that they knew what had been going on all these years. "The sooner we get it over with, the better," she said in a voice that projected more confidence than she felt.

The moment they hung up, Laura got out the draft of the note she and Jake had been working on and filled in a meeting time. Then she read the whole thing over once more.

Dear Judge Ketchum,
You picked the wrong person to humiliate. Probably you thought my death eliminated me as a problem. I'm glad to inform you that I'm very much alive and well and have been digging into your relationship with the Ravenwood property over the years. I have information related to the toxic-waste dump site at the ravine. If you want me to keep the secret buried, bring your checkbook to the Ravenwood mansion at three p.m. Wednesday.

Laura deliberately omitted a signature. If her quarry wanted to think the note was from Julie Sutton, so much the better. Let him start to worry about what he was up against.

For the past two nights as she'd lain in bed, she'd pictured Ketchum's smug face as he gazed down at her from the bench. That had made her anticipate how good it was going to feel to make the judge sweat. Up till now she'd been the one trying to scramble out of the hole someone else had dug for her. Now she was going to push someone else over the edge.

Chapter Sixteen

Laura and Jake left for Garrett County at midnight so they could stop at Judge Ketchum's house and leave the note before driving to Ravenwood under cover of darkness—using the special infrared headlights Cam had provided. There was a three-car garage at the back of the house where they could park the van. But to keep from being spotted, they'd have to wait until daylight to set up the equipment Cam had put together.

Everything went according to schedule. Jake locked the garage doors behind them at four-thirty in the morning and then climbed into the back of the van, where Laura was sleeping on the mattress they'd sandwiched between the boxes of equipment.

She'd asked him to wake her when they arrived, but he knew she'd hardly slept during the past days of frantic activity. Now he decided she could use a few more hours of rest before the rough stuff began. Besides, the chance to lie down beside her was just too tempting to pass up.

When he eased onto the mattress, she snuggled against him. An automatic response to his body heat? Or did she know it was him? Closing his eyes, he inhaled her unique scent and pressed his chin tenderly against the top of her head. She felt so damn good, he thought as he lightly stroked her hair. He had to fight the desire to tip her head up, find her lips and kiss her awake. But this wasn't the time or place to start anything.

Besides, he was exhausted, too. And a little sleep wouldn't do him any harm, either.

It was still well before sunrise when Jake's eyes snapped open again. There was a fleeting moment of disorientation. Then he realized that Laura was moaning in her sleep. In the darkness, her small fists began to drum against his chest, as if she were trying to fight him off. Another dream. The first in days. Perhaps because she was back at Ravenwood again.

"Laura."

She didn't respond to him. But her head swung from side to side in panic. He knew whom she was fighting off.

Once, he'd let her suffer so he could get more information. This time, he couldn't allow the torture to go on.

Gently, he grasped her shoulders. "Laura, it's Jake."

"Please—no—"

"It's Jake. Wake up, honey."

Her face was pressed against the fabric of his shirt, but he sensed the change from sleep to waking. He wanted it to be a metamorphosis from panic to calm, but he could still feel the pounding of her heart.

"You're safe," he murmured, his lips skimming the top of her head, his hands enveloping her shoulders.

"The snow. The cold. Just like I always dream it." She forced herself to hold on to the images. "But this time was—I don't know—Julie was talking to me again. Warning me."

"About what?"

"Today. She was there in the swirling snow. And she was terrified, Jake."

"Didn't Dorian carry her out into the snow?" he asked softly.

"Yes. But that wasn't it. She was frightened for me. She wants us to leave before something terrible happens."

A chill that had nothing to do with the cold morning air had settled over his skin. "We can still call it off. The police can meet Ketchum."

All at once, their roles were reversed. Laura reared back and looked down at him. "It won't work. They won't get a thing out of him. We have to stay."

"But—"

"I'm okay now. I was just spooked. Dreams don't foretell the future."

"Laura—"

She forced an exaggerated smile onto her lips. "Don't tell me a big strong football player is panicked by a ghost."

"Don't get smart with me."

"I guess I'm way past getting smart." Before he could ask her what she meant, her arms captured his shoulders, and her warm lips touched his. Neither one of them was prepared for the power of the kiss. It drove away ghosts, drove away reason, drove away the fear they hadn't been able to talk about.

"You want me," she breathed.

"God, yes."

Now it was Jake who took control of the kiss. And Laura gloried in her surrender. They shifted on the narrow mattress, clinging to each other.

She and Jake were here together, mouth to mouth, breast to chest, hip to hip. And nothing mattered except the need to get closer to him still—as close as a woman could get to a man. Because if he walked away from her tomorrow, at least she'd have this one last time to remember.

THEY DIDN'T TALK about what had happened in the van. In fact, they didn't talk much at all except about where to string wires and set up hidden projectors and video cameras.

But by one o'clock they had everything working, including the link to the remote-reception station. Sighing, Laura brushed back the lock of hair that kept drooping across her eyes and looked out the window. She had expected to see the sun still shining brightly. Now she drew in a sharp gust of air as she realized that the sky had darkened to navy blue.

Jake turned, his face watchful. "What?"

"Look out there." She pointed to the window. "What do you think is going on?"

"I'll check."

A few minutes later, the word came back from their remote station that a freak snowstorm was hovering over the mountains.

So it was going to happen the way Julie had warned her. Icy fingers danced down Laura's spine. She knew the biting cold of a winter squall up here—from her dreams.

Jake must have seen the dead white of her face before she quickly turned away. "Honey, we're not going to get trapped. A storm can't dump that much snow in a couple of hours," he said soothingly. But she was tuned enough to him now to pick up his own uncertainties.

"Here comes the judge!" The warning crackled from a speaker hidden behind the drapes.

"He's over an hour early," Jake snapped.

"I guess he decided to get the drop on whoever showed up for the meeting."

They made a frantic last-minute check of the equipment before Ketchum's BMW pulled up in front of the house.

The final thing Jake did before withdrawing into the secret passage where they were going to hide was spray a cloud of Julie Sutton's Spring Meadow perfume into the air.

The scent made Laura feel as if she were choking. She hoped it had the same effect on the judge.

"You all right?"

"Yes," Laura lied.

Jake closed the panel and set up the protective barrier Cam had provided. "Show time, honey," he said as he pushed a button and a monitor gave them a picture of the front hall. Moments later, the front door opened and Warren Ketchum stepped into the mansion. They hadn't turned on any lights. The hall was as dark and shadowy as a haunted house on Halloween.

The setting was a perfect match for the judge's countenance. Even on a small black-and-white screen, he looked frightened—a far cry from the stern, imposing figure who had glared down on Laura from the bench. There, he'd appeared robust and vigorous. Now old age had bowed his shoulders and bent his body. Or perhaps it was fear that had doubled him over.

Pushing his glasses higher on his nose, he stood with his back to the door, apparently trying to quiet the shaking of his body. His left hand clutched and stroked a small bit of fur.

A rabbit's foot? Had he really stooped to that? But Jo had told them about his superstitions.

"He looks scared spitless," Jake whispered.

"Good."

The low-voiced exchange was cut off abruptly.

"Is anyone there?" Judge Ketchum bellowed with surprising force. When he stood up straighter, Laura caught a glint of gold around his neck. A fairy cross. Like the one that had saved her life. She hoped it didn't hold any special powers for him.

Laura swallowed around what felt like cotton batting in her throat and reached for a microphone. Jake stayed her hand. "Let him stew for a minute."

They watched as he took several cautious steps down the hall. "We don't want him to go the wrong way," Laura warned. But she still hesitated for several seconds. Would their elaborate scam really work? She was the star of the performance, and if she failed, the whole thing would blow up in their faces.

Jake sensed Laura's nervousness and moved closer to her, slipping an arm around her waist. "You're going to do just fine."

"I hope so." Laura cleared her throat and pressed the button that activated the mike in her hand. "In here…" she called in a soft voice. "I'm waiting for you in here."

On the monitor, Ketchum swung sharply around like a weather vane that had reversed direction in a windstorm. "Who is that?" he challenged. "Come out and show yourself, you coward."

Laura ignored both the question and the order. "Come in here…" she repeated in a slightly louder voice. There was a great deal of satisfaction in using the same technique that the killer had employed to lure her into the drawing room.

Another hidden camera followed their quarry down the hall. Before he reached the drawing room door, he slid his hand into his breast pocket and put away the rabbit's foot. Seconds later, he pulled out an automatic pistol.

Laura stifled a startled exclamation. He might be superstitious, but he wasn't going to trust magic to save himself.

Jake turned off the mike. "So much for Jo's intelligence. I thought she said he wasn't supposed to have a gun."

A firearm in the hand had done wonders for Ketchum's confidence level. Stiff-armed, he jumped through the drawing room doorway like a narcotics agent on a drug bust. "Freeze!"

"Lethal Weapon One and a Half," Jake muttered. The

words died in his throat as the gun swung directly toward the draperies behind which they were hiding.

Laura was pretty sure she could do something about that. Quickly, she slammed against one of the control buttons in front of them. Behind Ketchum, the doors banged shut and the lock clicked into place with the finality of a prison door clanking shut.

Again, the judge whirled. With a squeal of mingled anguish and rage, he fired a burst of shots into the doors, splintering the wood.

"He's out of control," Jake whispered. "It's happening too fast."

"Then let's get him to start talking." Laura clicked on the microphone again. "Bullets can't kill a ghost," she taunted. As she spoke, Jake activated a holographic projector. In the next second, the translucent image of a woman seemed to float eerily out of the door that Ketchum had just shot.

The apparition wore a white robe. Blond hair wafted out behind her and her arms were flung wide, as if to beckon the judge into her cold embrace. It was a recorded image of Laura. But with the right makeup, she looked a lot like the young Julie Sutton.

"Go back. No. Go back," the judge screamed, his fingers gripping the fairy cross around his neck. Gibbering in terror and confusion, he stumbled away from the apparition, firing another barrage as he went.

The bullets went right through the flickering image that kept advancing toward him, until, at the last second, it winked out of existence.

Ketchum sagged against the back of the sofa, panting and clawing the velvet fabric for support. His face had turned the color of cobwebs. Sweat stood out like blisters on his clammy skin. "Where are you? I smell your perfume. Where are you?"

Laura kept silent.

"Go away, do you hear? I didn't do it. I didn't kill you," he screamed.

"But you know who did! You know. You know. You know." The accusation came from every corner of the room, echoing from half a dozen speakers.

"Let me out of here. Leave me alone." He ducked down, holding up his fairy cross as if it were a shield.

Jake activated another projector. This time, the Julie Sutton image came sailing at Ketchum from another angle.

The victim ducked, dropped the talisman, covered his head with his hands and began to moan.

"Tell me about the murder," Laura intoned as Jake turned up the lights so that the judge was spotlighted like the lead singer in a rock group. And he was going to sing, all right. "Tell me! It's the only way to save yourself from my revenge."

"You know it wasn't me. Dorian did it. I didn't even know he was going to."

"What did you think was going to happen?"

"I thought you'd be too frightened and humiliated to talk."

They had him babbling now. And it was all being recorded on videotape.

"Talk about what?"

"Fairbolt. Their army contract. You tricked us. You pretended you were coming up here for fun and games. But you were snooping around—digging up secrets. You found out about the toxic-waste dump. You were going to ruin everything."

Ketchum had slid down to a heap of quivering flesh on the couch.

"And what about you? You found out about Fairbolt's business up here when you transferred the deed."

"No. Dorian asked me to set it up for him. He needed me. I was proud of that."

Laura kept the verbal pounding coming hard and fast, not giving her victim time to think. Ketchum must have been storing this stuff up for years like the poison chemicals in the ravine. "Who? Who are you talking about?

"Dorian," he choked.

"That's not his real name."

"But it's what we all called him. All the fraternity brothers. We used to ask him if he had a picture hidden in the attic—a picture that got nasty looking while he stayed the same."

"Like a picture of Dorian Gray."

"Yes! He was so rich. We kidded him that he could buy anything—do anything. We acted like it was a joke, but we whispered about it in secret because we were all afraid of him, too," the judge gibbered on. "He's capable of anything. We used to think he got us drugs and girls because he wanted to be everybody's best friend. But it wasn't like that. When you accept something from him, it gives him power over you."

"Who is he?"

"Please. I can't tell. I can't tell. He'll kill me. Or worse." Ketchum was sobbing now.

"Where did he get his money?"

"His family. They were some of the original investors in Fairbolt."

Laura and Jake exchanged glances. He was answering all their questions but the most important one. "It's ironic that you're protecting Dorian. He's tricked you again. Why do you think you're here?" she jeered. Recorded laughter filled the drawing room. Ketchum clamped his hands over his ears and curled into a tight ball.

"Did he kill Emma Litchfield?"

"Yes."

"Did he kill Andy Stapleton?"

"Shut up, you fool!" The roar of protest didn't come from the man huddled on the couch. Laura and Jake had been focused on the judge. Now they watched in horror as the door Ketchum had shot at shattered and splintered under the impact of a heavy boot propelled by powerful leg muscles. The knob and lock came flying across the room and landed on the rug several feet from the judge.

"You're not going to ruin everything now, you miserable coward. Not when we're finally going to get out from under this mess." The promise was spoken by Sam Pendergrast, who stepped into the room and stood looking around intently.

"Sam!" Laura's exclamation carried across the open mike and was broadcast to the room.

"That's right. And Laura and Jake. The two investors who couldn't leave well enough alone." His piercing gaze seemed to pick out each of the projectors and microphones they had carefully hidden.

He was holding a dagger in his hand. The same dagger Laura had found in the box. No, that was impossible. Police Chief Hiram Pickett had the knife with the murder evidence. Unless he'd given it back to the rightful owner. Or had Sam stolen it back?

With the speed of a man half his age, Sam Pendergrast advanced on the quivering judge. Somehow, Ketchum found the will to resist. He raised the gun, but before he could fire, Pendergrast knocked the weapon out of his hand.

"You swore to live by the sacred dagger. Now die by it!" Then he was slashing down with the knife. With a grunt of fear, Ketchum ducked to the side. The two men went at each other, and Ketchum's glasses went flying across the room. The fight couldn't last for long, not when Sam was in so much better shape.

Jake snatched the microphone away from Laura and threw a toggled switch on the console in front of them.

"Cam? Come in Cam. As they had since the beginning of the show, the words should be going out to the remote station Cam and Evan Hamill had set up down the road at the Slumbering Pines. But there was no answer. Not even static.

"Cam, are you picking us up?" Jake tried adjusting several dials. Still no answer.

He swore. "I can't raise him. I think that bastard Pendergrast damaged the transmitter." He grabbed Laura's arm. "Time to bail out."

Laura cast one last look at the monitor.

Pendergrast had raised the knife again, and Ketchum was trying desperately to keep it from plunging into his neck.

They couldn't save the judge. Could they save themselves?

"Come on!" Jake stood up too fast, whacking his knee against the control console. He grimaced in pain.

"You're hurt."

"I'm all right. Let's get out of here." He gave Laura a little push toward the other end of the passage, and she started moving, listening to make sure he was following.

When she reached the exit, she stopped short. "I don't know how to open the door from this side!"

"I hope I do."

Jake squeezed past her and felt for the mechanism. The door slid back on the noiseless tracks.

Laura's mind was racing. If Sam had cut off their transmission, then he'd probably also disabled the van. But they could hike to the motel through the woods, the way Jake had come up last week. That was their best bet. Or had Cam, Hamill and the police team already started on their way when they'd lost communication? There was no way to know. And no way to warn them about what they'd find.

Laura glanced at the window, and an exclamation of dismay tore from her throat. The only thing she could see was a solid wall of swirling white. The blizzard Julie had warned her about had moved in with supernatural swiftness.

Nobody was coming to help them now. And there was no way they were going to make it through the woods to safety because they wouldn't be able to see more than two feet in front of their faces.

They were trapped!

Chapter Seventeen

Jake followed Laura's frozen gaze, silent as he contemplated the enveloping whiteness and the roar of the wind tearing at the roof and windows. Then he squeezed her arm. "We'll be okay. There must be tons of places in the house to hide. Other secret passages. Stuff like that. And Cam's got four-wheel drive. He and Hamill are probably already on their way up here."

"Right." There was no use dwelling on the obvious flaws in Jake's reasoning. Any hiding places in the mansion were probably already well-known to Sam Pendergrast. And if the reinforcements arrived, they'd have no idea where to look for anybody. Laura pressed her lips together. She'd put a lot of energy into convincing her friends and Hamill that this crazy scheme would work. Now it looked as if she was going to be hoist on her own petard.

"I don't know how much time we have before Sam opens the panel down there," Jake said. "Or how fast he can get around the electronics equipment and the bullet-proof shield. So you get out of here. Find Hamill. I'll hold the bastard off."

A bolt of emotion shot through Laura as the impact of his words hit her. It was almost like being hit by lightning and miraculously surviving. A few days ago Jake had told her he didn't know how much he could care. Now he was saying he'd risk his own life to save hers.

"Jake, we're in this together."

His voice was low and urgent. "Laura, I'll only slow you down. This damn knee of mine has been bad news every step of the way."

The words only strengthened her resolve—and the feeling of elation coursing through her. Despite the terrible danger, she'd just learned something precious. "I'm not going anywhere without you. If you want to make a stand in here, we'll both stay."

Jake muttered a few choice expletives.

"But I vote we go," Laura continued. "And we're wasting time arguing."

"Yeah." They turned and started rapidly down the hall.

When Laura didn't hear footsteps directly behind her, she risked a glance over her shoulder. Sweat had broken out on Jake's forehead, and he was limping badly. His left knee looked as if it wasn't going to support his weight much longer.

"Go on—"

She dropped back and shoved her shoulder under his arm. There was no way she was going to leave him to the killer pursuing them.

"You go ahead," he insisted. "I want you to."

"No."

He didn't spare any more breath. Together, they stumbled down the hall. When they reached the turn, Laura hesitated. Earlier in the day, they'd locked the doors to the main stairs to keep Ketchum where they wanted him. The keys were still in the control room.

"Either we climb out a bedroom window and take our chances in the storm or we squeeze past the hole in the burned part of the house," Jake said.

Laura wondered if Jake could make the climb and what

their chances were outside. But the other alternative wasn't very attractive, either. "We can't get by that hole."

"I'm pretty sure there's enough room. I remember thinking that the floor wasn't cut all the way to the edge. If we watch what we're doin' and keep our backs to the wall, we'll be okay."

Somewhere in the distance, above the moaning of the wind, they heard a crash. The electronics equipment falling to Sam's angry onslaught? If so, he'd be on the second floor pretty soon.

Jake gritted his teeth and picked up speed as they moved down the hall. But when they reached the end of the corridor, the door was nailed shut.

"Damn!" Jake glanced over his shoulder as if calculating their chances of going back the other way. They were both flushed and gasping for breath. At this point, neither one of them could win a forty-yard dash.

"I should've been prepared for that." Without further consideration, he rammed the barrier with his shoulder. When the door didn't give, he muttered a curse and redoubled his efforts. On the second try, the door groaned, gave and sent him tumbling forward into the corridor.

"Close it," Jake gasped as he pushed himself to a sitting position. "Maybe he won't figure out what happened."

Laura eased the damaged door shut and leaned against it, sucking in lungfuls of the dank, stale air and fervently wishing she were somewhere else.

Since the first time she'd bumbled in here, she'd been wary of the place. Now she felt as if she'd deliberately walked into a death trap. With the door shut and the storm outside, there was very little illumination. And the light that reached the hallway was eerie—a continually shifting aura of swirling snow making odd patterns on the floor and walls. Above them, the wind tore at the burned shingles like a howling lion, sending in gusts of frigid air and snow.

However, the gaping chasm in the floor was more compelling than the roof. But at least Jake had remembered correctly; it didn't cover the whole surface. There was a narrow ledge of flooring along the right wall.

"Maybe whoever started the fire was trying to get warm," Jake quipped.

"Uh-huh." She reached for his hand to help him up and heard him stifle a grunt of pain as he came to his feet. She didn't ask him if he could make it to the other side of the abyss. They both knew he had to. Moving cautiously forward, they kept to the side of the flooring, feeling an all-too-familiar creaking and shifting under their feet as they reached the margin of the crater. But there were no further earthquakes.

Jake gestured Laura forward. "You're lighter."

By now she knew how his mind was working. "So maybe I'll get across—even if you don't?"

His harsh features softened for a moment. "We both will. Quit stalling. Or are you chicken?"

"Of course not! But I'm not a tight-rope artist. You're going to have to help me keep my balance." She reached for his hand and felt a surge of warmth as their fingers knit together. Let him think she needed his help, if he wanted.

As they began to inch toward the other side of the chasm, the wind shook the fire-damaged rafters above them and tore off more shingles. If they didn't fall into the hole on their own, maybe they'd be blown in.

How many minutes had ticked by? How much time did they have left? Maybe they really had fooled Sam about which way they'd gone. But what would he do when he didn't find them at the other end of the hall?

Laura's hands were icy, her pulse was pounding in her ears, and she was breathing in shallow gasps as they neared the three-quarters mark. *Please, we've made it this far. Let us make it all the way,* she prayed silently. *Both of us.*

Still, Laura could hardly believe it when she reached the firm ground on the other side. Jake was only a few steps behind her when the door through which they'd entered blew open as if a hurricane had swooped through the hall. But the door hadn't been seized by the wind. Laura watched as a grim-looking Sam Pendergrast stepped into the dank, dark hallway. He was holding the judge's gun.

"End of the line," he grated.

Jake turned so that his body was shielding Laura. For just a fraction of a second, he risked a look back at her. "Get ready to run," he whispered. Then he raised his head and looked Sam in the eye. "You're right. This is the end of the line. You've lost."

"No, I haven't."

"It's all on tape." Jake's words were bold, but Laura could feel the tension in his body. She knew what he was doing. Playing for time. And if that didn't work—if the cavalry didn't arrive—Sam's attention would be focused on Jake, so she'd have a chance to get away.

Her mind scrambled for alternatives and drew a blank.

"I'll take care of the videotape after I take care of you," Sam shot back.

"It was transmitted directly to the police. All they have to do is start interviewing Ketchum's fraternity brothers. You couldn't have bought them all off. Someone will tell the police which of the guys was called Dorian."

"Not the ones who count. Not the ones in my secret society will talk! Anyway I'll be out of the country before any of them cracks."

"The judge cracked!"

"Because you tricked him with your stupid haunted house show. The fool believed in ghosts. That's why he hadn't been up here since the night of that party."

Was there a note of desperation in Sam's voice, Laura wondered. Was he close to the edge? Could they get him to make a mistake? She racked her brain. Was there any detail—some tiny thing—that would make a difference? She thought back rapidly over what she knew about Sam Pendergrast, hoping for a flash of inspiration, like the kind that often came in the middle of a tense courtroom battle.

The tension worked now. A concept seemed to leap out at her. Night blindness! During Andy Stapleton's presentation, Sam had complained about not being able to see well in the dark. And it was getting darker by the minute in here.

Hope bloomed and withered in almost the same moment. Logically, Sam must have been the man Jake had chased that night at the motel. How come he'd been able to run away so rapidly without crashing into a tree or something? Because he'd been wearing special goggles. They weren't just a disguise. They had allowed him to see. And he didn't have them on now because he hadn't expected it to be dark at three in the afternoon. Maybe he couldn't see well enough to shoot accurately.

The reasoning had taken only seconds. Inching toward the far end of the corridor, Laura gave a slight tug on Jake's hand. If Sam noticed, he didn't react. Maybe they had a chance.

She was so preoccupied, that she barely heard the elements tearing and clawing at the damaged roof above them.

"Did Andy Stapleton double-cross you?" Jake continued the dialogue.

"I don't have to tell you a thing."

"I'll bet you didn't know that Julie Sutton left a box of incriminating papers. That must have been as shocking as realizing she was getting ready to blow the whistle on to the whole Fairbolt toxic-waste deal."

"Shut up." Sam raised the gun.

They had inched farther away—almost to a doorway right in back of them. Did they have a hope of throwing

themselves into the room beyond, Laura wondered. It was
a risk. But one worth taking, if she'd guessed correctly
about Sam. She squeezed Jake's hand, hoping he understood it was almost time to make their move. He squeezed
back, his eyes flicking to the doorway. He understood!

Every muscle in Laura's body coiled in readiness. But
before they could leap, there was a rush of movement near
the ceiling, just as when Jake had worked the projectors.
Now it was accompanied by a rending, tearing sound. Or
was it a shriek?

A stream of icy, swirling white swooped into the passage, arrowing straight toward the man with the gun. It was
a column of snow driven by the wind. But it looked in-
credibly like a woman with a long white dress trailing out
behind her, her arms outstretched—ready to pull Sam Pendergrast into her cold embrace.

Screaming, Sam held up his arm to shield his face and
bolted forward. Either he didn't see the pit, or panic had
made him stop thinking clearly. He screamed again when
he sailed into space. And again when the gun in his hand
went off with a muffled crack.

Then there was only the dull thud of a body hitting the
floor below.

"My God—what just happened?" Jake croaked.

"The roof. A piece of the roof ripped off. And the snow
came pouring in on Sam."

"Snow. That was all you saw? Snow?"

"No. I felt like Julie was there, too. As if she came back
to save us."

It was hard to believe the terror was really over. Laura
didn't quite take it in until Jake had folded her into his
arms. The tender gesture released the mix of emotions
brimming inside her.

"You damn fool," she muttered. "Don't you know what

it would have done to me if you'd gotten killed trying to save my life?''

He took her chin between thumb and forefinger and tipped her face up toward his. "I didn't have a choice. Standing in the hallway, knowing Sam was probably on his way up the stairs with the gun, I realized that if he killed you, I couldn't go on.''

"That's how I felt about you.''

"A man likes to hear that from his woman." Jake's voice was husky. "But it's not true. You're a survivor. You've already proved that.''

"Sure. I've been surviving. But meeting you made me realize I wanted a lot more.''

He held her tighter. "Oh, God, Laura. I realized today that that's the way I've been feeling for weeks.''

"Why didn't you tell me?''

"I guess I was a coward. Loving you was too scary. It wasn't just that I couldn't risk the pain I'd been through before. I couldn't risk your rejection.''

"*My* rejection!''

"Yeah. You'd been hurt, too. Suppose I admitted I love you, and you just thought I was saying what you wanted to hear. Or that it couldn't last. Like with your ex-husband. Or like your father.''

There were three important words Laura picked out from his sentences. "You love me?''

"Yeah." His voice was raw. "I love you, all right. I didn't plan it. I just couldn't help it.''

"Oh, Jake. I love you so much. The night we climbed out of Stapleton's office, I realized I couldn't help myself, either.''

"Oh, honey.''

"Jake—'' The next part was hard to say. But he had to understand. "When I started falling in love with you, I couldn't help being jealous of Holly. Of the way you loved her so much. Then, when I thought about it, I realized that if you ever loved anybody again, you'd make the same commitment. Because you're that kind of man.''

She could feel him swallow convulsively. ''Making a commitment. For life. That's why it was so hard. That's why I'm glad I finally could.'' All at once, he laughed. ''I feel—I don't know—brand-new. Reborn.''

They held each other as if they never planned to let go.

''I can't believe we're saying these things,'' Laura whispered, her face pressed against Jake's chest.

''Nothing like a brush with death to bring your life into focus.''

''All this time, I thought the most important thing for you was revenge.''

''For a long time, I thought so, too. I was wrong.''

WHEN THEY GOT BACK TO THE front hall, Cameron Randolph and Evan Hamill were waiting, obviously relieved to see the pair.

''Ketchum was still alive when we got there,'' Cam said. ''I think he was hanging on because he needed to set the record straight before he died.''

''Did he say anything about my father?'' Laura asked the question that had been hanging over her.

''He thought you'd want to know that he wasn't involved.''

Laura closed her eyes for a moment. ''That means a lot to me.''

''Jake's uncle wasn't in on it, either. It was really just Pendergrast. And what Ketchum told me matches with what Jo picked up in town. Once she asked the right questions, it was easier to get answers. Up until twenty years ago, Ketchum had a much worse reputation. Then he seemed to undergo a change for the better.''

"I guess it was the shock of knowing Sam had killed Julie," Laura said.

"According to the judge, Pendergrast's family money bankrolled Fairbolt," Hamill continued. "And he knew about the wide-open spaces up here through his good friend and fraternity brother Warren Ketchum. I think we can assume he organized the original investment deal to cover up the toxic-waste dump and keep the land out of circulation. That gave him a long-term tax shelter along with the possibility of making money on the eventual development of the property. But he didn't see anything wrong with making short trips up to Ravenwood to let his hair down. It was the perfect setting for the wild parties he'd acquired a taste for in college."

Jake nodded. "He sounds totally ruthless. The kind of man who used anyone and everyone for his own purposes. I guess he talked up the land deal as a great investment—neglecting to tell the other stockbrokers they were in for the long haul."

"But Emma must have found out." Jake glanced at Laura. "I've been thinkin' about her and your father. For a while, I was worried because I figured she'd been the mistress of whoever masterminded the Ravenwood deal. Now I guess it's pretty clear your father wasn't her only conquest. She had Sam hooked, too."

"Two ruthless people. You couldn't ask for a nicer couple."

"And I have the feeling Martha was green with envy. That's why she was stirring up trouble."

"Your analysis sounds pretty good," Hamill said, breaking in to the conversation. "The department got a search warrant for Emma Litchfield's safe-deposit box. She kept a coded notebook in it. The woman didn't trust anybody. But we knew she was getting regular payments from some-

one over the years. We just couldn't figure out who.''
Hamill looked at Laura.

"When Sam Pendergrast came in the door wielding that
knife, everything fell into place,'' Cam said, picking up the
narrative. "The trouble was, we knew we had to get up
here fast—in the middle of a snowstorm."

"Was Andy Stapleton in on it?'' Laura asked.

"Believe me, we've investigated Stapleton back to kin-
dergarten. There's no evidence that he even met Pendergrast before he got interested in Ravenwood. It looks like
he was the wild card—a sharp operator looking for resort
land in the path of development."

"And Sam had to go along with Stapleton's proposal
just like everyone else until he could figure out what was
going on,'' Laura speculated. "Maybe Emma was threatening to spill the beans to Andy unless she got more money
from Sam. I guess his first plan was to kill her with the
chandelier. Then when she didn't want to sit where he'd
suggested Andy put her, he took that place himself to allay
suspicions later. When his first attempt failed, he must have
decided the so-called bad blood between me and Emma
gave him the perfect opportunity to kill two birds with one
stone. But I guess he was shook up when he saw us with
the box. He had to get it away from me in case it had any
incriminating evidence." She paused for a moment.

"What about Pickett?'' Jake asked.

"Nothing's been pinned on him yet. Arresting you so
fast could just be a case of misguided zeal, although that
doesn't rule out the possibility of his getting some kind of
payoff in the Julie Sutton case. But you can be sure everything that went on up here will be under investigation
now."

"He didn't give Sam back the dagger?'' Jake asked.

"No," Hamill told them. "It's a twin to the one from
the box. According to the judge, they were both part of a

set that was used in some kind of secret rituals a group of the fraternity brothers initiated. Swearing an oath of allegiance in blood, I think. Sam had the new one specially made.''

Laura shuddered. ''Fraternity rituals! That's hard to believe.''

''It wasn't all of the boys. Just the ones who wanted to suck up to Pendergrast,'' Cam clarified.

''So how much did you get on tape?'' Jake asked.

Cam looked pleased. ''Everything. Including Pendergrast's attack on the judge.''

''But I thought we'd lost you,'' Jake said.

''You couldn't raise us, but I had a fail-safe backup system for your transmission. I left Jo back at the motel, monitoring the broadcast. She's probably mad as hell about missing the action.''

''No. She's decided she's content with a ringside seat.'' The voice of Jo O'Malley boomed over the speaker in the hall.

Cam laughed. ''That's my wife. How did you get back on the air, sweetheart?''

''Hooked the walkie-talkie into the main unit in the van down here. I'm learning.''

Jake looked meaningfully at Laura. ''Wife. How does that sound to you?''

''Awfully good.''

The speaker crackled. ''Katie and I were taking bets on how long you were going to last.''

''Me or him?'' Laura asked.

''Both of you.''

''Whatever.'' Jake looked at Cam and spoke in a whisper. ''Can you turn your darn surveillance system off, and give us a little bit of privacy?'' Without waiting for answer, he turned his back on the rest of the group and pulled Laura into his arms.

The door closed behind Hamill and Cam, but the man and woman on the couch didn't even notice.

After a long, passionate kiss, Jake nuzzled Laura's neck. "Marriage goes with commitment, you know. And if you accept the proposal, it's going to be for keeps."

"Oh, Jake. Yes." She reached for his hand.

"I'm glad. Because you don't have a ghost of a chance of getting away."

One of the lights beside the couch flickered out. Laura smiled. "Julie's leaving us alone, too."

"Yeah. Have you noticed the house feels different?" Jake asked. "Since she swooped in to save us, I mean."

"You really think it was her?"

"I don't know. It sure was perfect timing."

"Yes. And whatever happened back there, I think the ghost of Ravenwood is finally at peace," Laura murmured, before snuggling into Jake's arms again.

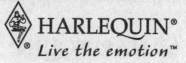

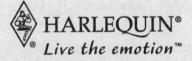

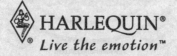

Harlequin Historicals®
Historical Romantic Adventure!

From rugged lawmen and valiant knights to defiant heiresses and spirited frontierswomen, Harlequin Historicals will capture your imagination with their dramatic scope, passion and adventure.

*Harlequin Historicals...
they're too good to miss!*